Quentin Smith is a medical doctor and practising anaesthetist with a background of writing magazine articles of topical or historical interest, usually with a discernible medical flavour. He served as the editor of a national anaesthesia publication for several years before devoting more free time to the enjoyment and pursuit of writing fiction. He lives in Durham with his wife and son.

The Secret Anatomy

of Candles

QUENTIN SMITH

Matador
9 Priory Business Park,
Wistow Road, Kibworth Beauchamp,
Leicestershire. LE8 0RX
Tel: (+44) 116 279 2299
Fax: (+44) 116 279 2277
Email: books@troubador.co.uk
Web: www.troubador.co.uk/matador

ISBN 978 1780883 922

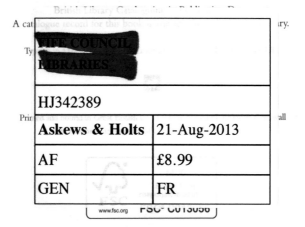

I dedicate this book to my family,
both near and far, for always believing.

Revenge is a kind of wild justice, which the more man's nature runs to it, the more ought law to weed it out.

Francis Bacon

ONE

Jasper did not yet know that his wife was already dead as he paced back and forth on the light brown, Purbeck marble floor of Durham Magistrates' Court. The iPhone he was holding to his ear clicked in to Jennifer's recorded message.

"*The Candles are out. Please leave a message after the beep.*"

He loathed that message, but he had to concede that Jennifer was right in taunting him that he was never at home long enough to change it. One reason for this was that the conduct of every court case was always the same – consuming, demanding, exhausting – and this case was no different. Jasper was an enthusiastic slave to the process and could literally disappear for days at a time without returning home.

With a grimace, he stabbed a finger at the iPhone and slipped it back inside his broad, pinstriped, charcoal suit. He stopped pacing, hands on hips, and stared at the large round clock on the wall above the entrance to court one. It was ten to four. Jasper was annoyed that he had made the call, annoyed that he had succumbed to sentimental distraction just moments before his crucial closing argument.

But his concern that he had not managed to raise Jennifer at all over the past four days was growing. She wasn't even returning his voicemail. Where on earth could she be? With a resigned sigh he realised that there was no time to dwell on this, as he had to concentrate on the cunningly contrived plan he had devised to save his client's case.

As Jasper glanced about the cavernous foyer, echoing with murmurs of gossip from scattered clumps of people dotted around like weeds in a fallow field, his eyes were drawn to the unmistakeable purple dress of his client, who resembled a plump, ripe cranberry. She was standing beside her mother and, quite unbelievably, cradling the disfigured baby in her arms.

"Damn it," Jasper hissed through clenched teeth. "I told you, don't hold the baby – give it to your mother."

There she was, in full view of the public just minutes before closing remarks and final jury deliberations, doing exactly what they had agreed she must not reveal to the world. She caught his eye and smiled, waving excitedly. He stared back, gesturing animatedly with his arms for her to pass the baby to its grandmother. Had they taken in a word of his careful instructions that would need to be carried out to the letter in just a few moments? Did she not realise how critical every nuance of his finely crafted performance was, especially in such cases where the evidence was so weak?

Shaking his head in despair, he took a deep breath and then sat down beside a worn, tan leather briefcase on the wooden bench straddled between court one's two entrances. Rubbing his greying temples with his left thumb and middle finger, he ran through his rehearsed speech silently, lips moving wordlessly and eyes staring blankly ahead.

Just then the increasingly familiar tic began to tug at the corner of his left eye, causing him to blink repeatedly as though he had a speck of dust in it. Quickly, the spasm began to spread to his cheek, distorting the contours of his clean-shaven face with warm and uncontrollable contractions.

Not now, he cursed, not moments before he needed to face the members of the jury, establishing close eye contact, connecting with them, and winning them over. He held out his left hand and stared at it, willing the noticeable tremor, which now also controlled his hand, to cease. But even spreading his fingers apart and tensing the muscles until his knuckles blanched was futile.

He closed the errant fingers into a clenched fist and with his head bowed forwards Jasper suppressed a scream of anguished frustration. What was happening to him? Why were these tics and spasms invading the autonomy of his body, mocking him? His moment of silent torment was interrupted by approaching footsteps clipping the shiny marble floor.

"Well, if it isn't Jasper Candle?" said a man's voice.

Jasper looked up, surprised, and annoyed to be disturbed. It was that awful man with sweaty palms whose name he could never recall. He too wore a charcoal pinstripe suit, the solicitor's badge, and worn but polished black brogues. Today he exuded an odour of garlic, no doubt from his lunch.

"I thought I'd catch you here. If you've got a moment, I must talk to you about the Edward Burns case. You really have gone too far this time, Jasper. How do you sleep at night, man, have you no conscience?"

Jasper took a deep breath as the spasms continued to corrupt his calm demeanour. He was accustomed to the vitriol and immune to the animosity, bordering on repugnance, that his colleagues directed at him. He accepted that his choice of clientele was not one that cultivated popularity amongst fellow solicitors.

Without responding to the inflammatory outburst he

3

gesticulated with his thumb in the direction of court one and the wall clock.

"I haven't got the lager and lime right now," Jasper said in a gentle accent that betrayed his east of London childhood.

"What?"

"Closing argument's in five minutes. No time to chat," Jasper said, avoiding eye contact.

"Typical," the man said, wrinkling his upturned nose and sniffing loudly.

Jasper produced a black business card from within his immaculate suit and held it out between index and middle fingers.

"Call my office."

Printed on the card in silver italics were the words: '*Jasper Candle, Compensation and Personal Injury Solicitor, Court Lane, Old Elvet, Durham.*'

The man stared at the card, seemingly transfixed by its unusual design, his mouth slightly open as if he was not yet done. Suddenly Jasper recalled his name, and wondered how he could ever have forgotten it.

Life imitates art, he thought to himself.

"I need to focus, Mr Ferret, excuse me," Jasper said dismissively, turning his body such that his displayed language of withdrawal was unambiguous.

He did not want any further distraction at this crucial time. It had been bad enough trying unsuccessfully to contact his wife and wondering where she was, and why for days he had not been able to reach her. But the last thing he needed at that moment was to become embroiled in a debate with his opposite counsel over the complexities of the death of Edward Burns. The next hour was crucial in wrapping up the present case, winning it against all odds for his client, and maintaining his unblemished reputation.

The iPhone vibrated against his chest and Jasper pulled it out immediately, poking at the screen with impatient fingers. But it was not his wife. It was from Stacey, his secretary.

"Hi Mr C. Can you talk?" Stacey said in a diminutive voice.

"Quickly."

"That American woman, Mrs Debra Kowalski, has an appointment to see you at 6pm. Her child has died, poor thing, and all she does is cry."

Jasper's eyes tightened almost imperceptibly, wrinkling the skin of his lower eyelids.

"Died from what?"

"Measles, I think."

Jasper's face registered surprise as he straightened up.

"I didn't know you could die from measles."

A brief silence ensued, before Stacey spoke again.

"Well, that's what she said."

Jasper rubbed his twitching face.

"Can't it wait until tomorrow?" he said, glancing at his wristwatch.

"She's called several times. I tried, but she won't wait."

Jasper clenched his teeth and pulled a face, as a sudden spasm jerked his arm violently and almost flung the iPhone from his grasp.

"Brad Pitt!" Jasper cursed.

He had taken to swearing at these involuntary movements, chastising them, as though they had assumed a personality that would respond to abuse and reprimand. Jasper cupped the iPhone in his palm to steady the tremor.

"What was that, Mr C?" Stacey said.

"Stacey, has my wife left any messages today?" Jasper looked down as he spoke, scuffing the polished tiles with the toe of his brogues.

"No, Mr C."

He paused.

"When last did she call… looking for me?"

"Ummmm… I don't remember, Mr C, not for a few days. I'll have to check the voicemail."

Jasper pocketed the phone and, taking a deep breath, glanced up at the wall clock. It was time to go in and execute his cunning plan. He had warned his opposite counsel repeatedly about the danger of not accepting his settlement offer, and now they were about to learn to their cost never to call Jasper Candle's bluff.

He picked up the leather briefcase, massaged the incessant tics around his left eye, adjusted his collar and cuffs, and marched into court one as though he owned it.

TWO

Jennifer retreated in shock to the safety of the pavement as the black London cab almost ran into her. Staring at her incredulously, the driver shook his head and hooted.

"I'm sorry," she heard herself say.

Jennifer turned around briefly and looked back up Harley Street with a dazed expression ironed onto her narrow face and sharp features. Even her eyes blinked slowly, indicative of the paralytic state of her brain. As she stared up towards the distinctive pinkish sandstone of number sixty seven, she could still hear his words echoing in her head, still smell the powerful sweet musk of his aftershave.

"I am so sorry to have to be the bearer of such bad news, Mrs Candle," he had carefully enunciated, his exotic middle eastern face exuding empathy beneath small letterbox spectacles.

In her hand Jennifer clutched the letter that he had given to her: the letter that had shattered her life.

"Take this as a summary of what we have discussed."

Jennifer recalled speaking to him as if from the depths of a bad dream, her voice echoing and alien to her own ears.

"Are you sure this isn't some kind of terrible mistake, Doctor?"

"I am so sorry," he had said, standing up in his impeccably

tailored Armani suit and offering her his hand.

Pulling the collar of her thick blood red coat tightly around her neck, she turned into New Cavendish Street and began to walk in the direction of Hyde Park. Soon she was away from the traffic in the vast expanse of the park, entering at Cumberland Gate and walking aimlessly along the many intersecting pathways. A group of students were playing football to one side, but she did not even notice them as they whistled their approval at her.

She walked further before stumbling into something that squealed.

"Watch it!" an old man cursed as she almost trampled his spaniel that had stopped to sniff a mole hill.

The dog yelped and sprang away to safety, before the leash tautened and terminated its escape. Rising up from the hem of Jennifer's red coat was a smear of mud from its frightened paw.

"I am so… I didn't see… please excuse me," she stammered, looking up at the wrinkled face of the old man.

He looked back into her vacant, swollen eyes, saw the tears streaking her cheeks and creased his eyebrows.

"You all right, love?" he asked, pulling the circumspect spaniel towards him on the leash.

"Yes… sorry."

Jennifer nodded absently, not even feeling the sting of the wintry chill on her face, and moved on.

She did not know how long she had walked, but eventually found herself standing on the stone bridge, staring into the brooding waters of the Serpentine. Ducks paddled about gracefully in the icy water, occasionally speeding up to chase down a crust of bread lobbed in by a samaritan on the bank. Stiffened fingers tinged with blue lifted and meticulously unfolded the letter on the stone parapet. Jennifer began to read it again, perhaps doubting her recollection of its contents, or hoping that it would convey a more benign message now than it had earlier.

Living with the shadow of this prophecy hovering relentlessly over her life had been difficult enough, but to discover now that her worst fears had materialised was heartbreaking. She felt crushed as a tear rolled down each blanched cheek, past pale, pursed lips and dropped on to the letter.

Jennifer stared into the depths of the dark water, drawn to its tranquil ripples, pacified by its calming expanse, leaning into its allure. In her mind she tried to imagine the despair that Jasper's father must have felt when he had received his letter and whether the water below Westminster Bridge had called to him that fateful day, just as it was calling to her now on West Carriage Drive.

A woman unhurriedly pushing a regal Silver Cross pram stopped beside her.

"Are you all right?" she enquired, touching Jennifer lightly on the shoulder.

Jennifer was startled and shrank back from the cold parapet and the sucking abyss beyond it, absently mumbling and nodding her head as she stared at the woman with wide eyes.

"I'm fine, thank you, just fine," she heard herself say softly and without conviction.

Walking away towards Albert Hall, Jennifer pushed the letter deep into her coat pocket, hoping to banish its contents from her thoughts.

THREE

Debra Kowalski cradled the toddler on her lap, resting her chin on his profusion of curly, blonde hair as he played with a gold locket hanging around her neck. Debra kept dabbing at her moist staring eyes with a balled up tissue in her hand. She was frightened and anxious, and clearly had no intention of letting the nurse, seated directly in front of her, anywhere near her child.

"I don't know what to do," Debra said through teary gasps.

They were sitting in a small austere clinic room: examination couch covered in starched white sheets to one side; desk with computer centrally placed to the other; walls adorned with charts and posters of various parts of the human body. The air was rank with the overpowering odour of Savlon, a smell Debra had never forgotten since her brief spell as a dental nurse.

Dressed in a navy blue uniform, the nurse leaned across to her desk and pulled a clean, crisp tissue from a box and offered it to Debra. Her plump, round face fringed by black bob-styled hair smiled sympathetically above a rectangular white identity badge which read 'Yvonne, Practice Nurse.'

"Well, you've come this far, and you did discuss all of this with Dr Potter at length last week, and I do believe that you know it's best for young Ollie here," Yvonne said, trying to engage the little boy's attention with a coy smile and a wiggling finger.

But Ollie just curled up on his mother's lap, pressing into her bosom and staring suspiciously at the nurse. Debra was clearly torn, biting on her lower lip first one side and then the other until she could feel it hurting. She shifted her weight from one leg to another and by doing so seemed to move Ollie further from Yvonne's reach.

"I am so confused right now. My husband died only three months ago, he had leukaemia you know, and Ollie is all I have," Debra said in her Bostonian twang, instinctively hugging the little boy tightly.

"You did tell me, Mrs Kowalski, a terrible loss for both of you," Yvonne empathised, pausing and taking a breath before continuing. "Perhaps, though, you should think that there is even more reason now to protect little Ollie with the MMR vaccine."

Debra nodded her head, but her body language betrayed her inner uncertainty. Tears had streaked her cheeks like railway tracks and those that had not dried dripped occasionally on to Ollie's head.

"It's just that I'm so messed up, you know, I can't think clearly, what with Harry's leukaemia and all. I'm so worried about doing harm to little Ollie right now. After everything that Harry went through, you read so much conflicting stuff about vaccines and their complications. I'm terrified of doing something that I cannot undo."

Yvonne sat quietly, drumming her fingertips together rhythmically in her lap as she considered the frightened American woman sitting before her. She had spent the past fifteen minutes with them and her clinic was now running behind. It was difficult not to feel frustration over the woman's indecision and she wondered how best to tackle Debra's intransigence.

"I just can't help thinking of all those children who have had complications of the MMR – autism and all that – especially now that I've lost Harry. I can't replace Ollie," Debra continued through bubbling tears.

"To be honest, Mrs Kowalski, as I'm sure Dr Potter told you, Ollie here is at far greater risk if he does not have the MMR vaccination than if he does, far greater risk. Measles is a dangerous disease if you're a young unvaccinated boy, like little Ollie. People forget that all too easily."

Yvonne was getting somewhat impatient now and stood up from her swivel chair, enjoying the sudden return of circulation to her legs as she stretched slightly.

Debra took a deep breath and stared out of the small window at patients trying desperately to find parking in the crowded car park behind the surgery. The sun emerged from behind a grey cloud and filled the room with a burst of warmth. Suddenly, she kissed Ollie on the forehead, gave him a tight squeeze, and looked up defiantly as she sniffed away tears.

"Do it now, before I change my mind. I know Ollie's father wanted him to have it. I'll do this for Harry."

With this final act of resolve, Debra suddenly dissolved into tears as the nurse hurriedly primed her tiny syringes with vaccine.

She couldn't decide whether she was taking control by submitting to this invasion of her precious son's body, or surrendering to the unknown and the unpredictable. As the tiny bundle of golden curls began to cry with the first injection into his exposed thigh, Debra cradled his head against her breast and kissed him.

"I will look after you so carefully, my love. Mummy will never let anything happen to you. Not anything, I promise."

The words, heavy with sincerity and emotion, glided off Debra's motherly tongue sweetly, with an ease that would make them all the harder to forget when remembering became too painful.

FOUR

Jasper stood up and walked over towards the jury. He smiled at them, not frivolously, not whimsically, but just enough to exude some warmth and humanity. A long, highly polished brass rail ran along the length of the jury benches, and Jasper liked to leave his finger prints all over it by the end of a case. Walking up to the jury he wrapped his hands authoritatively around the polished rail. He did this as much to study the faces of the jurors staring back at him expectantly, as he did to hide the tremor which had still not subsided in his left hand.

He had always found that analysing the composition of the jury was a crucial factor in formulating his closing argument. The evidence and facts of the case had to speak for themselves, but this was his opportunity to strike at the jurors' personal vulnerabilities.

"What exactly is it that you need to consider in this case?" Jasper said eventually, making eye contact with all the young female jurors.

There were quite a few young women in the jury and that was good, as they themselves might be mothers and would identify easily with his client's position. There were also some older jurors, both men and women, perhaps grandparents, and he always felt that raw, emotive issues with the capacity to shock resonated amongst more mature members of society.

There were very few middle aged working people, those who perhaps would not immediately identify with his client or the emotive shock he had planned, the ones who would be cool and objective. These jurors were his major challenge in winning over this jury with his closing argument.

He turned around and walked back to stand in front of his client. She was a round, plump woman with straight blonde hair that cascaded over her shoulders on to her hibiscus purple dress. Her chubby cheeks turned rose pink as she felt the glare of the jury directed at her.

"My client, Miss Courtney Green, has just been through one of life's most natural and normal experiences by bringing a baby into this world."

Jasper turned back to the jury and addressed the women.

"I'm sure many of you have been through this yourselves, one of life's most rewarding and exhilarating experiences. But not only that, it is a life event that brings with it great responsibility and expectation for young mothers, who suddenly have to care for their helpless little babies."

Jasper turned and glanced over to the first row of the public gallery where, immediately behind Miss Green, he was pleased to see his client's mother sitting holding the newborn baby, as he had requested. The tics twisted around his left eye and began to drag up his cheek and the corner of his mouth. Jasper rubbed the side of his face in a desperate attempt to suppress the intrusive distortion, or at least to hide it.

"So, put yourself in Miss Green's position. She was sent home from hospital with such a debilitating injury that rendered her incapable of performing these basic responsibilities and expectations, things we all, and you all, will take for granted."

Jasper wanted to return to face the jurors but he was concerned that the tics and tremors would become evident and distract them from focusing on his elaborate performance.

"You have heard from the defence counsel that Miss Green had an injury to her left arm as a child, and that she attended physiotherapy as a teenager for pain in that arm. We do not dispute any of that. But consider Miss Green's situation as it affects her now. Her arm has not troubled her in recent years and was perfectly functional when she went into hospital to deliver her baby."

"Counsel."

Jasper stopped, in disbelief that the judge had interrupted his speech. He turned to face the judge.

"Your Honour?"

"Approach please," The judge said, gesticulating with a bent index finger. "Not you, counsel," He said to the defence barrister, who too was standing up, waving at him to sit down.

Jasper walked right up to the judge's bench.

"What is it Your Honour?"

The judge leaned forward discreetly, peering over the top of his gold rimmed bifocals that were perched halfway down his beak-like nose, and lowered his voice as he spoke to Jasper.

"Are you all right, sir?" He casually brushed a finger down the side of his face.

Jasper realised that the judge was questioning the contortions visible on his face, and perhaps the tremor of his hand. He smiled, though within he was seething with frustration and embarrassment at his infernal condition.

"I am fine, Your Honour. It's nothing at all, if anything perhaps lack of sleep. I'm barb-wired."

"What?"

"I'm tired, Your Honour," Jasper explained.

The judge stared closely but quite impassively at Jasper without displaying any reaction. Jasper wondered for a moment if the judge's craning nostrils were trying to detect the whiff of alcohol. Jasper tried not to breathe, though he did not know why as he had not been drinking, not yet. All of a sudden the judge sat back in his ornate seat.

"Continue, please."

Jasper smiled, bowed slightly and retreated to the safety of his bench. The tics continued to tug at his cheek.

"As I was saying, Miss Green was admitted to hospital with a normal arm and now, as a result of repeated and traumatic attempts to establish intravenous drips, some of which were allowed to leak undetected into her arm instead of into the veins, she has a painful inflamed arm." He paused. "But it doesn't end there, does it?"

He glanced at his client, reminding her of their cue, and she quickly unfolded her chubby arms to reveal the cumbersome splint and strapping that was wrapped around her forearm. Then she tried to pour water from the small jug in front of her into a glass, struggling with one hand to complete the simple task. She fumbled with the tumbler and Jasper, as planned, stepped forward to help her, eventually pouring water into the glass for her. He took his time, ensuring that everyone was watching. Though she had not spilled a drop, he pulled out his handkerchief and dabbed the surface of the bench.

The defence barrister thumped his pencil down on his legal pad and sat back as he folded his arms. He rolled his eyes to the heavens and exhaled loudly.

"Move it along please, counsel," The judge said patiently, motioning with his hand.

"Yes, Your Honour. Miss Green's disability has significantly hampered her ability to care for her newborn baby. She has found basic natural functions such as breast feeding, bathing the baby, changing nappies, even cuddling the infant extremely difficult, due to the pain and weakness in that afflicted arm."

Jasper looked across at the jurors. He certainly had the attention of the young women and most of the older jurors seemed to be moved by her plight. Next, he looked over at the grandmother who was holding the infant, and nodded to her slightly. He wanted the infant to be made visible, he wanted it either to smile or to cry because he needed the jurors to see its mouth open wide.

"Now, any mother would find the inability to provide these basic mothering tasks very distressing, after all, who can be certain exactly how much this will affect the vital mother-infant bonding process. But Miss Green's little baby needs even more care, for he left hospital with a significant disability to overcome."

Jasper paused, waiting for the sound of crying as the baby was displayed on the grandmother's lap, like a stage prop.

"This is my client's little baby, needing to be cared for by its grandmother … "

With that the infant let out a blood curdling cry and, with mouth wide agape, revealed to the whole jury a massive cleft lip and palate, a deep, dark gouge that snaked back from beneath its nose into the depths of the mouth. To the uninitiated this unfortunate defect is quite disturbing, and the effect on the jury was better than Jasper could have scripted himself, especially all the women, young and old alike, who gasped and stared.

He watched with satisfaction as many jurors sat back in

their chairs, their faces betraying their horror, a few covering their mouths with cupped hands. What parent could not be moved by the sight of a poor little infant, so unfortunately disfigured?

The grandmother produced a bottle of formula milk and, as she had rehearsed beforehand with Jasper, tried to pacify the infant with a feed. But, with the eyes of the court watching her every move, milk leaked out from the baby's mouth and through its nose as it spluttered all over her floral patterned dress. The poor infant appeared to be in great distress. The grandmother stood up, apologised and excused herself, making a very public exit, followed closely by every eye in the courtroom. Miss Green was visibly upset and emotional, covering her face with her splinted arm.

Jasper approached her and quietly reassured and comforted her. He was pleased. It had all gone very well.

Then he turned again to face the emotionally charged and apparently shaken jury. He approached them slowly, hoping that his continuing facial distortions would not interfere with his carefully orchestrated performance.

"Miss Green has her time cut out, members of the jury. Her poor infant is going to need so much extra care in the months and years ahead. She is starting out with a significant disadvantage, as a direct result of this debilitating injury. I will remind you again that many aspects of this injury were avoidable. As you have heard from the evidence presented in this courtroom, there were failures in obtaining senior help to site her intravenous drips, and failures in detecting fluid leaking into her arm."

He turned again to look at Miss Green, and then back to the jury.

"Members of the jury, I thank you for your time in listening to all the evidence about the unfortunate plight of my client. I am confident that you will make the sensible choice, the right choice and recognise that Miss Green cannot cope with her duties as a mother, as a result of her injury."

Jasper quickly clasped hands to quell the sudden crescendo of uncontrollable movements in his left arm. He smiled warmly at the jury, but inside he wanted to scream. Enough. Enough.

FIVE

Debra almost dropped her cup of tea upon hearing that fearful little word. The four women sat huddled amiably around a small unstable table beneath the ancient vaulted stonework of Durham Cathedral's undercroft café, exchanging stories about the school their beloved children attended. Aromas of fresh coffee and cinnamon warmed the friendly atmosphere.

"Well I can't believe she never complained. I would have if my child had wet his pants in class because he was too afraid to ask the teacher for the toilet!" Catherine announced haughtily, finishing off the last of the chocolate cake in front of her.

"She should not be a pre-prep school teacher, she doesn't have the soft touch needed with little ones," Tamara agreed, nodding and glancing around at the other faces for support.

"The children are petrified of her. Petrified!" Angie repeated slowly for effect, her eyes stretched theatrically wide.

"Oh, did you hear there's an outbreak of measles in the reception class?" Catherine butted in nonchalantly, to a startled reception from everyone assembled.

Debra's heart began to pound as she felt the blood draining from her face and the cup of tea almost slip from her grasp. Ollie was in reception class.

"Measles?" Debra repeated in faltering disbelief.

"Incredible, isn't it?" Catherine said gleefully, nodding at each of her friends in turn around the table, as though she enjoyed delivering shocking news.

"Who has measles?" Debra questioned, barely able to hear her own voice over the rushing of blood in her ears. Inwardly, she felt as though she was discussing Ebola Virus or some rare and extremely fatal tropical fever.

"I've heard that little Seamus has been off with it, you know the boy whose mother runs the coffee shop beside the cinema?" Catherine said.

"The one who doesn't shave her armpits?" Tamara asked.

"I don't think they believe in deodorant either," Angie said, nodding.

The others nodded as they leaned forward, ears pricked for the juicy gossip.

"And Seamus' sister Zoe has it, the girl with glasses, and I heard that Mr Wright, the student teacher from Australia, caught it as well. He was quite ill, Jackie told me."

"I read somewhere that you can be very sick from measles," Tamara said.

The silence at the table was broken only by Angie sipping noisily on her tea.

"But how, I mean surely everyone has been vaccinated?" Debra barely managed to speak through her dry mouth.

They all shrugged their shoulders in unison.

"Mine were both vaccinated with the MMR," Catherine said.

Angie leaned in and began to whisper, as though divulging a sworn secret that could endanger all of them.

"I don't think Zoe or Seamus were vaccinated, you know."

Debra's heart began to pound even faster as she heard things that could mean only one thing: her precious child was in danger.

"But why ever not?" Tamara asked.

"The parents were dead against the MMR."

"I know the type you mean," Catherine said, leaning back in her chair and nodding.

"So they could have brought measles into the school then," Tamara said.

"Has everyone here had their kids vaccinated?" Angie asked.

They all nodded and murmured approvingly.

"So we should all be all right then?" Debra ventured cautiously, seeking confirmation that their children would be safe from the plague. Her eyes were large, filled with apprehension and beginning to look moist.

"You OK, Debs?" Catherine asked, placing a hand on her shoulder.

Debra was struggling to maintain her composure, trying to contain the fear that something dreadful could happen to her precious little son, the only surviving memory of her husband.

"I couldn't bear it if anything happened to Ollie."

All the women joined in with encouragement and warm touches of reassurance.

"He'll be fine, Debs, he's had the vaccine and anyway, it's only measles, children get it and shrug it off in no time. You don't need to worry yourself," Tamara said.

Debra wiped her eyes self consciously, smearing her mascara, and delicately cleared her nose, embarrassed by her show of emotion in front of everyone. All she wanted to do was rush over to the school and remove Ollie from the germ infested environment, to protect him from potential harm, as she had promised to him that she would do.

But it was already too late.

SIX

Jasper hurried towards Elvet Bridge, pausing briefly as he felt his iPhone vibrate, to admire the majesty of Durham Cathedral's eleventh century Norman architecture, just visible above the tall beech trees on the river banks. Basking in the setting sun, the sandstone crenellations on the cathedral bell tower glowed against a pastel blue sky beside Durham Castle, home to his former student college.

He squinted at the iPhone. It was a message from Stacey.

Where are you, Mr C? Mrs K waiting. No calls yet from Mrs C.

Where on earth was Jennifer? Jasper thought to himself, once again reminded that he had not yet managed to contact his wife. It was as though she had fallen off the edge of the world. He dialled Jennifer's number and was directed to voicemail.

"*The Candles are out. Please leave a message after the beep.*"

He sighed with a frown etched on his face, examined his wristwatch and walked briskly into The Swan and Three Cygnets, where he was instantly enveloped by the jovial early evening atmosphere of people chatting, laughing and drinking beer. In the background The Beatles sang 'Maxwell's Silver Hammer' and underfoot he crunched potato crisps that had escaped beery mouths.

Staring intently around the room, Jasper's eyes quickly found their prey. He snaked his way through groups of youthful revellers, most of whom were wearing clothing adorned with 'Boat Club', 'Regatta' and related insignia indicating that the local student rowers were out in force.

Sitting in an alcove that overlooked the river and the ducks swimming about on its calm surface was a very large man in a well-worn brown leather jacket. He was lifting a pint glass of Black Sheep ale to his face with stubby fingers that were strangled by heavy pewter rings.

"Guv'nor," The man acknowledged, as Jasper sat down opposite him on an upholstered stool. "Here for a few short ones?"

"I have an appointment, this will have to be quick," Jasper replied curtly.

The fat man nodded and the smile that creased his bristly pear shaped face lifted his pierced earlobes.

"Aren't you going to have a... "

"What have you got on the surgeon, Lazlo?" Jasper interrupted irritably, leaning forward into Lazlo's beery personal space.

Lazlo put down his glass and made a horizontal sideways sweeping motion with both arms.

"Nothing. Mr Daniel Keys is clean."

"Cobblers, Lazlo. Nobody is that clean. Edward Burns is dead and this fellow operated on him just ten days earlier. There's got to be something on him," Jasper protested.

"He's clean, I'm telling you. No priors, no mistresses, no pendings," Lazlo shrugged almost apologetically and lifted his Black Sheep.

"Look Lazlo, I use you because you're supposed to be good,

and I don't pay you what I do to tell me this Brad Pitt."

Lazlo was not shaken by this outburst and held Jasper's fiery gaze with steady, measured eyes.

"I'm not good, guv, I'm the best."

Jasper's gaze faltered and suddenly he looked desperate.

"God, I really need a gay and frisky right now, fancy another pint?" Jasper asked, as he fumbled in his trouser pocket for change.

"Never say no, guv," Lazlo replied.

Returning with two drinks, Jasper sat down and gulped a large mouthful of Chivas Regal. He savoured the warmth on his tongue and tilted the heavy tumbler this way and that, as he studied the swirling amber liquid caressing a trio of ice cubes. Almost instantly he felt the oppressive fog that surrounded him lift on welcome malted wings.

"I do, however, have something very interesting about the circumstances surrounding Mr Edward Burns' death." Lazlo's pierced earlobes bounced on his ample cheeks as he spoke.

"Nothing to do with the surgeon?" Jasper asked, raising his eyebrows.

Lazlo shook his huge head slowly and paused, savouring the moment and a mouthful of beer.

"What if I was to suggest that Edward Burns' death had nothing to do with his surgery, or his medical care, or his nursing care?"

Lazlo watched as his words settled on Jasper.

"Are you absolutely mad? Have you gone Bohemian, or something?" Jasper ridiculed with a twisted face.

"What if I was to suggest that Edward Burns may have been the unfortunate victim of a member of the general public?"

Jasper guffawed, but could not disguise his curiosity. He

stared at Lazlo, weighing up this new development in his mind.

"Do you have a reliable source for this… extraordinary suggestion?"

"I had to get a matron very drunk."

"Put it on your expenses," Jasper said, trying to appear nonchalant, before relenting. "Well come on, out with it."

Lazlo made placatory gestures with his hands and sat forward, suddenly unable to contain his excitement as he prepared to deliver his grand opus.

"A few days before he died, on a Saturday night, the hospital was full and a new patient admitted from a care home with pneumonia was housed on Edward Burns' surgical ward."

Jasper was perched on the edge of his stool, leaning forward and listening intently to Lazlo speak.

"This new patient had gastroenteritis, you know, the squirts… "

"Yeah yeah, tommy guns, I get it," Jasper said irritably.

"Exactly, guv, diarrhoea. Anyway, this spread around the ward like a bad rumour and poor old Edward Burns got it. He began spewing his guts out into a bowl, and hey presto, his surgical wound broke down, then it got infected, and… "

"As a result of that he's brown bread." Jasper finished.

"Now he's brown bread, guv'nor," Lazlo repeated, leaning back and tucking into his Black Sheep.

The two men sat in silence for a moment enjoying their drinks.

"I need a lot more information on this other patient and I need to know who is responsible for admitting patients to the ward, who makes these decisions, et cetera."

"Of course, guv," Lazlo nodded.

Another pause as both men considered this unexpected development.

Jasper rubbed his chin and watched through the window as the ducks took evasive action from a doubles canoe on the river.

"I wonder if it's possible to hold a fellow hospital patient responsible?" Jasper thought aloud.

"If not the patient, then perhaps the person who decided to admit that patient to the ward?" Lazlo suggested.

Jasper snapped his fingers and pointed them at Lazlo.

"That is a very good line of thought. Pursue that, don't pull any punches. Get your matron drunk again if you have to."

Lazlo nodded.

"Do you still think we should go to this AA meeting tomorrow night?" Jasper said eventually, studying the melting ice cubes in his Chivas.

"Absolutely," Lazlo said, pointedly arranging his beer glass on the small table beside four empty glasses and gesturing towards them. "We agreed, and let me ask you guv, is that a single scotch?"

Jasper hesitated, looking at his glass.

"I would Arthur Scargill with a single. This is a triple, Lazlo, and I take your point."

"Tomorrow night it is then," Lazlo said.

Jasper suddenly felt the spasms returning to his face, pulling, twisting, teasing, testing his patience. He didn't want Lazlo to see him like this so he moved a hand up to rub his face discreetly, realising too late that it was also twitching. There was only one thing to do. Jasper downed the rest of his whisky and stood up to leave.

"Did you win in court today?" Lazlo said.

"What do you think?"

"You always do, guv."

"I have to go, a new client awaits," Jasper said, clutching his twitching arm to hide the involuntary spasms.

Lazlo raised his glass in salute and rubbed his hands together.

"Excellent. More work for me then, I hope."

"Tomorrow night I want to know everything about that patient with the tommy guns," Jasper said as he turned to leave.

SEVEN

Dr Potter slowly pulled back the lime green T-shirt emblazoned with a smiling Tyrannosaurus to reveal the pale, spotty skin of Ollie's abdomen. The muscles driving Ollie's laboured breathing contracted rhythmically and fast.

Debra watched closely as the doctor's gentle fingers exposed more of Ollie's skin to reveal further fine, red spots. They were everywhere on his hot little body. She held her clenched left hand to her mouth and chewed on the knuckle of the index finger, afraid to breathe.

"You're such a good boy, Ollie. Tell me if I tickle the dinosaur," Dr Potter said in a soft and mellifluous tone, as he began to auscultate Ollie's chest with his stethoscope.

Dr Potter was middle aged, bald on top but fringed with a finger of black hair above each ear and small, round, gold rimmed spectacles that made him resemble a chemistry professor. The brightly coloured bowtie might have completed the picture were it not for the Disney characters that exposed him as the practice children's doctor.

But Ollie wasn't interested in Dr Potter's friendly banter or Pinocchio chasing Pocahontas on his bowtie that day. His listless brown eyes just stared straight up at the ceiling, as though deeply distracted by more important matters.

Debra's petrified eyes studied Dr Potter's every reaction,

preying on every miniscule and subconscious response.

"What is it, doctor?" she suddenly said, rejecting the raw knuckle from her mouth.

Dr Potter took a deep breath and removed the stethoscope from his ears. He didn't meet Debra's concerned stare, trying instead to elicit a smile or a response from Ollie's flushed little face. He failed; Ollie just panted and stared. He didn't even object, only moaning slightly when Dr Potter inserted an aural thermometer into Ollie's ears to measure his temperature.

"He's very hot, Mrs Kowalski, 39.8 degrees Celsius. We must try and cool him slightly first."

"What do you mean, first?" Debra asked anxiously, her voice rising as her throat began to close in, making her feel breathless. Already her chest felt like it had a ton of lead pressing on it.

Dr Potter turned now to meet her eyes, but Debra looked away towards Ollie as he lay without protestation on the examination couch beneath his lime green dinosaur T-shirt.

"Can I?" she asked, motioning towards him.

"Yes, yes of course."

Debra picked up Ollie and held his hot little body tightly in her arms. His head flopped limply on to her shoulder as he moaned and cried slightly.

"Is it measles?" Debra asked.

Dr Potter nodded and drew breath to speak.

"How can it be measles, he had the MMR two years ago?" Debra continued.

"I do think he has measles," Dr Potter said slowly, measuring his words carefully. "What concerns me though is that he might be developing complications."

"Oh God, no, no!" Debra wailed weakly, shaking her head

violently in disbelief. "This is not supposed to happen… "

The room began to spin around her and spots began to infiltrate her field of vision. Debra was acutely aware of the sweaty limp bundle she cradled in her arms, but beyond that everything was blurring and merging into a spinning, chaotic nightmare. She felt the warmth draining from her face at the sudden fear that her fragile world was crumbling beneath her feet.

"I want to bring Ollie's temperature down while we wait for an ambulance to take him to hospital. I think it's best if we admit him to the children's ward right away for tests." Dr Potter continued.

But Debra was silent, no crying, no hysterical tears, no sobbing as her lily white body crumpled on failing legs. Dr Potter managed to rescue Ollie from her spent embrace as she folded untidily upon herself on the blue, carpeted floor.

EIGHT

Thirty years previously

Jasper slouched on the sofa with muddy legs outstretched, his eyes flicking between his socked feet and his father's hairy face. Jasper had left his football boots at the door of their semi-detached house, but hadn't had the energy to remove his soiled school socks.

"What's for dinner, Mum?" Jasper yelled in the direction of the kitchen. It sounded and smelled like she was crisping bacon, but whenever he was hungry all home cooking smelled like bacon to Jasper.

"So, you didn't make the team?" Jasper's father blurted out in a strong Cockney accent, a scowl carved into his face.

"No, Dad."

"You disappointed?" his father asked, raising his tangled, hairy eyebrows.

"Of course I am. I've been training for weeks."

"Did you train Marquis de Sade?"

"Of course I trained hard, Dad. I wanted to be in the team, didn't I?"

Jasper was familiar with this routine from his father and felt his irritation rising.

"Obviously you didn't try Marquis de Sade enough, son. If

you really wanted it you would have put in more effort."

"I tried, Dad."

"No son, you didn't try hard enough. I've told you before that success only comes to those who really work at it. Nothing for nothing in this old world."

Jasper's gaze was now fixed on his mud stained socks. He knew by now when to submit.

"It's just like when you missed out on being a prefect, you were gutted. But as I told you, if you had wanted it enough and worked hard enough at getting it, you would today be a prefect in your school."

Jasper's father played with and stroked the black beard under his chin as he spoke, his eyes never leaving Jasper's face. Just then his father's forehead began to twitch and pull up his great hairy eyebrows. His mouth pulsed into a twisted pout several times, somewhat like a sea anemone closing in on its prey. Self consciously his hand shot up to rub his face from side to side.

"It's all about what's in here, Jasper," his father said leaning forward, patting first his head and then his chest as he spoke. "If it's strong enough in your crust of bread, and in your jam tart, if you want it bad enough and work hard enough, you'll make it happen. It's only ever about effort."

Jasper nodded passively.

"Yes, Dad."

This seemed to be the wrong thing to say to his father.

"It's not about agreeing with me, son, it's about getting off your bottle and glass and putting some effort into things. There's no such thing as bad luck, or good luck in life. Only how much you want something and how far you're prepared to go to make it yours. So far I have only ever seen you come up short."

Though his legs ached from running all afternoon at the team trials, Jasper did not feel that he deserved to have a tired body any more. He no longer felt worthy of being exhausted.

"If you know what's good for you, son, you'll take my advice and put some real effort into life in the future, or you'll always be a loser."

"Dinner's ready, boys. Egg, bacon, and chips!" said Jasper's mother, as she emerged from the kitchen carrying three plates.

"Tent pegs and Jagger's lips, my favourite, Evie," said his father, slapping his meaty thighs before standing up and walking unsteadily towards the table.

"I want to study to be a lawyer," Jasper suddenly blurted, surprised by his unprompted outburst.

His father turned casually and fixed Jasper with a mocking stare as his head twisted demonically to one side a few times. Then he chuckled in a lightly amused way.

"You, a Tom Sawyer? For someone who couldn't even make prefect, or the school football team, you should be more realistic, son."

Jasper could no longer enjoy eggs, bacon and chips after leaving home. The heady aromas were too powerful to shut out and the memories they inevitably conjured up simply too unpleasant.

By the time Jasper received notification just six months later that he had been accepted to read law at the prestigious University College of Durham University, his father had already died. It was rather sudden and unexpected, but even so Jasper had found it difficult to mourn. He was filled with regret, however, regret that his father had not lived long enough to see him achieve his ambition. It was as though he did not want to see Jasper succeed, selfishly leaving this world just weeks before Jasper's acceptance at university to pursue his dream. Far more than sadness, Jasper felt the overwhelming need to prove his worth as he boarded the northbound east coast train at Kings Cross Station, bidding an impatient farewell to his tearful mother. On the train he binned the egg and bacon sandwich she had made for him.

NINE

The woman waiting in Jasper's office made an immediate impression on him. Wearing beige slacks and a loose fitting white blouse finished with a simple lace trim around the neck, her tall, slender frame matched Jasper's in height, but smelled of rose petals.

"Please, call me Jasper. I am sorry to keep you waiting," Jasper said, extending his hand.

"Debra Kowalski," she said, holding his hand softly.

Beneath a low fringe of blonde hair a pair of large, grey-blue eyes swam between teary lids, blotching carefully applied eye make-up. Jasper found himself staring at her, touched by her engaging fusion of beauty and sadness. He felt her warm hand slip out of his.

"Coffee, tea?"

"No thank you," she said.

Jasper ushered her into his office before returning to the reception where Stacey, standing behind an expansive chrome and glass desk, was carefully pulling a black coat over her black buttoned blouse.

"How'd it go today, Mr C?" Stacey asked, pursing her lips to smooth the black lipstick she had just applied.

"Good. Majority decision in our favour, just awaiting the damages now."

Stacey was in her late twenties, of a pale, creamy complexion, with emerald green eyes under pencil thin black eyebrows and long straight jet black hair. She claimed to be a Goth, but had agreed to tone down her dress sense whilst at work. Jasper said that at work she should look like a conservative Goth, then wondered if he meant a liberal Goth.

"Lazlo called," she said rifling through papers on her desk.

"Yes, I saw him at The Swan."

"Oh."

"I will probably finish late tonight and sleep here," Jasper said.

"Again?" Stacey frowned.

"Will you please bring a couple of almond croissants with you in the morning, and pick up a new white dicky dirt from Greenwoods – size seventeen remember."

"A what?" Stacey made a face.

"A shirt, haven't you learned anything working with me for five years?"

She tipped her head and dropped the lipstick and hairbrush into her small, black leather handbag.

"Thanks Stacey," Jasper said with a warm smile.

But the smile was corrupted by muscle tugs around the corner of his mouth and cheek. Embarrassed, Stacey pretended not to notice.

"I did find a message from Mrs C."

"Yes?" Jasper's eyes widened and he looked at her expectantly.

"But it was from several days ago, saying she was off to London for an appointment in Harley Street."

"Harley Street?"

Stacey shrugged and moved to the door.

"Good luck with Mrs Kowalski. She's very upset."

*

Debra Kowalski was sitting in a leather high back chair, taking in the eclectic mix of furnishings in Jasper's office, when he returned. Behind an immaculately neat cherry wood desk topped with burgundy leather inset hung several framed certificates. In the corner stood an imposing drinks cabinet in matching cherry wood which was open, displaying crystal-cut glasses and several spirit bottles. Half way between the desk and the cabinet in a square terracotta pot stood a large, spiky cactus with side branches resembling a policeman directing traffic.

Jasper caught Debra's gaze currently directed at the single bed in the far corner that was made up and covered with a midnight black quilt, courtesy of Stacey.

"I often work late and sleep in my office," Jasper explained, as he slumped into his throne-like desk chair.

Debra sniffed and quietly blew her nose into a small crumpled tissue, held in a tightly clenched fist.

"Stacey told me a little about your background. I am really sorry for your loss."

Debra's face screwed up with emotion and she held a balled fist against her chest.

"I am so angry, yet so empty inside at the same time. I have lost everyone, and everything."

Jasper felt her gentle, lilting, east coast American accent soothing him. He let her regain her composure, then leaned forward on his elbows and pressed his fingertips together.

"How can I help you?"

"I have come to you because I was told you are the best, and I want justice for my son."

Jasper nodded but said nothing. He lowered his arms and then folded them as he became aware of the coarse tremor in his left hand.

"I met Harry when I came over as a graduate student to research dental health in the severely mentally disabled. Harry lectured in English literature at Durham University and we married a year later. My parents died long ago and I made my life here with Harry. We were very happy."

Debra paused and looked down.

Jasper used the silence to remove his jacket, revealing bright red braces cutting into a loose fitting white shirt, and draped it over his chair back. Pulling open the top drawer of his desk he produced a dictaphone.

"Do you mind?" he asked, "I take terrible notes."

Debra nodded distractedly.

"I struggled to maintain a pregnancy and it took so many years before one finally made it into the second trimester. Then, following a series of nose bleeds, Harry's leukaemia was picked up. Chemotherapy almost killed him, and I didn't think he would live to see his son born."

Jasper felt the warm tics pulling at his left eye. Fortunately Debra spent most of the time gazing into her lap, but nevertheless he felt compelled to rub his brows repeatedly. The self conscious awareness of his outward appearance at such close quarters to his client was making him uncomfortably moist beneath his shirt.

"You know, I could never explain to Ollie that his father had died. He was too young to understand and even remember Harry. As a consequence we have never grieved together, it has always been just me suffering, with little Ollie playing at my feet. He was such a precious child, my only living flesh and blood, my only memory of Harry. I promised him I would keep him safe, Mr Candle, no matter what, and I failed him."

Debra tried to stifle tears, swallowing hard and wiping her puffy eyes with the tissue. When she spoke again it was with a blocked nose.

"Despite my apprehensions about the MMR vaccine I took Ollie to have it. Harry believed in it and so did all the medical advice, so I trusted them. But it didn't save him, and I just don't understand why."

This time she sobbed and even Jasper felt a pang of sympathy for the grieving mother cloying at the back of his throat. Suddenly he wanted a whisky.

"Would you care for a drink?"

In the midst of a noisy nose blow, Debra looked up at Jasper in astonishment.

"I beg your pardon?"

"I keep whisky in my office. Would you like one? It may help."

Debra was taken aback by this suggestion.

"Well, OK," she replied.

"Neat, ice, water?" Jasper asked as he clinked crystal glasses together at the cabinet.

"On the rocks, please."

Seated back at his desk with the warming reassurance of Chivas lingering at the back of his mouth, Jasper was ready to continue.

"What happened to Ollie?" he asked.

Debra hadn't touched her whisky yet.

"Ollie was exposed to a child with measles at school and

despite having had his first MMR vaccine, he became infected. He got really sick and ended up in ICU with… "

Debra began to sob again. Jasper wanted to reach out and touch her gently on the shoulder.

"I'm sorry," she said, forcing herself to continue. "He developed encephalitis, and… he did not… recover."

Jasper looked down at his glass while Debra wiped and cleared herself. He was moved by the sadness in her voice and wondered if it was because it resonated so close to home.

"Do you have children, Mr Candle?"

The suddenness of the question surprised Jasper and he stumbled to an answer.

"No, not yet, unfortunately, no God forbids."

Jasper felt her eyes observe the bed in his office and he realised what conclusions she might be drawing from it. If only it was as simple as that.

"To lose a child as young and vulnerable as Ollie is the greatest burden of guilt and failure imaginable, Mr Candle. It is indescribable. And it's worse when you know that his death was avoidable, caused by someone else's irresponsibility."

Jasper's attention was immediately heightened.

"What exactly do you mean?" he asked, leaning forward.

"It's obvious, isn't it? A boy in Ollie's class, a boy whose parents had knowingly denied him the MMR vaccine, brought measles into the school. If that child had been vaccinated, as he should have been, this would not have happened. They effectively killed Ollie."

Debra's penetrating gaze held Jasper's for the first time.

Jasper scratched his head as his brain processed the permutations of her allegations. Was it against the law not to vaccinate a child? Was an unvaccinated child, or its parents, guilty of endangering members of society? Had a crime been committed? After all this was no trivial outcome, a healthy young boy was dead as a result. Could it be proved that the accused was responsible? These thoughts tumbled about in Jasper's head as he tried desperately to recall any pertinent legal precedents.

"This is quite an allegation, Mrs Kowalski," he said finally.

"My only son is dead. The boy who infected him, and many others at the school, is still alive. His negligent parents have a lot to answer for, in my opinion."

Jasper nodded thoughtfully and drained the last of his Chivas. Suddenly his arm jerked and swept the glass off his desk, sending ice cubes tumbling across the dark blue carpet. He felt Debra's eyes on him and wondered what she must be thinking. He decided not to even attempt an explanation and boldly ignored the incident. Wishing to shorten the awkward hesitation, he quickly met her eyes and continued.

"I am not even certain if it's compulsory for all children to be vaccinated in England, or whether any laws have been broken? I need to do some research into vaccination law and I will have to investigate, painstakingly, the events leading up to your son's illness. This would be a complex case, Mrs Kowalski, be under no misapprehensions about that."

"I want someone to pay for taking Ollie from me."

"This is a case quite possibly without precedent. I can make no promises."

"But can you help me?"

Jasper's gaze was held by her resolute and determined eyes. They had a power and intensity that disarmed him.

"I will do my very best. Help you I certainly can. What I cannot be certain of is the likely outcome, not until I have done more research."

"But what can you do for me, Jasper?"

It was the first time she had called him by his name. He liked how it sounded.

"In the normal course of events, if we prove our case, there will be the satisfaction of apportionment of blame. Verdicts will attract compensation which, though money can never replace Ollie, seeks to acknowledge your suffering. But most of all I can help you find closure through this process, closure that helps you to regain your life and begin again. I believe closure is essential in this process."

Jasper knew that this was going to be one of the biggest challenges of his career. From the outset he did not know whether he could even build a case against anyone, let alone a three year old boy. But he pitied Debra Kowalski's desperate situation, and he almost felt her pain.

"What's this other boy's name?" Jasper asked.

"Seamus Mallory."

*

It was late when Debra left and Jasper helped himself to more Chivas to quell the increasing irritability in his facial muscles. He reflected on the whisky glass incident, a worrying and socially embarrassing development. He banished concerns of potential professional consequences from his mind, not permitting himself to think that far.

Lying down on his black quilted corner bed, he picked up his iPhone. No calls from Jennifer. He dialled their home.

"*The Candles are out. Please leave a message after the beep.*"

Terminating the call, he dialled her mobile and was diverted to mailbox.

"Hi Jen. Been another long day, but you'll be pleased to know, a successful one. Be home soon. I'm not sure… where you are. Everything OK?"

He paused.

"Call me. Love you."

Why had Jennifer been down to Harley Street in London, he wondered? She had never mentioned anything when they had last spoken. And where was she now? Perhaps she had gone on from London to visit her sister down in Esher. His shoulders rolled in a brief contorted paroxysm and he cursed out loud.

"Brad Pitt, damn this chicken plucking thing."

Perhaps he too should see a doctor, he thought, staring at the cactus that never moved.

TEN

Jasper twisted self consciously in his chair, a padded leather high back, one of ten arranged in a very voyeuristic circle. The chair beside him was empty and Jasper kept glancing at it and then at his watch. His chair was positioned in front of the bay window in the large room and he liked to think that it was for the purpose of admiring the view behind him that the rest of the group looked constantly in his direction. But, of course, there was also the real reason why they were all looking at him.

"Welcome everyone. It's gone six thirty already, so we should begin," said a small man wearing a brown plaid jacket, green knitted tie and a warm fuzzy beard like a chipmunk. A simple white badge pinned to his lapel read 'Dr Montgolfier'. He pulled a pair of horn rimmed spectacles off his face and looked around the group, sucking on the curved end of the frame.

"We have a new member tonight and I would like to welcome him to our session," he continued, smiling broadly and gesturing towards Jasper with outstretched spectacles.

Jasper managed a weak smile and stared back at the varied faces leering at him from the accusing circle of chairs. He wondered if he seemed to them as unusual and weird as they looked to him. What on earth was he doing here? And where the hell was Lazlo, this was all his idea?

Jasper became aware of a patient silence and then realised that everyone was still peering at him expectantly.

"Well, introduce yourself and tell us a little about you," Montgolfier said, replacing the spectacles on his nose.

Jasper cleared his throat and, with a final nervous glance at the empty chair, faced the group.

"My name is Jasper. I am a little too close to fifty for comfort. I am a lawyer."

The group smiled in response and some made encouraging sounds.

"That's good, Jasper. Get it out," Montgolfier said rather patronisingly, with a phony grin.

"Well, here I am, for help, I guess. A friend and I agreed to do this together, but… he is… I'm not sure where he is," Jasper stumbled, waving a hand towards the empty chair.

Ripping his spectacles off his nose again and crossing his legs, Montgolfier leaned forward.

"Are you married, Jasper?"

"Yes."

"Are you happily married?" a raspy voice from Jasper's left asked.

"Now Brian, that's a little personal for the first five minutes," admonished Montgolfier, shaking his head with disapproval.

Jasper managed a weak smile and felt his face beginning to twist and pull under the spotlight. He rubbed, and he massaged, but he knew the corruptions would not dissipate.

"Don't mind Brian, he just knows the ropes," the counsellor said. "What kind of lawyer are you, Jasper?"

Jasper rubbed his twitching eye.

"I am a compensation lawyer, you know – negligence, hospital claims, accidents – that sort of thing."

"Like an ambulance chaser?" Brian's throaty voice cut in.

Jasper nodded meekly, not wishing to make eye contact with Brian.

"Don't worry, there are no doctors in this group," Montgolfier said jokingly as everyone laughed, breaking the nervous tension. "Apart from me that is." More laughter.

Jasper crossed his legs and folded his arms, closing up self consciously.

"Any children?" the counsellor asked.

Jasper's shoulder twitched twice and then rolled forwards. He had to move quickly to disguise the demonic contortion and began to feel perspiration breaking out on his upper lip.

"No, we've not managed any."

Jasper began to squirm under the interrogation. He had had misgivings about this right from the start and had only agreed to attend because Lazlo had been so persuasive and insistent.

"Right. So you must be a very busy man then."

Jasper wasn't sure if it was a question or a statement.

"He doesn't look happily married," Brian's gravelly voice interjected again.

"Brian, why don't you start now by telling Jasper a little about yourself, then we'll quickly go around the circle so Jasper knows everyone," Montgolfier said, returning the spectacles to his nose and flicking over a page on his clipboard.

Jasper felt a weight lift off him as the spotlight turned to another member of the group. The tic on his face was spreading and now his lips were curling ever so often. He could feel the perspiration under his arms and shifted about in his chair.

"I'm Brian, I'm forty one, and my wife left me for the

bricklayer who was building her a new kitchen. So now I live above a chippie on my own. I drink a bottle of wine a day, which is better than a month ago when it was a bottle of gin every day. I put that progress down to this group therapy with Dr Montgolfier and my new friendship with Mandy. Thank you, Mandy."

Brian looked warmly across the circle towards a petite woman with freckles and long, straight, orange hair. As all the other faces turned towards her she blushed deeply. Jasper cringed and cursed Lazlo.

"I think this illustrates that each one of us has stress points that can weaken under strain and why our dependence on alcohol can become a subterfuge. Now you know too, Jasper, why Brian asked you about your marriage?" Montgolfier said, pointing the frames of his spectacles first at Brian and then at Jasper.

Jasper nodded with a small forced smile.

"So, would you like to attempt Brian's question now, Jasper?" Montgolfier said.

Jasper avoided Montgolfier's intense but friendly eyes, glancing instead at Brian who sat smugly with arms folded.

"Am I happily married?" Jasper repeated the question, gazing down at his hands as they trembled in his lap, aware of the twitches eroding the dignity of his face. The question ricocheted about in his head and for a brief moment he became oblivious to the group staring at him. Normally he was the one asking difficult questions of others, manipulating their emotions and exploring their weaknesses.

He returned to the discomfort of his situation, under the scrutiny of strangers, with all his physical peculiarities on display for the leering group to gossip about. Worse than all of this, however, was that he felt unsure how to answer the question. He did not even know where his wife was, or who she was with, so an answer would be very speculative.

"Brad Pitt! I don't need this."

Jasper jumped to his feet and walked out of the room to a stunned silence. He was not embarrassed, but as multitudes of spasms rippled across his face and arm, in a satanic violation of his body, he felt uncomfortably hot with prickly humiliation.

*

Later that evening as he sat at his desk pouring over legal statutes, searching for legal cases involving vaccination disputes, Jasper noticed two messages awaiting him on his iPhone. The first was from Montgolfier.

I am sorry you felt the need to leave this evening's session. I am concerned about you, particularly in light of certain physical signs you were displaying. If you do not wish to return to group therapy, which is entirely at your own discretion, please take my advice and seek a medical opinion. I urge you not to ignore the problem.

Jasper deleted the message and savoured the glow of a mouthful of Chivas. He scrolled to the second with a deep frown. It was from Jennifer's sister in Esher.

Hi Jasper. I've been trying to get hold of you. Please call me, I'm concerned about Jennifer. Charlotte.

Jasper stared at the message without moving a muscle, except for the twitch of his left eyebrow, glancing at his wristwatch. It was 9pm.

"Sod it!" he said aloud. He could not understand why Jennifer would not call him herself. Why would her sister call when he had left countless messages for Jennifer over the past few days?

Jasper's fingers attacked the iPhone as he dialled Jennifer's number in frustration. It rang nine times before clicking to voicemail.

"Brad Pitt!" he muttered, staring at the cactus and taking another large mouthful of Chivas.

The afterglow of his reflective moment was interrupted by a loud knocking on the door to his offices.

ELEVEN

Magnus Burns was a tall, wiry man with a hawkish nose and a tousled mass of grey hair. He wore a knitted cream turtle neck shirt beneath a tailored, platinum Karl Lagerfeld suit, smelled of powerful musk and the only thing missing was a conducting baton in his hand.

Jasper ushered him in and offered him a drink.

"No, I don't want a drink. I want to know what is happening about my father's death."

Magnus spoke in manicured English, with just a hint of Teutonic inflection.

"There have been some interesting developments," Jasper said, pouring more whisky for himself at the corner cabinet.

"I have been away with the orchestra in Berlin and have just returned this evening, but I have heard nothing from you, Jasper."

Jasper returned to his desk and sat behind it. Magnus paced up and down on the plush blue carpet, turning every six or seven paces, and rubbing his chin as he did so.

"Our investigation is still underway, Magnus. There is a lot to discover about what happened."

"What do you mean, discover? What about my father's surgeon, this Mr Keys, surely you must concentrate there?"

Jasper shook his head and sat forward, parting his hands in the air.

"He's as clean as a Partick Thistle."

"I beg your pardon?" Magnus said.

"We can find no fault with the surgery, no fault with his medical care, and it does not seem likely that the surgeon is the root cause of your father's death."

Magnus' piercing blue eyes glowed as a puzzled look crossed his tanned face.

"But how can this be? My father had surgery, then suddenly died from major complications a few days later. He was a fit man, Jasper, as I recall anyhow, how else can something like that be explained?"

Jasper wagged his index finger.

"There are so many other aspects to consider. Patients in hospital are not just at the mercy of the surgeons, you know."

"What are you saying?"

"Let me explain. We have uncovered the fact that your father may well have been the victim of an outbreak of gastroenteritis on the ward. If so, that had absolutely nothing to do with his surgery."

"What?" Magnus said in disbelief. "Gastroenteritis? And you think this may have been the cause of his death?"

"We're looking into this possibility very seriously."

Magnus digested this unexpected revelation quietly, then sat down with a submissive creak from the leather chair in front of Jasper's desk.

"You know, I was not close to my father when he died. Apart from the fact that I travel a lot with the orchestra, we had fallen out over my second wife. Too many years passed during which we barely spoke. Life is filled with regrets, Jasper, as I'm sure you understand, and I regret not making amends before it was too late. I feel that this course of action is my only way of doing so now."

Jasper felt himself resonating with Magnus on this issue of paternal discord, for he too had not been close to his father when he had died. But closure had been more elusive for Jasper, because there was seemingly nobody to blame for his father's death, something which Jasper now pursued on an almost daily basis – blame, retribution, and closure.

"I can understand how you feel, Magnus, I will do all I can to help you resolve and close this painful chapter and to find a peace you can live with," Jasper said.

"Do you know who is responsible for the outbreak of gastroenteritis?" Magnus asked.

Jasper took a deep breath and sank back into his desk chair, cradling his whisky tumbler in cupped hands. That question really summed up both the strength and the gaping weakness in his case. Who indeed was responsible for the outbreak of gastroenteritis? Could it be whittled down to one person? An old patient with dementia from a care home would not make a likely defendant, whilst class actions were always so cumbersome and complex.

"I'll get to the bottom of it, that I promise you."

Magnus held Jasper's gaze.

"Where there is a will, there is a way." Magnus suggested.

"That's what my father used to tell me," Jasper replied with a thin smile.

"Thank you, thank you so much. Do you have enough money from my initial advance?"

Jasper gestured nonchalantly.

"Don't worry. I'll get Stacey to check in the morning, if we're running short she'll be in touch."

Jasper suddenly noticed something as he and Magnus moved on to discuss the orchestral tour of Germany. For once, his hand was not trembling. He put it down to the Chivas and submitted to another malty mouthful.

Lying back on the black quilted corner bed, Jasper dialled Jennifer's number again. The call was re-directed to voicemail.

"Friar Tuck!" Jasper cursed.

TWELVE

Dr Potter had metamorphosed from soft and cuddly children's doctor into uncompromising, unyielding professional adversary. He still wore a brightly themed Disney bowtie, but now the round, gold rimmed spectacles perched halfway down his nose created the impression of intellectual determination rather than eccentric affability. His smooth, bald pate reflected the bright fluorescent light from the ceiling, as he sat with hands clasped defiantly in front of his face.

"Yes, of course I recall the name Ollie Kowalski," Dr Potter said. "But I also recall the name Jasper Candle."

Jasper tried to appear friendly and relaxed as he sank into the chair in front of Potter's desk, but he hated surgeries, the smell of antiseptics and the possibility of unwanted revelations. The anatomical diagrams on the walls only served to remind him that beneath his unwanted and uncontrollable muscular spasms lurked a sinister labyrinth of body parts, amongst which lay the cause of his affliction. He wanted Potter to like him, to become talkative, informative, but he was frightened that the spasms and tics, which were totally beyond his control, might betray something to the ever watchful eyes of the astute doctor studying his every move.

"I'm only here on behalf of my client, Debra Kowalski, in which respect I am here exclusively to learn more about measles and vaccines, Dr Potter," Jasper replied.

"That may be, but your reputation precedes you, sir, and it is not reassuring from my perspective."

"We are both on the same side here, Dr Potter," Jasper said with an embracing gesture. "You treated Ollie when he was desperately ill, now I am trying to help his mother understand how and why Ollie got measles in the first instance."

Potter considered Jasper with a look of deep distrust and suspicion.

"I don't know how you talked my secretary into giving you an appointment, but knowing that you operate on a strictly profiteering basis I certainly hope for her sake that no money changed hands."

Jasper held his hands out in a gesture of clemency, then withdrew them quickly as he noticed the worsening tremor in his left hand.

"Please, Doctor, I am here only to learn about the medical condition that so tragically took Debra's, that is Mrs Kowalski's, only son from her. I have no axe to grind here, you have my word."

"A lawyer's word," Potter scoffed. "Okay, you've got twenty minutes."

"Thank you."

Jasper sat forward, not wanting to waste a precious second.

"Firstly, Ollie had been vaccinated with the MMR vaccine, right, so how did he then become infected with measles?" Jasper asked.

He had decided not to jeopardise his welcome further by pulling out a dictaphone, so Jasper sat instead with a yellow legal pad perched on his crossed knee. He looked uncomfortable and the pad shook erratically from the trembling in his left hand.

"Ollie did receive the first dose of MMR vaccine when he was around two years, quite correct. This is normally followed by a booster before the age of five. Some children will be fully immune to measles after the first MMR, but a significant minority may be vulnerable to developing measles if exposed to it before the booster."

"What sort of minority?"

"Let's say around ten percent," Potter said.

Jasper scribbled and sensed Potter's analytical gaze staring at the writhing in his wrist and hand.

"You see, vaccination works in two very different and important ways. Firstly, it protects the individual from developing the disease, but almost more importantly it reduces the pool of disease circulating in society, thereby reducing the likelihood of any individual becoming exposed to measles." Potter said, using his hands animatedly as he spoke.

"Is that what is called herd immunity?" Jasper asked.

Potter sat back with a wry smile and wagged a finger at Jasper.

"You see, Mr Candle, that is precisely the sort of insightful question that makes me uneasy about you."

Jasper managed a dismissive chuckle and shrugged his shoulders coyly.

"So vaccination doesn't necessarily prevent a child from developing measles?" Jasper said.

"Ollie was very unlucky. A healthy boy, vaccinated at the right time, ninety nine times out of a hundred would be perfectly safe. Circumstance played cruelly against the poor boy; if he hadn't come into contact with measles at such close quarters in school, it is very unlikely that he would ever have got measles."

"Yes, the boy at school with measles," Jasper mused, sucking on his pen. His mouth suddenly contracted into a series of three or four pouts that closed around the pen and pulled at his cheek. Jasper pulled the pen from his mouth and scratched at his cheek self consciously.

"He wasn't vaccinated with MMR," Jasper said.

"The boy with measles?" Potter asked.

"Yes."

"I wouldn't know. Is it relevant?"

Jasper paused.

"Is childhood vaccination compulsory in the UK, Doctor?"

Pushing his gold rimmed spectacles further up his bony nose, Potter sat forward.

"Now that is exactly the kind of question I expect from a compensation lawyer. That is where the money comes into it."

Jasper ignored the remark.

"Debra Kowalski is very interested to know if her son died because of someone's negligent failure to vaccinate their children with the MMR vaccine. I see this as relevant to the health of the wider public, Doctor. How many other children out there are at unnecessary risk?"

Potter sat back, surprised and caught unprepared by Jasper's retort. Jasper decided to press home the slight advantage he perceived.

"I am struggling to see where the rights of an individual actually infringe on the rights of society. Surely there must be a boundary, if not legal, then at the very least ethical?" Jasper said.

Potter tapped his fingers together thoughtfully in front of his face, his eyes not moving from Jasper's reassured gaze, albeit corrupted occasionally by obtrusive tics.

"You're into deep waters here, Mr Candle, very controversial ones too. Vaccination is not compulsory in the UK, not currently anyway, but the issue is very divisive."

"Meaning the law might change?" Jasper asked.

"Meaning the rate of MMR vaccination uptake is falling, probably because of negative publicity causing parental concerns and mistrust. Doctors and politicians are debating how to increase uptake and in many countries, yes, vaccination is compulsory."

"So challenging the existing laws would be well timed," Jasper remarked, ~~scribbling untidily on the legal pad~~.

"You'd face a mountainous task to change public health policy."

"With sufficient effort, application, and determination… " Jasper said, almost hearing his father's voice echoing in his head.

Potter glanced at his watch.

"Is there sufficient reason for parents to refuse the MMR? I mean, is measles a dangerous disease?" Jasper continued quickly.

"Measles is a more dangerous disease than many realise. A child with measles has a one in 3000 chance of dying, the risks of anything similar from having the MMR vaccine is one in a million. To me, as a health professional, this is a no brainer."

"Except, Doctor, that Debra Kowalski wants to know why her vaccinated child died from measles."

Potter reflected on this for a moment, studying Jasper thoughtfully, before adjusting the spectacles on his nose and leaning forward.

"Notwithstanding your primary motivations here, Mr Candle, I believe you are quite possibly on the right track.

History tells us that there is a potential public health time bomb ticking out there. In the 1970's, misconceptions about whooping cough vaccinations led to a massive drop in uptake, producing a huge pool of unprotected children. Cases of whooping cough soared into the thousands, and dozens of children died as a direct result."

"Do you think that gives me sufficient ethical mandate, in your eyes, to pursue this case of possible negligence?" Jasper asked, trying to hold back his sarcasm.

"Ethically, perhaps so, but to pursue an individual for negligence in a case like this is, I would imagine, without precedent. You're in unchartered waters, Mr Candle, and I can't decide whether I find the notion despicable, or admirable."

Jasper smiled.

"Despicable I'm quite accustomed to, Doctor. Admirable, on the other hand, would be unusual."

THIRTEEN

Jasper cradled a paper cup of steaming coffee in both hands as he rested his elbows on the worn stone parapet of Prebends Bridge. The 250 year old tri-arched sandstone bridge across the tranquil waters of the River Wear languished between the dense canopies of golden beech and oak trees that formed a collar on each bank beneath Durham Cathedral's majestic spires. Jasper's eyes drifted lazily towards the rolling figure of Lazlo, who was trying to heave his bloated body across the bridge with a semblance of speed towards him.

"Morning guv'nor," Lazlo said cheerily as he wheezed to a halt.

"You bar steward, you dental flosser, you Khyber Pass you," Jasper retorted, with barely more than a twitch of disdain across his face.

"Sorry, guv, something very important came up."

"You stood me up, you bottomless pit."

"What was it like?" Lazlo asked cautiously, trying to strike a placatory tone as he stood beside Jasper and placed his huge arms on the parapet as he tried to catch his breath.

"It was hell," Jasper said, turning away from Lazlo to drink coffee. "And it was your idea."

"Sorry guv."

"Friar Tuck Lazlo, how could you do that to me?"

Lazlo lowered his head, realising he should give Jasper a moment to calm himself. His eyes wandered down the stone wall in front of him and came to rest on the engraving bearing Sir Walter Scott's infamous description of Durham Cathedral.

Grey towers of Durham
Yet well I love thy mixed and massive piles
Half church of God, half castle 'gainst the Scot
And long to roam these venerable aisles
With records stored of deeds long since forgot

"I was drinking with the matron again last night," Lazlo said eventually, with his head still bowed as he contemplated Scott's deeply etched words.

Jasper stifled a snort.

"So I went to AA and you went drinking. Bloody marvellous."

Lazlo let Jasper vent his anger and waited for it to subside.

"What did she say?" Jasper asked after draining his coffee.

Lazlo looked up, but Jasper was gazing across the flat water at a group of white T-shirt clad rowers being put through their paces.

"As a general rule, medical admissions do not go to surgical wards."

"Because they try and keep them apart?" Jasper asked.

Lazlo nodded his huge fat head and the single broad pewter band that he wore through his right ear lobe wobbled.

"Surgeons don't want sick patients with infectious diseases near their recuperating surgical patients. Stands to reason, I suppose."

"I can see that. So what happened in Edward Burns' case?" Jasper said.

Lazlo exhaled loudly and turned to Jasper.

"We know that the hospital was very full that night, emergency admissions do not get turned away… "

"Why not?" Jasper interrupted.

"They can't refuse to treat the sick, guv, that's what they're there to do," Lazlo said.

"Even at the expense of risking other patients in the hospital?"

Lazlo was used to this devil's advocate adversarial role that Jasper always assumed, as though he was arguing a point in court.

"Who is going to decide which patients should be turned away, guv?"

"More to the point, Lazlo," Jasper said, turning to face him for the first time with a glint in his eye, "who decided to admit that sick patient to a surgical ward, against procedure?"

Lazlo inclined his head and raised one eyebrow.

"Well, I've not established that any procedural rules were broken, not yet anyway. A sick patient needs a bed in hospital, guv. Hospital policy is that you make space where you can."

"Tell that to Edward Burns' family. I had his son in my office last night wanting to know why we haven't sued anybody yet."

Lazlo paused.

"Who do you think we're after in this case, guv?"

Jasper shrugged his shoulders and turned away to look down the river towards Framwellgate Bridge. Beneath them, eight oarsmen synchronously powered their lacquered spruce rowing boat with practised splashes through the Prebends central arch.

"I initially thought we'd be after the surgeon: after all, Edward Burns died from complications of his surgery. But it seems he's in the clear. We could sue the sick, old patient who brought gastroenteritis on to the ward… " Jasper trailed off as he considered his words.

"That would be impossible." Lazlo said.

"Why?"

"She died."

"From tommy guns?" Jasper's eyebrows creased into a questioning v-shape.

"She had a stroke."

Jasper's iPhone began to ring in his pocket. He ignored it as he stared intently ahead.

"What we need to know is who made the decisions to place her, as a clear and evident contamination risk to all the surgical patients, on that ward. Was it a casualty doctor, a matron, a duty manager? Somebody must have made that decision. Magnus Burns wants to know who it was and I want to know who it was."

"Your phone, guv," Lazlo said, pointing at Jasper's jacket.

Jasper brushed him off and shook his head.

"You need to find out who made that decision."

A familiar tic began to curl the eyelids on the left of Jasper's face; once, twice, three times, then a violent inclination of the head towards his shoulder.

The phone stopped ringing.

"There is another side to this, guv."

Lazlo turned towards the river, watching the eight oarsmen receiving instruction from their coach, who stood straddling his rusty old bicycle on the riverbank. He could not hear what the coach was saying, but there was a lot of jagged gesticulation.

Jasper wanted to say "yes" but the word wouldn't come out,

as though he had developed a sudden immutable stammer, paralysing his speech. A panic rose quickly within him as he realised the word he so wanted to say was stubbornly trapped inside of him. A tic ravaged his face and he rubbed at it with a balled fist.

"Edward Burns wasn't the only patient to become infected with gastroenteritis on that ward," Lazlo said.

Jasper shot a penetrating look across at him.

"Five patients were affected by it, as well as several nurses and a junior doctor," Lazlo said slowly for effect.

Jasper rubbed his face in vain. He wanted desperately to leave the meeting, to escape with his dignity intact, but he could not tear himself away from Lazlo's revelations.

"What's more… are you all right, guv?"

Lazlo had tried to ignore the facial spasms and occasional twisting of Jasper's neck, but he could no longer pretend he had not noticed that something was amiss.

"It's nothing, just…" Jasper stammered, lowering his head in embarrassment.

"What guv?"

Jasper took a deep breath, stared skywards, and then concentrated on speaking slowly.

"I'm… cream crackered, that's all. I need a… good night's… Bo-Peep."

"When last did you go home, guv?"

Jasper made dismissive gestures with his hands and turned away.

"What else… did you find out?" Jasper said.

Lazlo hesitated as he considered the unusual movements that Jasper was trying so hard to conceal.

"Oh yes, Edward Burns was located in bay four on the

ward, and the old lady with gastroenteritis was in bay one, a good fifty feet and several walls and doors away."

Jasper absorbed this information without revealing anything.

"You're saying it was the ward staff... who spread the infection throughout the ward... and to the other patients?" Jasper managed to say, in a slow and thick voice.

"Who else?"

"That's surely very poor... hygienic practice." Jasper mused.

"Few would disagree with that. Have you seen all the advertising in hospitals these days, urging everyone to wash their hands?" Lazlo said.

"Did the ward staff effectively cause Edward Burns' death then?" Jasper suggested.

Jasper's phone rang again. He pulled a face of intense frustration, then suddenly realised it might be Jennifer. Extracting the phone from his breast pocket he stared in deep thought at the illuminated screen.

"Important?" Lazlo asked.

"It's just Stacey, I'll call her in a moment. I want you to find out everything about hygiene policy on the wards, Lazlo. They have a term for the nursing of infected patients on hospital wards which is supposed to prevent the spread of contagious infections." Jasper's voice was coming back to him.

"Barrier nursing," Lazlo said, deadpan.

Jasper began to pace up and down, extending an index finger as he thought.

"It could be important to establish which one of the ward staff was the first to catch the tommy guns from that patient. I want to know about how the barrier nursing failed and how so many people subsequently became infected. I also want to know who made the decision to admit that sick patient to a surgical ward."

"Anything else, guv?" Lazlo said sarcastically, with a subtle shake of his meaty head.

Jasper ignored him, continuing to pace up and down. Did the repetitive movement ease the tics, he wondered, or did it just help to hide them?

"There'll be a lot of closing of ranks," Lazlo said.

"I hope you and this matron get on really well. You'll need an insider."

Lazlo scoffed.

"I'm going to need more than that. It'll be like trying to break into Fort bloody Knox."

"I'm moved to tears, I am," Jasper said placing his elbows on the stone parapet, the left arm twitching as though an electric current was torturing it. "And that's not all, I have another assignment for you."

Lazlo rolled his eyes.

"Another job?"

"Yes," Jasper replied, without hesitation. "I have a new client whose three year old son died from measles. The boy attended Bailey School and the mother says he caught the measles from another boy at school called Seamus Mallory."

Lazlo had pulled a notepad out from his jacket pocket and was scribbling furiously with a stubby pencil that almost completely disappeared between his fleshy fingers.

"I need all of this information confirmed, as well as whether the Mallory kid had been vaccinated with MMR."

"M – M – ?" Lazlo repeated as he scribbled.

"MMR – measles, mumps and rubella. It's a standard pre-school vaccination. Got it?"

Lazlo nodded.

"I'll do my best, guv."

Jasper studied his phone as he tried in vain to rub away the distortions on his face and neck. He read the message from Stacey.

Mr C, your wife's sister has been calling and calling, she's trying desperately to reach you. She sounds very upset and says it's urgent. And another thing – Mrs K is in hospital. Please call back.

Jasper froze and wondered why on earth Jennifer's sister was so persistent in trying to reach him. He had not spoken to her for at least a year, not since last Christmas when he was obliged to thank her for yet another set of braces she had sent, probably at Jennifer's behest. Her calls must be about Jennifer, what else could they be about? Jennifer was staying with her, was she not, so why did Jennifer not call him back herself? Had something happened to her?

Suddenly, the unanswered phone calls and lack of contact over several days struck a chord of concern deep within Jasper and he felt his heartbeat increase.

"Everything OK, guv?" Lazlo asked.

Jasper nodded as he scrolled through his missed messages and found the one he had ignored on the bridge minutes earlier.

"Mrs Kowalski is in hospital," Jasper said absently.

"Mrs who?"

"The mother of the three year old who died of measles."

"Why?" Lazlo said.

Jasper did not answer as he listened to the missed call with a look of disbelief crossing his face.

"Jasper, it's Charlotte here. I've been trying to contact you for

days. I'm really worried about Jennifer, she's not been returning my calls and I haven't spoken to her for a week. I was expecting a visit from her after her trip to London but she never turned up. What's going on? Has something happened? Is she all right? I'm so worried about her, please call me."

Jasper felt the colour drain from his face. All this time he had thought Jennifer was staying with her sister. Until now, he had not thought too much of the fact that she was not returning his calls; he too had not exactly been terribly attentive recently with court cases demanding his attention. But the fact that she was not returning even her sister's calls, for she and Lottie were close, was very out of character for Jennifer.

"What's the matter, guv?" Lazlo asked again.

Jasper paused as the facial tic twisted his face and pinched his eyelids together.

"Something's wrong."

"Mrs… er… whatever her name is?" Lazlo ventured.

"No, my missus. Jennifer has been uncontactable for too many days now. I must find out where she is."

"Is she not at home, guv?"

"I haven't been there for quite a while, Lazlo, but she's not answering the phone."

Suddenly Jasper began to move, walking purposefully across the bridge. Lazlo stared after him, a frown creased into his ample features.

"Where are you going, guv?"

"Home. I need to go home, Lazlo, something's not right."

Lazlo pocketed his notepad and short pencil and began to lurch across the bridge in pursuit of Jasper.

"I'm coming with you, guv."

FOURTEEN

Dr Timothy Potter listened intently as the speaker on stage explained in passionate detail his concerns over the impending vaccination crisis. Potter was attending a national meeting on current challenges facing General Practitioners in the United Kingdom. The speaker, standing behind a gleaming glass and chrome lectern, was none other than the chairman of the British Medical Association.

Professor McAndrews was a short, slightly overweight man dressed in a black suit. His vocal delivery was measured, emphatic and struck right at Potter's heart.

"As GP's you are facing an outbreak of measles on a scale never before seen in this country." McAndrews said, indicating a graph projected on to the enormous white screen behind him.

"In 2007, there were 990 cases of measles, in 2008 there were 1350, and in 2009, you will see an estimated 1600 cases."

Potter scribbled frantic notes on a pad in his lap. His gold rimmed spectacles were balanced halfway down his sharp nose, enabling him to both peer over them to see Professor McAndrews and the screen and also to focus on the notes balanced on his legs.

"Almost all cases of measles are in children who have not received the MMR vaccine, this is currently estimated to be one in five children across the UK."

McAndrews paused and studied the attentive faces in his audience. He gripped the podium with both of his hands and rocked slightly on his heels, as though he were riding a steed, his quick eyes active beneath a learned head of greying hair.

"The irony of this situation we all face is that the seven years leading up to this impending catastrophe saw worldwide deaths from measles fall by seventy five percent, due to the success of international vaccination programmes."

He paused again and leaned forward even closer to his captive audience.

"Do you know how many children died worldwide from measles in those seven years? I'll tell you, ladies and gentlemen, it was 197 000. 197 000! I'd like to see that figure printed in tomorrow's tabloids."

He drank a little water from a glass on the podium before continuing.

"Now, I know that each and every one of you in this audience today wants to know what can be done to head off this impending measles epidemic. I'm going to tell you what I think should be done."

Potter scribbled, unable to take his eyes off the startling figures up on the screen and thinking all the while about Ollie Kowalski and even about Jasper Candle's visit to his surgery just days earlier. Following that visit he had seen this meeting advertised and suddenly felt compelled to attend.

"We do not have to re-invent the wheel here, we simply need to follow the established models of so many other countries: the USA, Spain, Australia. Yes, ladies and gentlemen, I believe we must move to make childhood vaccination… compulsory."

A hushed murmur emanated from the audience and

several delegates thrust their hands high in the air. McAndrews picked them out one by one with a raised forearm.

"I know what you all wish to ask me. How would we ever hope to police a compulsory vaccination programme? Well, the answer is very simple. Childhood vaccination, and in this specific case, MMR, becomes a pre-requisite for admission to school. It becomes a health and safety issue for the paramount safety of all children at school. No MMR, no entry to school."

Potter found a wry smile creeping across his face as he thought of Jasper Candle's analytical remarks in his office. The lecture ended to rapturous applause and an announcement of a coffee break. Potter rose quickly, grabbing awkwardly at papers and pencils falling off his lap. He was desperate to catch Professor McAndrews during the interval.

Potter managed to corner the ever popular professor cradling a cup of coffee and trying to devour a crumbling Danish pastry with as much elegance as possible. Up close, Professor McAndrews was even shorter than he appeared behind a podium, which is where most people only ever got to see him. Potter weaved in between the bodies of delegates, packed like sardines and cradling cups of tea and coffee. The room was filled with the smell of coffee and the murmur of dozens of conversations blurred into one.

"Professor?" Potter said with raised eyebrows, hoping to invite an audience with the great man.

McAndrews gesticulated and mumbled behind lips encrusted with sticky pastry. His sharp eyes darted down to Potter's lapel badge, identifying him by name and area of practice.

"I'm Timothy Potter, from Claypath in Durham."

"Yes, I know," McAndrews said, pointing at Potter's badge with the half eaten pastry and a sardonic smile.

"If I may, Professor, I have a very interesting situation developing back in Durham. One of my patients died recently from measles encephalitis…"

"So tragic and unnecessary, but this is what the public don't realise will happen ever more often," McAndrews interrupted, nodding his grey head.

"The thing is that I've had a visit from a medico-legal solicitor, a compensation lawyer, who is considering a case of negligence against the family of an unvaccinated child who infected the victim with measles."

McAndrews raised his eyebrows but said nothing as he chewed.

"I'm not sure if there is a precedent for such a prosecution under vaccination law, is there?" Potter continued.

McAndrews wiped his mouth on a small serviette and managed to spill some coffee into the saucer.

"In the USA it is not unusual, there were 800 prosecutions in one year alone in Maryland. In England, however, you'd have to go back about 100 years."

Potter was surprised, as he did not think there had ever been prosecutions in England against individuals who had failed to vaccinate. His outward astonishment prompted the professor to continue.

"It was 1903, the Ashton vaccination prosecutions."

"And the outcome?"

McAndrews chuckled and sipped at his coffee.

"The public outcry was such that it effectively marked the end of vaccination prosecutions. A typically emotional and sentimental reaction, just as has happened in recent times with the misguided and damaging media campaign against MMR. Of course, much has transpired since 1903 and worldwide successes of vaccination programmes like polio and smallpox have firmly established vaccines as safe and effective in improving human health."

It was a noted behaviour of professors that, whenever they spoke to anyone, there was an instinctive tendency to lecture. Potter merely nodded affably in agreement.

"Well, his timing is very appropriate. We need ninety five percent of children to be vaccinated to maintain herd immunity safely. Latest figures I have indicate MMR vaccination levels down at eighty five percent. Too low, Timothy, too low, dangerously low. An epidemic is inevitable and almost unavoidable at this stage."

"Do you think Parliament will back a compulsory vaccination programme?" Potter asked.

McAndrews smiled wryly and reached into his suit pocket, producing a small, white card.

"Democracies have their weaknesses, I'm afraid. Please give my card to this solicitor and feel free to give him a copy of my lecture as well."

And with that the professor turned to another group demanding his attention, their meeting summarily terminated. Potter pocketed the card thoughtfully. In a strange and inexplicable way, he found himself emboldened by Jasper Candle's involvement, a notion that both encouraged and displeased him in equal measure.

FIFTEEN

The drive to Jasper's house took about fifteen minutes, ending in a winding country lane outside Durham. He lived on a steep hillside that overlooked the River Browney as it snaked peacefully through verdant hedgerow lined pastures on the river's fertile flood plain. A single, small lane lined with neatly kept Georgian brick homes wallowed peacefully in the midst of rural idyll.

"I've never seen your house before, guv." Lazlo remarked, nodding in approval as Jasper's black Audi TT crunched to a halt on the gravelled drive.

Jasper turned off the engine and stared at the house for a moment. The curtains were drawn, the white panelled garage doors shut, and it appeared as if nobody was home. The front lawn was neatly manicured and trimmed along the pathways, exuding an impression of tranquil normality, while all around them birds twittered in the chestnut trees that swayed harmoniously in a gentle breeze.

But Lazlo's inquisitive eyes missed nothing; at a glance he knew that the postcard suburban bubble was not what it appeared to be.

"Look, guv," he said, pointing towards the doorstep.

Jasper's edgy eyes followed Lazlo's sausage-like index finger to the collection of milk bottles standing guard beside the coir mat. One, two, three, four, five pint bottles, he counted.

"A pint a day?" Lazlo asked, turning to Jasper, who sat ashen faced in the driver seat playing nervously with the car keys.

Jasper nodded, biting his lower lip that had begun to pull sideways rhythmically.

"And a daily newspaper," Jasper said.

Protruding from the letterbox were several rolled up newspapers with a few mail items tucked randomly in between.

Jasper opened the car door and crunched on to the gravel, his footsteps the only sound disturbing the tranquillity of the breeze and the chattering birds. The crisp winter air smelled of moss and wood smoke that curled from neighbouring chimneys. On a whim, Jasper pressed the remote control that operated the garage door. It clattered into life and began to rise noisily. Hearing Lazlo climb out of his car, Jasper turned towards his investigator and from the grave look on Lazlo's face his unease grew even deeper.

"Give me the keys, guv," Lazlo said.

Jasper watched in astonishment as Lazlo's meaty hands reached inside his spacious, brown leather jacket and extracted a compact black pistol.

"Lazlo?" he queried, as a look of puzzlement washed over his face. His movements felt thick and slow, his brain stuck in treacle, but despite this his heart was beating incredibly fast.

"You didn't see this," Lazlo said, glancing at the illegal pistol and shaking his head, "now, please give me the keys, guv."

Jasper turned and looked into the open garage, which revealed Jennifer's matching silver Audi TT. He winced, unable to rationalise the contradiction – Jennifer's car was home but she was not. Jasper began to walk to the front door, lurching slightly and fumbling with keys in his pocket. Lazlo drew level with him beside a pair of standard white roses and placed a restraining hand on his shoulder. Their eyes met silently for a moment.

"The keys, please guv."

Lazlo's fleshy hand was waiting, palm up, in front of Jasper.

His eyes darting between the small, oily smelling Beretta pistol and Lazlo's palm, Jasper was suddenly overcome with a sense of bewilderment.

"What's going on, Lazlo?"

"I'll have a look and we'll see," Lazlo said in a calm, reassuring tone.

"I want to go inside," Jasper said.

"I'll go in first, guv."

After what seemed like minutes, Jasper finally dropped the keys into Lazlo's palm with a deep sigh, feeling his face dissolve into a staccato salvo of warm tics. This time, though, he did not have the inclination or self awareness to rub them or attempt to cover them.

Lazlo moved smoothly to the front door and fiddled with the keys, his great bulky frame filling the neat white timber portico. Finally, a key opened the door and he cautiously pushed it open, gripping the Beretta tightly, though he did not know why. Lazlo didn't go far, he just stood and stared.

"Well, what is it?" Jasper asked. His voice was tight and flat.

Lazlo turned back to the pallid face of his boss who was staring at him expectantly, fear visible in his pained eyes. His face bore a look Jasper had never seen before.

"Don't go in, guv."

Lazlo took a step back but was too late to stop Jasper, who suddenly rushed forward and barged in. Jasper's thumping heart was in his throat and he felt a dragging sensation deep in his bladder, as though he could soil himself at any moment.

The sight that met Jasper in his beige carpeted hallway almost knocked the breath right out of him. A visceral moan wheezed from his throat as it closed in on him. His knees weakened and he felt his bladder yield.

"My God! Oh my God! Jennifer, what have you done?"

Hanging hideously from a rope was the engorged body of Jennifer Candle. Jasper stared in horror and disbelief. His eyes travelled from the rope, tied crudely to the landing banister, down to her glazed, staring eyes, swollen purple-black face and tongue, framed by clean, straight, golden hair. The rope twisted her head grotesquely to one side above a sleek, red, knee length dress, her once shapely legs discoloured and blotchy from the lividity of pooled blood no longer able to defy gravity. Finally, his eyes came to rest on her lifeless feet pointing towards the floor. One fluffy slipper had fallen to the carpet and lay in a pool of oily straw coloured body fluid that dripped off Jennifer's painted toenails.

"I'm so sorry, guv," Lazlo said softly, rather sheepishly tucking the Beretta back into his jacket.

"Why? Jennifer, why did you do this?" Jasper cried, finding it difficult to breathe.

The central heating was on and in the dry, contained heat the smell of fresh decay was almost tangible in the stagnant air. Jasper stared with disbelief at his wife's body, trying to recall when he had last held her warmly in his arms. He could not remember and now it was too late.

"We should go outside, guv."

Jasper kept looking up at her face, at those hollow, empty eyes staring at him, accusing him perhaps. He was overcome with a rush of remorse and guilt that sliced deep into his heart. Suddenly Jasper turned and rushed outside, bending over the manicured lawn as he retched and dripped sour, coffee flavoured vomit.

Lazlo took a few steps into the house and glanced around, looking for something, anything, he did not know what. But there was nothing, no sounds, no mess, no indication of a disturbance. The house inside was perfect in every way, not a single thing out of place.

The investigator in him suddenly kicked in and he decided that he must look around before the police arrived. Walking through the rooms, his eyes searched for anything unusual. In the spotless kitchen he found a cold cup of tea beside the kettle whilst the milk in an adjacent jug had curdled and separated.

The master bedroom upstairs was neat, the emperor size bed made up and the gold quilt untouched In the en-suite bathroom he found evidence in the toilet bowl of vomit that had not been flushed away.

But search as he did, Lazlo could not find a note or a letter anywhere.

SIXTEEN

"He's a private investigator, I'm telling you," Mandy said.

Mandy was dressed in a light blue tunic, with red and black pens protruding from a breast pocket beside a post-box red plastic fob watch. Her yellow lapel badge read 'Staff Nurse Mandy Shaw'. She emitted an overpowering smell of sweet perfume.

"How do you know that?" Billie said, leaning her beach ball frame back in the reclining desk chair in her small office. The dark blue tunic strained at every crease around her midriff.

"I saw him coming out of this solicitor's office, not just once either."

Mandy's ink black hair was pulled back from her overly tanned face and tied tightly at the back of her head. A pair of white, narrow framed spectacles were pushed right up her thin, shapely nose, accentuating her hazelnut eyes.

Matron Billie Gibson shook her head with a wry smile on her round face.

"You've an overactive imagination, girl," she laughed.

"What have you told him?"

Billie's smile vanished.

"What do you mean?"

"I know you two have been out. My Stevie saw you with him at The Shakespeare on Friday night."

Billie's face flushed slightly and her assured gaze faltered.

"Lazlo is just a guy, a good laugh, that's all."

"How did you find him?" Mandy persisted, leaning forward.

Billie hesitated and looked across towards the piles of light brown patient case notes bound with elastic bands on her desk. In the centre stood a single framed photograph of a boy of around twelve years, with the same spherical build as his mother.

"Actually he found me…"

"There! I told you, he's after something. I bet it's to do with Mr Burns. You know how the managers have been all over us about that case, wanting to know everything." Mandy said triumphantly, wagging an index finger knowingly in the air.

Billie opened her mouth to speak but paused for a moment.

"I really think you're jumping to conclusions, Mandy."

Mandy shook her head dismissively.

"I just know he's an investigator and Stevie agrees with me. What does he talk about?"

"Whatever, all sorts of stuff. We like the same sort of beer, the same music, we both love food and…"

"Does he ask about work?" Mandy said.

Billie screwed up her face. Her small button nose wrinkled up and took ten years off her features, aged by deep worry lines around her forehead and eyes and framed by black hair streaked with grey invaders.

"Sometimes, I suppose. But he's interested in me, so why would he not want to know about what I do?"

"Have you asked him what he does?" Mandy said.

"Something to do with the council, housing I think."

"What, with binoculars in his car and a camera with a long lens?" Mandy said dismissively.

"How do you know that?" Billie asked.

"Stevie."

Mandy contemplated her senior colleague for a moment, the fire of determination still burning brightly in her face.

"Have you two…?" Mandy asked quickly and with a cheeky smile, making twirly motions in the air with her index finger.

Billie blushed warmly.

"That's none of your business," Billie said with mock seriousness, before bursting into shy laughter.

Mandy covered her open mouth with her hand and sat back in the hardback chair.

"Oh my God. You won't even remember what you've told him then."

"Of course I do," Billie protested.

Mandy shook her head slowly from side to side.

"Pillow talk, Billie. Everyone gives away secrets in bed. What has he asked you about?"

Billie shifted uncomfortably in her seat and thought for a moment before replying.

"We have talked about procedures on the ward, hygiene and stuff, how we practice barrier nursing… oh my God…"

"Does he know about Edward Burns?" Mandy said, leaning forward and narrowing the gap between her and Billie.

Silence as Billie's deadpan face revealed nothing of the frenzied chaos in her brain. Suddenly she lowered her head.

"Yes," she barely whispered

Mandy gasped.

"Shit, Billie. I'm telling you, they know, he's digging for evidence."

Billie's expression was now sombre as she bit the inside of her cheek thoughtfully. Had Lazlo simply been using her to gather information? Had she perhaps compromised herself and her staff by taking him into her confidence? Desperately she tried to recall some of their conversations in her mind as she felt a cold shiver dance up her spine. Was it even remotely possible that she and her staff could be held responsible for the death of a patient, for Edward Burns' death? She had been worried, but now she was scared.

SEVENTEEN

Debra Kowalski stared indifferently at her arms as she contemplated the question. She was sitting up in a very neatly made hospital bed, with the sheet and woven powder blue blanket pulled up to her waist, her arms lying limply at her sides. Debra studied the clear plastic intravenous tube that snaked its way down to her wrist, entering her pale, silky skin through a pink cannula. On the other arm she wore a light green identity bracelet bearing her name, date of birth and hospital number in hand written block lettering.

"Why did you do it?" Dr Montgolfier had asked her. "Why did you swallow all those pills?"

Her mind was too numb to think clearly and her head seemed to hang forward slightly, barely defying gravity. Debra breathed in deeply, aware of little beyond the insipid smell of starched linen and floor polish. The stark white room looked and smelled as bland and sterile as she felt inside.

"This room needs flowers, don't you think." Debra said eventually, continuing to stare at her flaccid arms.

Dr Montgolfier crossed his chocolate brown, corduroy clad legs, pulled the spectacles off his nose and sucked one of the curved ends. In the breast pocket of his dark green tweed jacket, a pair of silver pens peeped out.

"Do you have family in America?" he asked, glancing down at the notes in his lap.

Debra shook her head.

"My parents died long before I came to England, and I am an only child."

"What about extended family?"

Debra pulled a face of disapproval.

"Somewhere in the mid west, but we were never close. I doubt they even know I've lost Harry, let alone…"

Montgolfier replaced the spectacles on his nose and flipped over a page of the notes in his lap.

"Why did you go to the Bailey School yesterday?"

Debra shrugged like a petulant teenager. She wondered whether the fluid dripping into her arm was reversing the effects of the powerful tablets she had swallowed and what would happen if she pulled the tube out. Would the tablets once again exert their soporific effect?

"I suppose I wanted to see that boy," Debra said in a monotone drone.

"Seamus Mallory?"

Debra nodded.

"You blame him for the death of your son?"

Debra looked up, her piercing eyes narrowing and glaring at Montgolfier. It was the most animated that he'd seen her.

"Who else is there to blame, Doctor? He is the boy who infected my Ollie with measles, which you know is the reason he… was taken from me."

"I know about the terrible loss you've suffered, Debra. I'm trying to understand why you blame a three year old boy."

"And his parents," Debra said quickly.

Montgolfier sucked his spectacles again and frowned.

"His parents?"

"They chose not to have him vaccinated with MMR, that is the reason he caught measles and brought it into the school. It's reckless, don't you think, irresponsible, a decision that endangered all the children at school."

Montgolfier took a deep breath as he made a brief note.

"I want you to know that I understand your pain and the grief you are suffering from the loss not only of your son, but of your husband also. I am just not sure that pursuing a course of revenge is going to help you to come to terms with it all."

Debra held his gaze.

"It's not revenge, Doctor, it's closure. That's what I desperately need."

Montgolfier pursed his lips and nodded thoughtfully.

"Do you not think it is wrong that a child and his parents can be allowed to play Russian roulette with the lives of other children? Is this acceptable behaviour in a civilized society?" Debra added.

"My concern is not society's problems, it is your problems, Debra," Montgolfier said gesticulating at her with his spectacles.

"I've been to see a medico-legal solicitor who deals with personal injury claims like this, who assures me that I will find closure through this process. He thinks I have a good case, a worthy case," Debra said.

"I just think that pursuing this protracted course of action keeps the wounds raw, keeps the hurt fresh and in the present. Is that going to help you?"

Montgolfier seated the spectacles on his nose, then adjusted them and peered into the case notes.

"I can't forget my husband and beautiful son, Doctor, if

that's what you're implying. Pretending that nobody is to blame is certainly not going to give me a normal life again. I have lost everything and I will do anything to honour their memory. Closure, Mr Candle told me, is a very valuable end result of apportioning blame."

Montgolfier looked up suddenly, removing his spectacles again.

"Jasper Candle?" he surprised himself by saying.

"Do you know him?" Debra asked.

Montgolfier suddenly realised he was at risk of breaching confidentiality and cursed his unguarded outburst.

"I've heard of him," he said casually, looking away.

"They say he is the best, that is why I went to him."

Montgolfier sucked his spectacles and played with his beard.

"I don't doubt that, Debra. I just want you to consider whether blame and retribution is the route to the closure that you seek. Hope is a good thing. Revenge, on the other hand, I'm not so sure about."

Debra leaned back on the pillows behind her, twisting her wrist back and forth as she studied it.

"To answer your earlier question, Doctor, about the way I felt yesterday, seeing that boy so carefree outside the school, running to his mother, laughing, and knowing that they took my Ollie away from me without a thought, let alone a consequence. I was overcome with a sense of desperation and emptiness that I have never experienced before."

"Did you really want to die, Debra?" Montgolfier asked.

Debra flopped her arms back on the blanket, palms turned upwards submissively.

"When I saw Seamus with his family, I realised I have

nothing left to live for. There is no fairness in what has happened to me and as a result I have lost everything."

"Surely no-one is that alone in life, Debra. Do you really feel that way?"

Debra shrugged, her empty eyes having once again lost their fire.

"There are no flowers in my room, Doctor, are there?"

EIGHTEEN

Jasper was still sitting on his front door step when the police pushed Jennifer's body out of the house on a steel gurney. She was zipped up in a black body bag that quite effectively masked the smell of ripe death. He had been unable to go inside the house while Jennifer was still hanging from the landing, preferring to sit outside and stare ahead at the falling golden chestnut leaves, and beyond that at the blackbirds picking worms out of the fields across the river.

Lazlo had made him a mug of coffee, which he still held between cupped hands, the coffee untouched and now cold. Milling around everywhere were the ghostly white shapes of the scene of crime officers, dressed in white protective suits collecting forensic evidence.

"Fresh cuppa, guv?" Lazlo asked.

Jasper looked up with empty eyes that seemed never to blink.

"I'd prefer a large Chivas."

Lazlo took the coffee mug, nodding. Jasper watched as the SOCO gathered items together into sealed plastic bags. One dusted the front door for finger prints, another used a small vacuum cleaner on the hallway carpet.

"Why are they bagging the rope like it's evidence?"

Lazlo paused, surprised that Jasper, a legal man, should ask a question with such a manifest answer.

"They'll look for trace, guv, fingerprints, DNA, that sort of thing."

"Why? She hanged herself."

"Procedure, you know that guv."

"I bought that rope, Lazlo, there's a roll of it in the garage. My DNA will be on it. My DNA is all over this house."

Lazlo nodded. His boss was rambling, his eyes still staring blankly ahead, trying to deal with what they had been forced to see earlier.

"I'll get that scotch, guv."

An officer wearing a knee length tan overcoat sat down beside Jasper. He held a notepad in his hand and pulled a well chewed pen out of his mouth as he flipped the pad open.

"My name is DCI Roscoe, Mr Candle. We met earlier and I wondered if I could quickly run through some details before we leave?"

Roscoe had very short cropped hair, such that it was not possible to tell whether it was black or brown. His easily visible scalp glistened and revealed a lengthy scar that crossed his skull from above the right ear to his forehead.

Jasper nodded, feeling the tics now in control of his arms, left shoulder and his face, inhabiting his body with brazen impunity at this time of immense personal weakness.

Roscoe stared at Jasper's involuntary spasms out of the corner of his eye, unsure what to make of them.

"Would you like me to call your doctor for you, Mr Candle. Perhaps some sedatives might help you get a little rest?"

"No," Jasper said, as Lazlo returned and handed him a generous tumbler of Chivas with three ice cubes. Jasper took it without looking at Lazlo and gulped a mouthful. "This will help."

Roscoe looked away and shrugged.

"You and your friend, Mr Lazlo, discovered your wife's body at about 11.15 am, correct?"

"He's a work colleague," Jasper said, savouring the glow on his tongue.

Roscoe raised his eyebrows and looked up from his pad.

"Was it around 11.15am, Mr Candle?"

"I don't remember the exact time, but more or less," Jasper said.

Roscoe scribbled in the pad.

"And the house was locked with no indication of forced entry?"

"We let ourselves in with my keys."

"Do you want this, guv?" a SOCO asked from behind them, holding aloft a laptop in a large, transparent plastic bag.

Roscoe twisted his body around to address the officer.

"Yes, take it to the station to be examined."

Jasper too had looked around.

"That's my laptop," he said.

"Does it contain confidential client information? You're a solicitor aren't you?"

Jasper met Roscoe's eyes and shook his head.

"No, that's all at work."

Roscoe smiled broadly, perhaps falsely.

"Well then you have nothing to worry about. We'll return it."

Jasper raised his eyebrows and sighed resignedly, disliking the discomfort of having his home invaded and probed.

"When did you last see your wife?"

Jasper became aware of his hands shaking as the ice cubes clinked in the tumbler, but he didn't care.

"I'm not sure, several days ago at least."

"Where have you been staying?"

"In my office. I've had court cases and I work late."

"Alone?"

"Mostly, I have a secretary who works fairly long hours too, and there's Lazlo, of course."

Roscoe's pen made scratching sounds on the pad, ending up being chewed in his mouth as he pondered.

"When last did you speak to your wife?"

Jasper's head writhed to one side away from DCI Roscoe and he struggled to control and straighten it.

"I've been trying to contact her for days. I thought she was in London with her sister. I should have…"

Roscoe stared at Jasper's facial contortions with a curious intensity.

"Should have what?"

Jasper lowered his head and shook it from side to side.

"I should have tried harder."

"What did you last speak about?" Roscoe asked.

Jasper looked up, lifting the tumbler to his twitching lips again.

"I am trying to remember our last conversation, but… I can't."

Roscoe looked across at Jasper as an experienced officer assessing the husband's emotional responses, looking for inconsistencies and suggestions that he was faking it. Body language was so difficult to fake, ask any poker player, and in spousal deaths the partners are implicated in an unsettling majority of cases.

"I hope you don't mind me asking, Mr Candle, but did you and your wife get along? Were there problems?"

Jasper shrugged and pursed his lips.

"I didn't think there were any major problems. I do work hard, I'm away a lot, but…"

"How long have you been married?"

Jasper tilted his head backwards as he calculated, his lips moving soundlessly.

"Fifteen years, give or take."

"Had you had any arguments recently?"

Jasper shook his head sadly. Perhaps they should have; any form of communication would have been preferable to nothing and could even have been a prelude to something beneficial which might have prevented this desperate act.

"Do you have any idea what might have prompted this?" Roscoe asked, slightly more compassionately.

Jasper continued to shake his head.

"I will figure it out though, that's what I do," Jasper said eventually.

The determination in Jasper's voice made Roscoe straighten up.

"Did you find a note or a letter from your wife?"

This was the hurtful part for Jasper and he buried his face in the tumbler of Chivas. Why had Jennifer not even felt moved to explain to him why she had done this, what her darkest final thoughts had been? That not only hurt deeply but was rather humiliating too. He shook his head.

"I'm sorry to have to ask you these questions at such a tragic time, Mr Candle. I'll leave you now, sir. Oh, one last thing, can I have the contact details of your wife's sister please?"

Jasper pulled out his iPhone, found Charlotte's details and showed it to Roscoe, whose pen scraped across the notepad. Jasper was distracted by the sound of the ambulance doors shutting loudly. He watched in silence as the vehicle, emblazoned with bright yellow phosphorescent diagonals, pulled away slowly off the crunching gravel drive beneath the autumnal chestnut trees.

That was his marriage, over, not at all how he had expected it to end.

Roscoe stood up and stuffed the notepad into the breast pocket of his trench coat like a used handkerchief.

"Do you regard suicide as unlikely without a note?" Jasper asked without looking up, staring intently at the melting ice cubes in the tumbler.

"Nothing is unlikely at this early stage, Mr Candle. We're very open minded in these cases."

This is the excellent foppery of the world, that when we are sick in fortune, often the surfeit of our own behaviour, we make guilty of our own disasters the sun, the moon, and the stars.

William Shakespeare

NINETEEN

Lazlo leaned over Stacey's desk, his simian knuckles pressed flat against the polished glass surface of her neatly kept desk. Stacey's fingers were rattling the keyboard and her concentrating face reflected the luminous glow of the computer monitor in front of her.

Lazlo lifted a huge arm and plucked the white earphone out of her ear. Stacey was startled and lifted her arms defensively as black mascara-enriched eyes widened in her pale face.

"Sorry Lazlo, didn't hear you."

Lazlo shook his unshaven swede of a head.

"How do you hear the telephone ring?" he said, gesturing at her earphones.

Stacey lifted the phone out of her lap and flicked it from side to side in the air.

"Vibration."

Stacey was looking particularly Gothic, with a deep shade of eye liner and midnight lipstick accentuating the emerald glow of her green eyes.

"How is he?" Lazlo asked, inclining his head towards Jasper's office.

A pained expression creased Stacey's young face as she spun round in her seat and placed her elbows on the desk.

"He just works, Lazlo. Works, and drinks scotch."

Lazlo nodded and rubbed his stubbly double chin with a meaty hand.

"Is he getting any sleep?"

Stacey shrugged.

"He hasn't been home since… you know. He's been living here."

"He hasn't been home at all?" Lazlo said in astonishment.

Stacey shook her head slowly from side to side. Lazlo remained silent, looking at Stacey's flawless youthful complexion.

"Can I go in?" he said eventually.

Stacey stood up, straightened her jet black figure-hugging dress and walked over to the closed door of Jasper's office. She lifted her arm and prepared to knock on the panelled door, but then sheepishly held her knuckles back and turned around to face Lazlo.

"You go in," she said with a child like shrug of her shoulders, "and take this with you please. It came today."

Stacey picked up a brown A4 envelope off her desk and gave it to Lazlo, who raised his eyebrows and then heaved his frame over to the door, entering after a polite rap on the wood.

Seated at his desk, Jasper was poring over papers scattered from corner to corner. His tartan braces creased a starched white shirt that he wore without a tie, top button undone.

"Ah, Lazlo," he said looking up briefly. "What brings you here?"

"Guv'nor," Lazlo said touching his forehead and sinking into the creaking chair in front of Jasper's desk.

He dropped the A4 envelope on to the desk. Jasper lifted

his eyes and looked at it. His left eyelid twitched its wretched dance, occasionally pulling the entire cheek into the foray.

"Today's post," Lazlo pre-empted, folding his arms across his bulbous belly.

"Care for an Engelbert Humperdink?" Jasper asked, walking over to the drinks cabinet in the corner.

On it, several empty bottles of Chivas mingled with others still glowing with ample amber nectar. Jasper had clearly stocked up.

"No thanks, guv, I'm working."

"So am I," Jasper said.

Lazlo winced slightly as he hadn't meant his refusal of a drink to sound like an admonishment. Jasper sat down and drank from his tumbler, the only sound in the whisky and cheese smelling room being the clink of ice cubes.

"How are you doing, guv?"

Jasper stared at the envelope, his only visible reaction being the tics that ravaged his face and the occasional subtle twist of his head to one side. His left hand trembled too, but by keeping it below the desk it was easier to hide.

"I'm not exactly… Patty Hearst, you know, but I'm keeping myself busy."

Jasper forced an insincere smile and then attacked the envelope, ripping it open with his index finger before studying the contents. His eyes scanned the pages in silence as Lazlo looked around the room. The bed in the corner was unmade, with two empty pizza boxes and a photograph of Jennifer, smiling within a silver-framed portrait, lying on the carpet beside it.

"It's from Dr Potter, how about that."

"Who's he?" Lazlo rasped.

"He's Debra Kowalski's GP, treated her boy. I went to see him recently about the case."

"Interesting?" Lazlo asked, nodding his head and raising his eyebrows.

"It's all about vaccinations and the law. I never expected him to be helpful. Funny that."

Lazlo continued to nod in silence, both because he was unsure what to say and also because he was concerned about Jasper.

"You sure you're OK, guv? Anything I can do for you?"

Lazlo unclasped his hands and then clasped them again, looking awkward and uncomfortable. Jasper leaned back in his reclining desk chair and lifted the Chivas to his mouth.

"I'll be fine, Lazlo. It's a bottomless pit now, but I've been through this before and I know what to do."

Lazlo frowned.

"Been through this before?"

Jasper sighed deeply and clasped his hands behind his head as he leaned back.

"I've never told anyone this, not even the old trouble and strife. When I was a law student I had a serious relationship with a girl in my class, quite a mother of pearl she was. We were planning our engagement."

Lazlo listened intently but uncomfortably, unaccustomed to such revelations from his boss.

"I was favoured to win the law medal, but I became distracted by this… I did say she was quite a mother of pearl, didn't I?"

Lazlo nodded. "You did, guv."

"Mmmh… well anyway, I took my eye off the ball and my head out of the books and, well… I didn't get the medal."

Jasper paused, his eyes staring into the distance as he seemed lost in time. Only the facial distortions and occasional roll of his shoulder rooted him in the present.

"What happened, guv?"

Jasper was startled back from his reminiscences and regained eye contact with Lazlo.

"I broke it off, furious with myself and with her for coming between me and success. I did much better after that, but three months later she jumped off Prebends Bridge in the dead of winter."

A silence hung over the two men, broken only by the clink of ice cubes as Jasper immersed his face in the tumbler of Chivas.

"Of course I had to get to the bottom of why she had done this. Painstaking investigation led me to uncover that her father had been declared bankrupt in the weeks before her suicide. Her mother had a nervous breakdown, and…"

More ice clinked in Jasper's tumbler and Lazlo shifted uncomfortably in his chair. If he had ever heard a more convincing account of denial, then he could not recall it, Lazlo thought to himself.

"Perhaps I will have that scotch, guv."

"It has been my life's experience, Lazlo, that there is always a clear and unambiguous reason for everything. Look hard enough and you will find culpability lurking in the shadows of every event." Jasper said, as he walked over to the drinks cabinet. First he re-filled his own glass and then poured one for Lazlo.

"Ice or water?"

"Straight please, guv."

Jasper sat down again and placed Lazlo's Chivas on the

desk, cradling his own in his hands. The silence extended as Jasper stared into his drink. He loved watching the wispy curls of melting ice water mingle with the uncorrupted, golden, malty scotch, like a Tchaikovsky ballet in a glass.

"What terrifies me the most, Lazlo, is the possibility, however remote, that Jennifer may have ended her life because of me."

Lazlo sat frozen to his chair, quite unsure how to respond or even if he should respond. He chose to remain silent, afraid even to nod or move a facial muscle.

"So, as painful as it is right now I am determined to find out who or what is to blame for Jennifer's…" Jasper could not bring himself to say the word. "There will be a culprit, someone to blame for this, and I will find them." He continued, seemingly unaware of Lazlo's catatonia.

Lazlo swallowed a large mouthful of Chivas and then struggled to speak as, being more accustomed to Black Sheep ale, the scotch paralysed his vocal cords. He cleared his throat.

"If I can be of any help, guv…"

Jasper nodded his appreciation.

"As soon as the coroner's examination is completed I will have something to go on, of that I'm very confident. There'll be a rational and clear reason for all of this… business… you'll see."

TWENTY

The most striking thing about any autopsy room is not its white sterile austerity, not the unfriendly expanse of bleached floor and wall tiles, not the hostile frigid cold of gleaming stainless steel surfaces, nor even the presence of splayed naked human cadavers. It is the powerful smell of antiseptic and air freshener which incompletely suppresses the odour of refrigerated human flesh, a vivid memory association that is not easily forgotten.

Add to this the discordant clanging of metal instruments on stainless steel, the intrusive whine of power saws and it is the last place one would expect to find anyone eating.

"Case number 1167/53 is a healthy looking forty two year old female, one hundred and fifty seven centimetres tall, sixty kilograms…"

"Oh God, do that in English please," said Dr Whitehouse through a mouthful of sandwich.

Dressed in green scrubs and calf length white gum boots, Dr Sally Whitehouse was sitting at the white melamine work surface in the corner of the autopsy room eating a sandwich as she supervised the post mortem examination. Her crop of copper hair was tucked into an unflattering disposable green theatre cap.

"Uh… five foot… er… three inches, and weighing one

hundred and twenty… er… one hundred and thirty two pounds," said the pathologist, surveying the body on the slab in front of him. His face was obscured by a surgical mask, but revealed short black hair and bushy eyebrows as he spoke into the microphone suspended from the ceiling above the dissecting table.

"Thank you, Tom. Proceed." She smiled at him.

Tom bowed theatrically as if taking a curtain call.

"The body is clean, well groomed, with visible abrasions and bruising around the neck from a nylon rope. Distinct post mortem lividity is visible in the legs up to the thighs, as expected with the body having been found hanging vertically by the neck."

"Could she have died somewhere else, in a different position perhaps, and been moved?" Whitehouse said.

Tom hesitated and shifted his feet. "I… er… don't understand."

"The lividity, Tom," she said stabbing a finger at the cadaver's legs, "What does it tell you about her death?"

Tom took a deep breath as his face lifted.

"Ah, yes, if she had died in a position other than the one in which she was found, then the lividity might be distributed differently, because it is dependent on gravity."

Whitehouse nodded in approval as she chewed on a huge mouthful of sandwich.

"So does the pattern of lividity prove she died by hanging?"

"Er… no… it doesn't prove it, but it is… consistent… with that possibility," Tom said, emphasising the word 'consistent'.

Whitehouse smiled broadly without bearing her teeth.

"Excellent word that. Do continue."

Tom turned back to the cadaver and ran his eyes along the length of the dead woman.

"There is evidence of early saponification of fat and skin discolouration again... consistent... with death having occurred... how long has she been dead?"

"Aha!" Whitehouse mumbled through a mouthful of sandwich. "You have uncovered a major inconsistency. Elaborate please," she twirled her free hand in the air like a conductor.

Tom hesitated and gathered his thoughts, resting his gloved hands on the cadaver's knees.

"Saponification, which is the conversion of body fats to a soapy substance, usually occurs several weeks after death."

Whitehouse nodded, swallowing food.

"And how long has she been dead?"

"We don't know, exactly. The husband had not seen his wife for five to seven days, he's not sure."

"But certainly not weeks."

"He says not."

"How is this possible then, my young protégé?" Whitehouse said with a forced grin, before taking a huge bite out of her sandwich.

Tom paused.

"The husband could be wrong, or lying?" He offered tentatively, shrugging.

"Or?" Whitehouse prompted.

"Or... the house was sealed and the central heating on, set at around twenty four degrees Celsius... providing warm dry conditions that might accelerate the onset... perhaps?" He didn't sound certain.

"*Exactement,*" she replied with a flourish of her hand.

"Nevertheless, therein lies a point of potential great contention. We may never be absolutely certain from the forensic evidence alone of the time of her death, not without other clues and of course good old police work." Whitehouse said.

He nodded agreeably.

"What about mentioning the negative findings as well?" Whitehouse said, sizing up her sandwich for another hungry bite.

Behind her on the wall was a sign that read: *No eating in the autopsy room. No exceptions.* Tom turned back to the body and ran a gloved hand along the arms, turning each one over and pausing at the elbows.

"There are no other signs of injury, no defensive wounds, no puncture or needle marks, er..." Tom began.

"Have you checked under the fingernails?"

Tom raised a finger and stooped down to examine the lily white cadaveric hands.

"Good point. I always forget that."

He looked carefully.

"No signs of covert needle puncture under the finger nails."

Whitehouse crunched through the iceberg lettuce and waited for Tom to continue. He seemed frozen and eventually turned to her, shrugging his shoulders.

"Anything else?"

"I would take a scraping from under her finger nails for analysis and DNA, and then a vaginal swab for semen."

"But there was no suggestion of assault or rape?" Tom said.

Whitehouse wagged a finger at Tom and in so doing shed some lettuce out of her sandwich on to the tiled floor. She ignored it.

"Be one step ahead of the barristers or be destroyed in

court. Make a habit of doing it, Tom, then you'll never be caught out.

Tom scraped the fingernails into a container and proceeded to take a vaginal swab for semen.

"Right, let's open her up," Whitehouse said, picking up the next cheddar, lettuce and apple chutney sandwich from her clear plastic lunchbox.

The scalpel flashed and soundlessly carved a deep Y-shaped incision into the body from each shoulder down to the pubis. A power saw screamed and vibrated its way through the ribs. Tom carefully exposed the organs, examining each in turn as it slipped through his gloved hands like a blood-stained fish.

Then each organ was weighed before being stored in a white plastic container. Once emptied of its contents, Tom stared into the deep hollow of the eviscerated abdominal cavity.

"This uterus looks a little bulky to me," Tom said, turning this way and that to gain different perspectives.

"What age was she again?" Whitehouse said, walking over to join Tom.

"Er… forty two," Tom said, checking the tag tied to the body's right big toe.

Dr Whitehouse looked at the uterus and raised her eyebrows.

"I agree. Well, open it up… carefully!"

Tom cautiously incised through the dark red uterine muscle until its contents gradually oozed out.

"Oh God," he said quietly.

Tom's scalpel stopped, suspended in mid air in gloves stained with dark, old blood: dead blood.

"Has it been there long enough for her to have been aware of it, you think?" Tom said.

Dr Whitehouse nodded continuously, her eyes mesmerised by the uterus as her chewing slowed until it stopped.

"I need to speak to Mr Candle."

The half eaten sandwich hung forgotten in her hand.

TWENTY ONE

Jasper stumbled through the house, feeling like a stranger in his own home. Everything was familiar and yet simultaneously foreign to him; wherever he looked he was confronted by objects that evoked vivid memories. That was all the house seemed to represent to him now, a mausoleum of memories.

Like the three foot long hand-made wooden ship, HMS *Victory*, that he and Jennifer had bought while on honeymoon in Mauritius. Up until now it had been his pride and joy and he had loved walking into the living room and admiring it, displayed high on the mahogany mantelpiece. But as he stood and stared at it, he was overcome by the memory of that bright humid day when he and Jennifer had braved the dangerous road from Grand Bay and shared a scooter ride into Port Louis, leaving behind a spiral trail of pungent oil smoke. He recalled as if yesterday the smells of the market – fresh seafood, lobster, sweet chickpea delights coated in coconut and the ephemeral smells of curry, ginger and coriander.

"You like it, don't you?" Jennifer had said playfully, as he walked around the HMS *Victory*, minutely crafted to the exact hand knotted rigging, portholes and gun decks.

"It's over priced. Not worth it," he remembered saying, trying to sound indifferent.

That was the day that he had spent too much of their limited budget on an expensive lobster dinner on the beach, beneath swaying palm trees as moonlight danced frivolously on the calm ocean. Barefooted in the soft sand and wearing only swimwear, they had satisfied their hunger, first on tender, butter grilled lobster with chilled Chablis, then later, on the long, secluded jetty that reached out to the moonlight in the bay.

At the airport, a three foot long box awaited them when they left. Somehow, Jennifer had found enough money to buy the HMS *Victory*. All she said, with a finger pressed against his mouth, was, "Because I know how much you love me."

The words echoed around Jasper's head as he stared at the vessel, a haunting reminder of what he had once been to his wife. It made him uncomfortable and he walked away from his pride and joy. Then he was faced with the framed photograph of the two of them atop Mount Kilimanjaro, taken perhaps ten years ago. Nuzzled close together in their padded, bright red mountain gear they looked so happy. He remembered Jennifer's warm words whispered into his frostbitten ear.

"Can it get any better than this?"

He swallowed and turned the photograph face down on the polished, walnut side table.

Walking through the kitchen his eyes were drawn to the photograph of Charlotte's two young children, Jack and Charlie, held against the fridge door at a playful angle by a ladybird magnet. Jennifer had adored her nephews and had unofficially adopted them as surrogate children, a desperate attempt to plug a void that she and Jasper could not.

Since that fateful day two years ago, it had seemed to Jasper that nothing was ever quite the same again. The look on Jennifer's face had said more than any tearful words could have managed.

"They tell me that we will never have our own children, Jasper," she had sobbed.

"They?" he remembered saying angrily, "Who are they?"

She had cried wet circles into the front of his shirt as her hands beat his chest in futile frustration.

"The specialists I've been seeing. Dr Morrison, Dr Zoekaart and you know, the other one who does fertility."

"We'll get another opinion. We'll go to London. We'll…" Jasper had protested, grabbing her wrists.

"How many more, Jasper? I've seen them all, I've been to London as well. I didn't tell you, but Lottie arranged it for me."

"When?"

"It doesn't matter now. It's done."

Jasper tore his eyes away from the photo of Jack and Charlie, feeling the vice like grip of remorse closing in around his throat.

The house was packed with emotional time bombs, placed at intervals like landmines, ready to explode when least expected. Nothing was merely an item in the house any more, nothing was devoid of association and memories, nothing felt like his any longer.

Finding himself standing in their bedroom, Jasper was overcome by the stark emptiness left behind by Jennifer's absence. This was the area she had filled with her smile and laughter, her delightful perfumed smells, now it was silent and lonely. He wandered into the bathroom and stared at her toothbrush, the splayed bristles a reminder of her recent presence. The vanity mirror had visible fingerprints near the edge, almost certainly Jennifer's. They had been dusted by the SOCO's during their forensic examination of the house.

Jasper opened the cabinet and looked through her most

personal items that she would have used daily and would never use again. Opening some of her favourite perfumes, Jasper enjoyed their evocative scents as his mind re-lived joyous memories. Why had they allowed those good times to become just that – memories? A pang of remorse nauseated him as he reflected on the numerous missed opportunities, particularly more recently.

Suddenly, he froze, as his eye caught sight of a rectangular pink and white box behind her cosmetics. It was open and a foil blister pack of tablets protruded ever so slightly. Jasper felt the tic begin to tear at his face as he tried to understand what he was seeing. His mouth began to pull and soon his neck twisted to one side, always the left.

He picked up the packet with trembling fingers and read the date of the prescription. *Mrs Jennifer Candle, six month repeat.* It was current. He extracted the partially used blister pack and counted back the days. His mind swirled and nausea swept over him like a salty tide. This could not be.

He swung around and opened the small bin beneath the hand basin. Rummaging through tissues, empty toilet rolls, ear buds and cotton balls, he found an empty blister pack that matched those in the box. Jennifer had been taking these pills for some time.

He felt physically sick and dizzy with confusion, sitting down heavily on the edge of the copper slipper bath and covering his mouth with a trembling hand.

It made absolutely no sense. Why on earth was Jennifer taking the oral contraceptive pill?

TWENTY TWO

"The Candles are out. Please leave a message after the tone."
Jasper sat at his desk, cradling the iPhone against his cheek as though he was nuzzling it. Having spent months loathing that voicemail message, all he wanted to do now was listen to Jennifer's voice. He kept pressing redial, hanging on to her every mellifluous tone and nuance as the voicemail message played over and over in his ear.

The irony of the snuffing of this precious Candle ached deep within his conscience, piling on guilt that he was finding frustratingly difficult to deflect.

A gentle knock at the door disturbed his moments of self pity.

"Come," he said quickly, as though a pause would draw attention to his state of deep reflection.

Stacey entered the room apologetically, carrying a square of note paper. Her customary black attire was brightened by the splash of a sunflower yellow scarf draped casually around her slender neck. Perhaps she felt the need to detract from the sombreness of black in the office.

"Hi Mr C, you all right?" she asked with a cautious smile.
Jasper nodded and forced a smile in return.
"What is it Stacey?"
She approached the desk, stooping to pick up an empty

pizza box from the carpet before pushing the square of paper towards Jasper, past an empty whisky tumbler on the desk.

"Just a few messages for you, Mr C. Charlotte called again, but said it's not urgent. A Mr Ferret called, desperate for an appointment, something about Edward Burns ..." she shrugged her shoulders in response to the face of disapproval that Jasper made.

"What shall I tell him?"

Jasper stared at the note paper and sighed.

"Tell him my wife died."

Stacey shifted her weight uncomfortably, still too young to know instinctively how to handle her grieving boss.

"O... K," she said slowly.

"No, don't say that. Just say I'll get back to him," Jasper said, rubbing his forehead. He could feel the tics becoming stronger again.

Stacey nodded.

"Also a message from a Dr Whitehouse at the coroner's office, she said it is urgent."

Jasper sat forward, his eyes suddenly brightening up.

"Is there a number?"

Stacey leaned forward and placed a slender finger with a manicured black nail on the note paper.

"It should be there."

She turned to leave, pausing at the bed in the corner to pull the black quilt straight, then hesitated at the door.

"Can I get you anything, Mr C?"

Jasper was dialling the number on the note paper and looked up as he finished, pressing the iPhone to his ear.

"No, thank you, Stacey. Actually, yes, I need some new dicky dirts."

Stacey nodded at the door with a wry smile.

"That's shirts, right, white, size seventeen?" She raised her left eyebrow.

"You're a quick study," Jasper said, "and could I trouble you for some Eddie Grundies too, extra large?"

Stacey held up her hands and made a puzzled face, mouthing the word 'what'.

"Underpants."

She nodded again with a slight grin on her face and turned away to leave the room before pushing her head back around the door.

"Did you remember that Mrs Kowalski was in hospital, Mr C?"

Jasper clapped a hand to his forehead.

"Brad Pitt! Please call her and… what happened again?"

"Attempted suicide… overdose I think."

Jasper held up his hand and turned away from Stacey as the call was connected.

"Hello, can I please speak to Dr Whitehouse, my name is Jasper Candle."

TWENTY THREE

The office of the chief pathologist to HM Coroner, beyond the unmistakeable smell of formaldehyde, was not at all what Jasper had expected. The most vital and refreshing item in the stark square room was Dr Whitehouse's flamboyant head of copper hair, a matted mane of iridescent curls that seemingly threatened insurgence at any moment.

"Thank you for seeing me at such short notice," Jasper said, wiping the seat before sitting gingerly in the worn office chair.

The walls were adorned with certificates and commendations, all framed in plain black with a patina of dust and all hanging off kilter.

"I apologise for the state of my office, Mr Candle, it really is a work environment for me far more than an interface with the public." Whitehouse said, as she replaced several glass jars filled with gruesome grey lumps floating in formaldehyde on a wooden shelf.

Whitehouse wore a creased, white laboratory coat over her green surgical scrubs. Jasper couldn't help glancing at her yellow-cream gum boots as she sidled round the desk to her seat. They were flecked with blood and spatter – *surely an oversight*, he thought.

"Is the report on my wife ready yet?" Jasper asked.

There was a knock at the door and a woman burst in without looking up from the papers in her hand.

"That letter to Judge Goldberg for you to sign… "

She stopped upon seeing Jasper.

"Excuse us please, Karen, I'll attend to it later," Whitehouse said, smiling but annoyed.

In the corner stood an X-ray viewing box, its central panel illuminating the chest X-ray of some unfortunate victim. Visible even to Jasper's untrained eye was the opaque outline of a sharp instrument, resembling a letter opener, embedded deep in the chest.

The door shut quietly as the secretary exited.

"That's not why I called you," Whitehouse said, clasping her hands in front of her.

Jasper frowned and felt his heart skip a beat. Was this the prelude to unpleasant revelations about foul play?

"Is there a problem?" he asked, feeling the tics tugging at his cheek and the corner of his mouth, intruding on his pronunciation of certain vowels. He hoped she didn't think he was drunk.

"Mainly a few questions, Mr Candle."

'Mainly', he mulled over that word and wondered what further surprises awaited him. He watched her pull out a dictaphone from her desk drawer.

"Do you mind?"

He shrugged, aware how many times he had inflicted this on his own clients.

"Can you remember when last you saw your wife, Mr Candle?"

Jasper breathed out and placed his fingertips together meticulously.

"I have told the police all of this. Do you not have their reports?"

"It's not an interrogation, Mr Candle, I assure you. Please indulge me."

Jasper cleared his throat and adjusted his position in the uncomfortable square seat.

"I had spent at least four nights, maybe five, at my office. I often do this when I'm in court, it's easier with the hours I need to work," Jasper explained, rubbing his face with a self conscious hand.

Whitehouse frowned, ever so subtly, as she watched his facial display.

"Are you a barrister?" she asked cautiously.

He both nodded and shook his head.

"Solicitor, specialising in…" he hesitated, fully aware of how his occupation inevitably put medical staff on the defensive, "medico-legal and negligence work."

Whitehouse rubbed both her cheeks thoughtfully with the splayed thumb and index finger of her left hand.

"Jasper… Candle… yes, I have heard of you…"

He watched as she connected the dots in her mind.

"All good I hope," he quipped with a slight smile.

She did not reply but instead looked down at the notes in front of her on the desk.

"So, five days perhaps. Is that definite?"

Jasper felt his neck twist to the side and his shoulder roll demonically as his eye twitched. He cursed inwardly as he began to feel self conscious and on show, like a freak.

"I am not exactly sure when last I saw her. She left a message with my secretary to say she was going down to London, but I only received that message a few days later."

Jasper felt his tics deteriorate under scrutiny, as Whitehouse paused, formulating her questions.

"So, in other words, you don't know what your wife's movements were in perhaps... her last week alive?" Whitehouse said sharply.

Jasper recoiled somewhat at what sounded like a rebuke, what felt like a rebuke. Deep within himself, however, he acknowledged that he probably deserved it.

"I thought she was staying with her sister in Esher," he replied meekly, lowering his eyes and rubbing his face to assuage the twitching.

Suddenly a flash of anger penetrated his mind, shaking him into belligerent action.

"Why do you need to ask me this again?" Jasper said, looking at Whitehouse out of the corner of his eyes.

Whitehouse sat back and played with a Bic pen between the fingers of her right hand.

"We're trying to explain the inconsistency between the timeline of her likely death and the physical findings at post mortem."

Jasper frowned as he felt his left arm slightly defying gravity again. He had increasingly little control over its paroxysms.

"You're saying everything doesn't add up?"

Whitehouse shook her head, her tight copper mane moving *en masse* as though expertly choreographed.

"It can add up, I just want the known facts to be clear first before we draw conclusions."

"I'm sorry, Doctor, what are you saying here? Do you suspect something out of the ordinary?"

"We need to explain why it appears that your wife has been dead for longer than you say she has."

Jasper felt his throat close as his mouth pouted uncontrollably several times.

"Are you all right, Mr Candle?" Whitehouse asked.

Jasper just stared at her sky blue eyes as he rubbed his cheek.

"Do you not believe me, Dr Whitehouse?" Jasper said bluntly.

"It's not a matter of belief, Mr Candle, it's a matter of gathering the facts that will speak for themselves. I am not in the business of judgement, merely of establishing facts."

Jasper ruminated over her words, wondering if she was ridiculing him.

"There will be phone records, CCTV from her appearances on Durham and Kings Cross railway stations, and…"

Jasper trailed off as it hit him; Jennifer had been to see someone in London, the context of which could well be significant to her suicidal intent. He had to find out with whom and what the content of her meeting, or meetings, in London were.

"That will form part of the standard police investigative work," Whitehouse confirmed.

"When will the report be completed?" Jasper asked, trying to sound affable again.

Whitehouse hesitated.

"I'm afraid there is one other matter that I wished to discuss with you in person, prior to the release of the report, Mr Candle."

Her tone was such that Jasper could feel his neck hairs rising in step with a rash of facial twitches. He swallowed noisily.

Whitehouse made careful eye contact with Jasper before

she continued. Jasper held her gaze apprehensively.

"Did you know that your wife was pregnant?"

Jasper felt a buzzing in his ears and blood draining from his face. For a moment it felt as if he could not draw breath.

"What?"

"She was pregnant, about ten, perhaps twelve, weeks."

Whitehouse could see from the pallor in Jasper's face that he was shocked by the revelation.

"Did either of you know?" she continued.

Jasper covered his mouth with his left hand as a crescendo of trembling spread across his face like an electric shock.

"That's impossible. It must be a mistake."

"No mistake, Mr Candle. I am sorry to have to break such news to you under these circumstances."

She paused, looked down at the notes, then back up at Jasper.

"Why do you say it would be impossible?"

Jasper sank back into his chair and shook his head from side to side, his eyes staring ahead but fixing on nothing.

"We had been to every fertility specialist in Durham to try and conceive, they all told Jennifer she could not have children."

"These things can happen, in fact are well known to happen," Whitehouse said, sympathetically.

"No, Jennifer would have been ecstatic, this is all she ever wanted, all we both wanted, a family. It tore the heart out of us knowing that we would never be able to have one."

Jasper looked stunned, his face a pallid yellowish colour, both hands trembling now, though in the context of this revelation it may have seemed quite normal to Dr Whitehouse.

A silence enveloped them as Jasper's eyes stared into the

murky reaches of Sally Whitehouse's office, searching for answers. It was not the pathologist's job to explain everything beyond establishing the facts and Whitehouse did not venture into the complex arena of this evidently unexpected pregnancy.

"Would she have known?" Jasper asked, looking up sharply.

"Almost certainly," Whitehouse replied softly after a brief pause.

Jasper inhaled noisily and inclined his head to one side, as if contemplating the personal divulgence he was about to make.

"I found contraceptive pills amongst Jennifer's things and I cannot understand, nor explain, this. If she was infertile, why did she take the pill?"

The look of pain and confusion was written across Jasper's face and transmitted straight to Whitehouse's perceptive eyes. She rested her head in the palm of one hand and thoughtfully scratched her copper curls with the other.

"Perhaps she was not the infertile one?" Whitehouse said.

Jasper slumped back into his seat as though he'd been thumped in the chest. This was a possibility that he had never considered and the realisation of its potential consequences shook the foundations of Jasper's world. His face writhed, his mind swirled, but he did not know what to say.

"Are you all right, Mr Candle?" Whitehouse asked.

Jasper nodded, biting his knuckle to stem the tremor.

"Can you tell if the baby is mine?"

Whitehouse almost imperceptibly raised an eyebrow.

"Would you like us to do DNA tests?"

Jasper pinched his eyes shut, forcing out the painful possibilities from his mind. He felt himself nodding, stunned by the disbelief that this might have happened to him. Is this what took Jennifer away from him? Was he now chasing after the identity of a secret lover, a Lothario who had destroyed his life?

Pangs of guilt welled up from deep within him and mixed uncomfortably with swelling anger. Was this all his fault for being neglectful, insensitive to their plight? Or was it her fault? Or was it someone else's fault?

"We'll need some blood from you, Mr Candle, the rest we can take care of."

Jasper nodded, numb and reeling not only from what he now knew, but also from the apprehension of what might still be revealed.

TWENTY FOUR

Jasper walked briskly over Elvet bridge, past The Swan and Three Cygnets where he frequently met with his investigator. A frisky autumn breeze blew gold and orange leaves across the worn flagstones in swirling patterns.

"Lazlo, yes, it's me," Jasper said into his iPhone, pausing beside the stone parapet on the bridge.

"Never mind that now, we'll meet later at the Swan to discuss it."

He listened, watching rowers glide through the wind rippled waters far below.

"Lazlo, I need some urgent information. It's about Jennifer…"

Jasper rubbed his nose self consciously.

"Yes, my wife, who else? Can you find out more about a medical prescription she had?" Jasper said.

"Have you got a pen? It's a Dr Giordano, and he, or she, is not a local practitioner in Durham…"

He listened briefly.

"Yes, *not* a local practitioner," he repeated, emphasizing the word 'not'.

The rowers disappeared downstream, leaving behind them in the windswept water only a thin wake to indicate that they were ever there. Jasper watched as the water swallowed up the wake and extinguished all evidence within seconds. *How poetically apt,* he thought.

"One more thing, Lazlo. Could you look into whether Jennifer was leading a… a… er… double life?"

Jasper looked down as he said this. A mixture of humiliation and guilt chewed away at his insides.

"No, that is exactly what I mean, did she have a lover?"

His eyelids twitched and his left arm jumped spasmodically. For this reason, he always held his iPhone in his right hand now.

"I've got her mobile phone and her diary for you to go through…"

"Yes, of course it's bloody important you tomtit. Do you think I'd ask you something like this if it wasn't!"

TWENTY FIVE

Debra Kowalski lived on Dun Cow Lane, early Georgian, terraced houses that lined a narrow cobbled street close to the University Law Department and facing Durham Cathedral. It looked untouched by time, aside from passing students wearing the baggy apparel that constituted contemporary clothing. Jasper knew the street well from his days as an undergraduate in Durham.

A low energy light bulb, in its original gas lamp housing on the lime washed wall above Jasper's head, flickered into life just as Debra opened the door.

"Thank you so much for stopping by," she said.

Jasper stepped into the humble two up, two down home. He could smell dampness in the walls and musty old carpets on the floors, while all around him wood panelled walls were lined with shelf after shelf of books, from floor to ceiling.

Debra ushered him into the warm living room wearing what appeared to be a black track suit and slippers. She had lost weight since Jasper last saw her and her face looked drawn.

"My husband lectured in the English department. He loved books more than he did me, I think," Debra said, watching Jasper stare at the books.

They sat opposite each other on matching Fleur de Lys

patterned oatmeal sofas with a well-worn wooden storage chest between them.

"Are you… all right? What happened?" Jasper asked, unclasping and then again clasping his hands.

Debra brushed the fabric on her thighs as if wiping away fluff. She inclined her head to one side and shrugged ever so slightly.

"Dr Montgolfier thinks so," she said quietly.

Jasper felt himself stiffen in surprise at the mention of Montgolfier's name, then he frowned.

"What happened?"

Her eyes were downcast now, her mouth open to speak but no words came for a few moments.

"I… er… I just couldn't go on anymore."

Jasper was surprised at how this hit him in the chest like a well aimed punch and he wondered if she could sense the colour draining from his face. *Debra had survived but Jennifer had not,* was his immediate thought. Was it the fact that he was just inches away from someone who had stood on the brink of the very same abyss as Jennifer, or was it the perceived injustice of the outcome that unsettled him?

"Why?" he heard himself say. "Why would you do that?"

He realised that his tone had been a little sharp and he could see her composure melting slightly. As his head twisted to one side and his left shoulder rolled like dough in a bread machine he felt a pang of remorse, and of sadness.

"I'm sorry," he said quietly, "I didn't mean it like that."

"No, I'm sorry, Jasper," she said sniffing back emotion. "I'm really sorry to hear about your loss."

Jasper did not know what to say, but nodded as he grasped his left hand to stop it from twitching.

"Believe me, I know what it feels like to lose someone that close to you, and I know how difficult it is to… understand," she continued.

Jasper breathed deeply, trying to contain the tics that threatened his dignity, whilst biting on his lip to fight off rising melancholy. How deeply ironic, he thought, having come to visit a client and offer support, then ending up receiving it from her, a recovering parasuicide victim.

Jasper looked up at Debra and held her gaze, the pain visible in his bloodshot eyes.

"Can you help me understand why you would want to do such a thing?" he said.

Debra stared at Jasper through watery eyes, unable to break the pained connection between them as she perceived the extent of his probing plea. She shook her head and wiped her eyes gently with her knuckles.

"I don't think I can."

She paused and sniffed.

"Desperation has depths that are impossible to rationalise in the cold light of day," Debra said.

Jasper looked away, aware that his facial symmetry was being corrupted increasingly by the thoughtless demon within him. He could understand and possibly even accept Debra's desperate state of mind – having lost first her husband and then, to compound this, her only child – such torments appreciably leading to plunging despondency.

But was Jennifer desperate, was she trapped with no way out? If so, what was the underlying reason for her hopelessness? What was the reason for her perilous state of mind? He sensed the same nagging fear biting his conscience – was he the cause of her desperation?

"Perhaps you might find it helpful speaking to Dr Montgolfier?" Debra suggested, sniffing and wiping her nose with a tissue. "He really helped me when I wanted nothing more than to…"

"No," Jasper said quickly, too quickly, shaking his head, and then slightly softer, "Thank you."

Debra took a deep breath and studied Jasper's twisting face for a few quiet moments.

"Do you still feel able to pursue Ollie's case, Jasper?"

Jasper nodded, grateful for the change of tack.

"I am a professional, Debra, I will see your case to its conclusion. That I promised you when I first met you."

She nodded without a flicker of emotion on her face, deep in contemplation as her eyes held his.

"Is there any news?"

Jasper nodded, squeezing his errant, twitching hand until it blanched.

"Ollie's case will be the greatest challenge that I have encountered in my career."

Her face fell slightly and she inclined her head to one side.

"What are you saying?"

"I thrive on challenges, Debra, and there have been numerous positive developments in our investigations to date. I remain very optimistic, very optimistic indeed, and so should you. There are many influential people whom I believe support our case in principle. So, there is no need for any…" he stopped, unsure how to finish.

Debra smiled warmly and balled her hands excitedly.

"Would you like tea, coffee… a scotch?" she said, recalling the drinks cabinet in his office.

He smiled sheepishly.

"A scotch would be… welcome. Three cubes of ice please."

"You're a good man, Jasper, I sense this in you," she said, staring at him with a warm smile.

Jasper felt his insides turning as his conscience denied him this compliment. It felt as if Jennifer was watching him, judging him from beyond the grave. No: Debra was wrong in her compliment. He was not a good man.

✦

TWENTY SIX

Lazlo upended the crisp packet and poured the remnants into his gaping mouth, following swiftly with a generous mouthful of Black Sheep to wash down the crumbs.

"The doctor who prescribed those tablets for Jennifer, Dr Giordano, practices in Northallerton, guv," Lazlo said, wiping his mouth with the back of his hand.

"Northallerton?" Jasper said, wincing at Lazlo's eating manners.

Lazlo nodded as he licked and sucked his teeth clean.

"Why on earth would Jennifer travel forty miles to see a doctor?"

"Discretion? I dunno, guv. Here are her details," Lazlo said, handing a square of crumpled paper to Jasper.

Both Jasper and Lazlo shook their heads. Why would Jennifer not wish to see her usual doctor in Durham? Jasper buried his thoughts beneath a generous gulp of Chivas as he studied the scrap of paper.

Jasper sighed. "Anything else?"

"I saw the matron again. Did you know, guv, that there is a strict hand hygiene policy that covers each step in the process of contact between staff and patients in every hospital?"

"A strict policy?" Jasper said, raising his eyebrows. "What

does that mean? Imagine, if you can, that you're talking to a jury, Lazlo."

They were seated in The Swan and Three Cygnets at their usual small, round, brass plated table, away from a raucous group of students determined to outwit each other with increasing fervour and volume as the beers flowed.

Jasper recalled his days as a law student and his own baptism by barley and hops in these very same premises, all those years ago. He had been unmarried back then, having not yet met Jennifer, tragically analogous to his predicament now as he sat and watched the carefree students.

"Hands have to be washed or cleansed with alcoholic rub before entering the room, before patient contact, immediately after patient contact and upon leaving the room," Lazlo said.

"To prevent the spread of infection, no doubt," Jasper said.

"Exactly. It's a mandatory policy reinforced by regular training and by the presence everywhere of posters and placards reminding everyone to comply."

Jasper shrugged, unimpressed as he stared deeply into the amber liquid caressing the ice cubes in his tumbler.

"So what went wrong on Edward Burns' ward?" Jasper said.

"That is the question, guv."

Jasper stared at Lazlo expectantly, and then shrugged.

"So, is breaking this policy a punishable offence? Could it ever be, as in our case, a criminal offence?"

Lazlo bared his teeth and drew breath through them sharply.

"That's a difficult one, guv."

"How many people could potentially have spread this virus through the ward and infected Edward Burns?"

Lazlo sat back, pulled out a crumpled notepad from within his coat and flicked through the pages.

"Well, there are the nurses, the health care assistants, the caterers, the doctors, the cleaners, er... visiting staff... physiotherapists and the like, er... medical students, nursing students, er... visitors and relatives, mmmh... sometimes managers, maintenance staff..."

"Cheese and rice, Lazlo, this will be like hunting for a needle in the proverbial. It could have been anyone."

"It could, but we do know of seven staff members who also contracted the virus. Caught red handed, you might say."

Jasper nodded thoughtfully as he savoured the afterglow of the Chivas that lingered on his tongue.

"Do you have their names?" Jasper said, peering at Lazlo over his tumbler.

Lazlo paused thoughtfully and lowered his gaze for a moment.

"Lazlo?"

He looked up at Jasper.

"How far would you go with this information, guv?"

Jasper sat up straight, though a muscle spasm twisted his head to the left.

"What on earth do you mean? As far as I can, of course, as far as is necessary to get justice for Edward Burns and closure for his family."

Lazlo took a deep breath and fidgeted uneasily on his stool, rubbing his stubbly chin with a meaty hand. Behind them a sudden cheer erupted from a group at the dart board.

"It's just that... my informer has got wind of something, and is worried that she might become implicated in all this, and..." his voice trailed off.

Jasper stared at Lazlo, motionless but for the omnipresent tics, trying to understand his sudden reticence.

"Is 'your informer' involved in Edward Burns contracting the tommy guns?" Jasper asked, using his index fingers to sign quotation marks in the air.

Lazlo shrugged and shifted his weight uncomfortably.

"She is the matron in charge." Lazlo sucked his cheek, unwilling to meet Jasper's eyes.

Jasper picked up his tumbler off the brass-topped table and leaned back with a wry smile.

"Wait a minute, I get it," he wagged his index finger at Lazlo. "You've gone bloody soft on her, haven't you?"

Lazlo looked like a cornered school boy who had been caught bunking class.

"She's really helped us, guv."

"My Khyber Pass, Lazlo. This is business, damn it. A man is dead before his time and his family rightly want the truth. We're in the business of bringing those responsible to justice, remember, and I certainly don't pay you to mix up your pen and your pogo stick."

Jasper stared at Lazlo and inclined his head to one side, indicating his disapproval. Lazlo bit his tongue and refrained from answering. He knew better.

"Seven staff members contracted the tommy guns from that infected patient because they did not follow hygiene policy. I want their names."

Lazlo nodded.

"And, Lazlo, I'm still waiting for the name of the person who made the decision to admit that infected patient to Edward Burns' ward in the first place."

Jasper stood up to get another Chivas just as his face began to ripple and distort, as though something inside him was trying to get out.

"Brad Pitt!" he cursed under his breath.

Changing his mind he turned towards the door and simply walked out of The Swan, still holding the empty tumbler in his hand. Lazlo covered the stubbly folds of his lower face in a meaty hand as he watched Jasper in thoughtful silence, his eyes devoid of expression, while the darts players celebrated rambunctiously in the background.

TWENTY SEVEN

Jasper stared out of the window as the autumn countryside slid by in a blur of greens, oranges and browns. Raindrops streaked the window at a gravity defying angle of sixty degrees, swept across the glass by the 125mph wind.

Spread out on the table before him were three yellow legal pads, one marked 'Jennifer', the second 'Ollie Kowalski', and the third 'Edward Burns'. Jasper stared at the pad marked 'Jennifer', unable to focus and order his thoughts in the midst of simmering grief and confusion.

After several minutes, he buried this pad beneath the others and opened Ollie's pad.

"*Next stop is Northallerton in approximately seven minutes,*" announced the conductor's voice over the tannoy.

The carriage was almost empty except for a rowdy group of teenagers at the far end, who were tormenting a boy with a shaven head for wearing a Manchester United football shirt.

Jasper squinted at his own handwriting, a flamboyant swirling style always written in purple fountain pen ink. As a series of tics attacked his left eye, he wondered if he needed reading glasses.

He read from the leading page: *Ollie age three, in vulnerable window between first and booster MMR vaccinations. Seamus Mallory, premeditated avoidance of MMR vaccine by parents, catches measles (where?), infects Ollie at school (can we prove this?).*

Jasper paused, then unsheathed his fountain pen and began to drag the nib across the yellow paper in extravagant arcs.

Key points – do Seamus Mallory's parents' actions amount to reckless endangerment?

Does Seamus Mallory's infection of Ollie constitute involuntary manslaughter by virtue of neglect?

Can the reasons for consciously avoiding the MMR be used as a defence?

Jasper circled the last point with his fountain pen. He needed to explore what the factors and hence the Mallory's state of mind was in their decision not to vaccinate Seamus. He recalled Dr Potter making reference to a destructive media campaign that he felt was responsible for the decrease in compliance with MMR vaccination.

What are the Mallory's reasons for avoiding the MMR? he wrote beneath this, underlining it twice.

"This service will shortly be stopping at Northallerton. Please ensure that you take all your belongings. Change here for Scarborough," announced the tannoy.

Jasper closed all three pads in his worn, tan briefcase and briefly checked his iPhone, before pocketing it in his charcoal pinstripe jacket.

He could feel a knot of apprehension about the impending meeting, like a fist pressed under his ribs, because he did not expect the outcome to please him.

TWENTY EIGHT

Dr Giordano's surgery was in the centre of the little Yorkshire market town of Northallerton, resplendent in autumn hues from its numerous deciduous trees. Despite the leaden sky and incessant rain, Jasper felt the village ambience lifting his spirits slightly. A surprising number of people walked the paved streets, mostly huddled beneath glistening umbrellas.

Dr Giordano's surgery was easy to find, right beside the Northallerton Salvation Army office. The waiting room was busy, filled with sniffing and coughing children and parents trying to maintain order. Jasper was relieved not to wait long.

"Mrs Candle?" said a tall, dark skinned woman with a husky and distinctly Mediterranean voice, as she scanned the sea of faces.

Jasper stood up and walked over to her. Up close he could smell her expensive Italian perfume, as he nodded and prepared to introduce himself.

"I am Dr Giordano," she said with a cautious smile and a frown as she peered past Jasper into the waiting area. "Where is Mrs Candle?"

"I am her husband, Jasper Candle, can I please speak to you urgently about my wife."

Hesitantly, he was shown into a small consulting room with neutral colours on the walls, brown checked carpeting, a desk and an examination couch. Jasper found himself evaluating her, trying to understand what it was about Dr Giordano that Jennifer had trusted to help facilitate her lengthy deceit.

"This is a little… irregular, Mr Candle. Where is Mrs Candle?"

Jasper paused, never moving his gaze from her deep brown eyes.

"She is dead, I'm afraid."

Giordano sat back and stiffened, visibly straightening in her chair.

"I am very sorry to hear that, sir. How can I help you?"

Jasper's face tightened as he suppressed rising emotion, extracting the foil blister pack from his coat.

"I found these pills at home that you prescribed for my wife," Jasper said, passing the blister pack to Dr Giordano.

"If I may ask, sir, what happened to Mrs Candle?" Giordano asked cautiously, as she studied the printed label on the medication.

Jasper hesitated and then edged closer to the front of his padded chair.

"She… er… committed suicide." His eyes drifted down to the carpet.

"I am really sorry for your loss."

She stared at the blister pack of contraceptives in her hand, confused curiosity declared by a subtle wrinkling of the skin around her attractive brown eyes.

"I'm not sure why you have come to see me, Mr Candle. Are you a patient in this practice?" Giordano appeared a little flustered.

"No, no I'm not. We, er… I, live in Durham, so having a GP forty miles away would not make good sense. But obviously my wife thought differently, as she was a patient of yours."

Giordano shrugged warily in half hearted agreement as Jasper re-established close eye contact.

"Did you prescribe these contraceptive pills for Jennifer, Doctor?"

Giordano crossed her arms.

"Mr Candle, you know I cannot divulge that information to you. It is confidential between doctor and patient."

Jasper's face began to twitch and twist on the left side, pulling up the corner of his nose.

"But my wife is dead."

Giordano shook her head and hugged herself all the tighter.

"No matter, sir, that is the law."

"I am a lawyer, Doctor, and I have brought with me my passport for identity, our marriage certificate as proof that I am, or was, Jennifer's husband, and a letter from a pathologist confirming that a post mortem examination would be performed on her."

Jasper pulled a manila envelope out from his coat and held it out to Dr Giordano. She stared at it hesitantly, then took it and placed it on her desk without opening it.

"I don't know what you expect me to tell you, Mr Candle. Details of my consultations with every patient are confidential."

Jasper sighed and inched closer to the edge of his chair. The muscles in his left thigh suddenly began to ripple, causing his leg to bounce. This was a new development, Jasper realised, the twitching contortions having been confined to his upper body until now.

"I am trying to understand why my wife took her life, Doctor. These contraceptive pills I found do not make any sense," Jasper said, gesticulating towards the foil packet lying on her desk.

Giordano frowned.

"Why not?"

Jasper took a deep breath, as if filling his cylinders for a long haul up a steep incline.

"We had fertility problems and had seen so many specialists. We were desperate for children, but… they told us that a family would not be possible…"

A silence filled the space between them and Jasper sat back in his chair, trying to cover his bouncing leg with a trembling hand. He felt Giordano's eyes taking in his disobedient body, the resident gremlin that tormented him. What could he see in her eyes: intrigue, pity, disgust?

Giordano said nothing.

"At post mortem they found that she was pregnant. The impossible had happened, despite being on the contraceptive," Jasper said, turning his palms upwards and examining them with his downcast eyes.

"I understand this must be extremely painful and difficult for you, Mr Candle. Have you spoken to your own GP?" she said sympathetically.

"I don't need to speak to my GP," Jasper erupted, "I need to speak to you, Jennifer's GP, to find out why she asked to be on the contraceptive."

Jasper buried his face in his hands for a moment as he felt the facial tics rip his calm exterior apart.

"I just need to understand why she did it, what on earth drove her to do it… please Doctor… only you can help me."

He looked up at her, his eyes now bloodshot and pained, his face twisting this way and that.

Giordano appeared to be torn and shifted about awkwardly in her chair.

"I am sorry, Mr Candle. I would be breaking the law," she said softly.

"It's not a law, it's a code of bloody silence. Who can it harm, she's gone… there's just me left."

Jasper collected the foil blister pack and envelope from her desk, stood up unsteadily and walked to the door. His neck writhed and pulled his head to one side.

"Mr Candle," Giordano said, in a monotone secretive voice.

Jasper stopped, his hand pressing down on the door handle.

"Your wife has been seeing me for quite some time. She asked for the most effective and the most discrete contraception available."

Jasper stood as still as his demons would allow him without turning around to face her. The words hit him like repeated gunshots, each one penetrating deeper than the one before. He felt winded, dazed.

"She never told me any more than that, and I had no reason not to meet her request."

A swirl of emotions mocked Jasper, he felt both anger and sadness, confusion and determination, all manifesting in his left hand as it trembled on the door handle which also began to rattle.

"Do you have a doctor to see back in Durham, Mr Candle?" Giordano asked softly. "I can see you are in need of help."

Jasper lowered his head as he sensed the inevitability of facing his worsening physical idiosyncrasy.

"I am a medico-legal litigation lawyer, Doctor, I cannot see any doctors in Durham. They all know me, and they all despise me."

He knew he was issuing a cry for help and it embarrassed him, but the moment seemed right as he fumbled at the threshold of opportunity. A short silence ensued but he did not turn around and face Dr Giordano, preferring to hide his humiliation.

"If you would like to make an appointment to see me… "

It felt right, and Jasper breathed a deep sigh of inner relief. "Thank you."

TWENTY NINE

Jasper cradled the twelve gauge shotgun over his left arm, the weapon open at the breach. The heavy, cold steel of the Holland and Holland felt good against his skin. Squeezed into a green canvas hunting jacket and wearing knee length boots, he looked out over the expanse of green fields and hedgerows that fell away before him.

"Ready, Jasper?" said the plump red faced man beside him, his breath fogging the air around him.

Standing a head shorter than Jasper, but filling his brown leather hunting jacket with the importance of a weightier man, was Merrill Bradshaw QC. His round face had the cherubic look of a choirboy about it and his cherry red lips and cheeks could easily have been crafted with stage make-up.

Jasper nodded nervously as Merrill closed the breach of his shotgun.

"Guest's privilege," Merrill said, gesturing to Jasper.

"It's been a long time. You lead," Jasper said.

"OK."

Merrill shouldered his side by side shotgun and cocked the hammers on both barrels.

"Pull!" he bellowed with a surprisingly effective voice.

Fifty yards in front of them, a man wearing a bright orange fluorescent jacket raised his arm in acknowledgement and activated the spring loaded trap. Two clay discs shot into the sky, arcing across its milky, pale blue hues before dipping down towards Penshaw Monument, a distinctive half size replica of the Doric tetrastyle Athenean Temple of Hephaestus, prominent on a distant hilltop.

Merrill's shotgun tracked the discs before bursting twice with loud puffs of grey smoke. Both discs disintegrated.

"Good shot," Jasper said.

The acrid smell of cordite hung in the air and stung Jasper's nostrils. It had been years since he'd last been shooting and he had missed it: the fresh open air, the smell of meadows and trees, the solidity of a gentleman's shotgun and the unmistakeable danger of burnt gunpowder.

"So, Jasper, you're plotting legal action against a three year old, I hear," Merrill said with a deadpan face, as he opened the steaming breach of his shotgun and ejected the spent red cartridges.

Jasper shouldered his weapon and shouted "Pull!" He squinted down the barrel trying to obliterate the annoying twitches of his left eye as he tracked the spinning discs in the sky. He squeezed the trigger twice and was enveloped in a cloud of cordite smoke. Both discs continued to fly, untouched.

"The grapevine never ceases to surprise me," Jasper said, grinding his teeth.

"Bad luck old boy, you'll get into the swing of it soon."

Jasper ejected the cartridges and reloaded.

"The three year old was the vector for infecting our victim, but obviously parental responsibility would legally place his parents in the dock."

Merrill snapped the breach of his weapon shut and cocked it.

"Uh-huh. Pull!"

Jasper watched as his rotund friend dispatched the two discs with precision shooting.

"Does the case not interest the CPS?" Jasper asked as he assumed his stance. "Pull!"

Jasper could feel the rippling muscles of his left shoulder tugging the shotgun off line as he struggled to keep the trajectory of the discs in his sights. He wondered if Merrill was staring at his wavering weapon. Two shots in close succession and one disc sprayed fragments off its trailing edge.

"Bravo! You're getting into your stride again," Merrill said as though marvelling at a performance of Gilbert and Sullivan. "What are you thinking, Jasper, manslaughter by gross negligence I presume?"

Jasper looked across at Merrill. They had sat their bar exams together in a busy law firm in York, the two highest achievers of their year. Colleagues, friends and yet also academic adversaries back in those early exciting days. Merrill had gone on to join the Crown Prosecution Service while Jasper had pursued a legal career of private enterprise.

"Why not? Vaccination is widely accepted in public medicine as an effective tool to improve the health of society. Surely the decision not to have the vaccination against government advice constitutes a disregard for public safety, a careless and negligent act endangering others?"

Merrill lowered his gaze as he twiddled two fresh cartridges between his stubby fingers.

"An interesting proposition, Jasper."

Merrill nodded thoughtfully as he loaded and cocked his shotgun.

"Pull!"

Two more discs disintegrated in the pallid autumn afternoon light. In the distance a few grouse could be seen scrambling to safety in the bracken at the forest edge.

"But you would have to prove gross negligence. Not easy I should think."

"We do have a dead three year old boy. A good starting point for any jury," Jasper said.

"Mmmmmh," Merrill said nodding slightly. "Are you familiar with the Adomako Test, House of Lords, 1994?"

"Pull!" Jasper shouted, determined to improve on winging one disc.

He struggled to keep the shotgun pointing at the targets as the contortions of his face conspired to make the task even more difficult. Eventually Jasper simply closed his eyes tightly and pulled the trigger defiantly. Two blasts thudded into his shoulder and, miraculously, one disc shattered.

"Well done, old boy. To prove a case of gross negligence manslaughter you would have to satisfy four stages in the Adomako Test. First, the existence of a duty of care to the deceased, and I'm not sure that participating in a vaccination program can be legally defined as a duty of care to members of the public. Second, a breach of that duty of care which, thirdly, contributes to the death of the victim. Finally, the breach has to be considered as gross negligence to constitute a crime."

Merrill continued to stare at the uncontrollable fasciculations in Jasper's face and neck, which were like a bag of worms writhing beneath his skin.

"There are precedents," Jasper said, self consciously rubbing his face with a balled fist. "The whooping cough epidemic of the 1970's saw vaccinations fall and infections rise, resulting in many deaths – exactly what is happening now with measles."

Merrill turned towards the field and shouldered his weapon.

"Pull!"

Another two deadly accurate cordite bursts followed. Jasper's eyes stung, not just from the gunpowder smoke but from the indignity of so comprehensive a beating.

"I do see your point, Jasper, but I think there is some way to go before a jury will be convinced that an individual's decision not to be vaccinated constitutes as a crime against society."

"It is in many states of America."

Merrill nodded and inclined his head to one side. "That may be, and I'm not saying that there are not the makings of an interesting legal debate here, but…"

"Pull!" Jasper shouted, increasingly frustrated not only by his failure to convince his learned friend of the legal potential of his case, but also by his struggle to shatter even one clay disc with two barrels of lead pellets flying through the air.

Jasper squinted, willing the powerful writhing muscles to desist, but this seemed only to encourage their mutinous behaviour. As he squeezed the trigger, his left arm pulled the shotgun down violently; as a result the discharge was much closer to the ground than ever intended. The trap operator dropped to the ground in a fluorescent heap and Merrill gasped, his small lollipop mouth open wide.

"Good God, Jasper, you nearly shot Max."

"Brad Pitt! I'm really sorry," Jasper said, feeling both embarrassed and angry.

Merrill continued to stare at him, narrowing his eyes inquisitively.

"Are you all right, old man?"

Jasper let the shotgun fall from his shoulder as he stumbled back. He raised his arm in a placatory gesture to Max who was picking himself up off the wet grass and brushing mud and moisture off his clothing.

"I should stop. Cheese and rice, what am I thinking?"

Jasper sat down on one of the canvas director's chairs set out behind them and rested his forehead and eyes in the palm of an outstretched hand. Reaching into his shooting jacket he pulled out a hip flask filled with Chivas, hoping that its warming, malty nectar would ease his embarrassment.

"Well no more shooting for you if you're on to that stuff," Merrill said, easing his frame into the groaning chair beside Jasper. "Give us a swig."

Jasper could feel his friend's gaze upon him: a lurid, curious stare that would miss nothing as he passed the pewter flask over.

"Are you perhaps a little too close to this case, Jasper?"

Jasper rubbed his twitching temples between the thumb and index finger of the hand supporting his forehead. He could still feel the warm glow of the Chivas in the back of his throat.

"It's a good argument, Merrill. I know that there is a significant body of medical opinion out there that is firmly behind fundamental change to the vaccination system. The timing is right for judges to consider a unique case that will act as a catalyst for improvements to a failing system."

"You really believe all that?" Merrill said.

Jasper shot a look at his friend.

"You used to, my friend, what's changed?"

Merrill looked away and took a deep breath.

"You know what I'm asking myself, Jasper – what was the

mens rea of the defendants? The actions speak volumes as you point out, but what was their state of mind that led to that decision not to have their child vaccinated? Have you considered that, because the judge will?"

Jasper pondered this as he held out his hand for the hip flask to be returned.

"I know that if it wasn't for the failure of Seamus Mallory's parents to vaccinate him, Ollie Kowalski would not have caught measles from him and died. I will find out their *mens rea* and I will crucify them with it," Jasper said in a steely, sarcastic tone.

Merrill sighed and his round shoulders sank on his bulky frame.

"There are those who admire your determination, Jasper, and there are those who despise your methods. As a friend, don't walk into an obvious ambush and let your adversaries shoot you down. This is too big."

Jasper shook his head without looking up.

"Are you suggesting that I'm not up to the challenge, Merrill, or that the case of this three year old boy, who died as a direct result of someone else's reckless endangerment, is not worth pursuing?"

"What I'm saying is that you look like shit and I think you need some time away from this sort of thing. Take a break, go away for a week with your lovely wife, enjoy yourself."

Jasper looked up and turned slowly towards Merrill, his eyes now bloodshot and bleary. He lifted the hip flask with trembling fingers to his lips once more. Merrill straightened in his chair, sensing the intensity in Jasper's face as the tics ravaged the corner of his mouth.

"What is it, old boy?" Merrill said apprehensively.

Jasper felt his shoulder roll demonically and his left arm

convulse once, twice, as though he had been poked with a cattle prod. His mouth was open, but not for the first time, he struggled to form the words he wanted to speak.

"Jennifer... committed suicide... last week."

THIRTY

Dr Whitehouse was sitting at the white melamine worktop in the corner of the autopsy room, cradling a mug of steaming soup in both hands. Dressed in green surgical scrubs and white gumboots, as was her registrar Tom, they filed piles of printed papers.

"I don't know how you can eat that," Tom said.

Whitehouse looked at him from beneath her mass of copper hair with wide eyes.

"What, spicy parsnip?"

"No, I mean how you can eat in here, with the smell and the…" he turned towards the naked cadaver stretched out on a stainless steel autopsy table behind them.

She took one hand off the soup mug and clipped him on the shoulder.

"I don't even notice it anymore. Now, where were we?"

Tom rummaged through a pile of assorted papers in his lap as Whitehouse slurped noisily at her soup.

"Toxicology results for… Jennifer Candle."

"Ah, yes, an interesting one this."

Tom looked at her with an odd expression on his face.

"What, the suicide, rope asphyxiation in the hallway?"

She smiled.

"The husband, he's the interesting part. Well, out with it."

Tom read from the first sheet.

"Negative tox screen, no drugs, prescription or recreational, no alcohol, no… nothing it seems."

"Uh-huh. Vaginal swab?" Whitehouse asked from behind the huge mug.

"Er, it's here somewhere… negative. No signs of recent sexual activity detected, no semen…"

"Right, so there are no suggestions of foul play, no intoxication."

"Walks like a duck, quacks like a duck, probably is…" Tom began.

"Yes, suicide. Wait a bit, we sent off a foetal DNA match with the husband. Is it back?" Whitehouse jumped in, lowering her soup mug.

Tom thumbed through the papers and pulled out a pink sheet.

"Here it is."

Whitehouse was leaning right over, peering at the paper. What she read surprised her and her face hid nothing.

"Oh dear… Mr Candle isn't going to like that. He won't like that at all."

THIRTY ONE

Stacey placed a new white shirt on the corner of Jasper's desk, beside it a little pastry box and a paper cup of steaming coffee. She began to tip-toe out of the office when Jasper stirred beneath the ruffled black duvet on his bed.

"Morning Mr C," Stacey said, casting a shy look towards the bed.

The room smelled stale, inhabited; it felt wrong.

Jasper sensed her embarrassment. "Don't worry, Stacey, I'm wearing panoramas," he said in a voice thick with sleep.

This appeared to heighten Stacey's embarrassment as she blushed a bright ruby shade under her Gothic clothing and black hair. She paused at the door without looking in Jasper's direction.

"I half expected that you might have… slept at home."

A pregnant silence hung over them as Jasper sat up in the bed and rubbed his creased features.

"Not yet, Stacey, not yet. Thank you for the breakfast."

Stacey pulled the door open.

"Two messages, Mr C. A Mr Ferret is very persistent, he's called several times about Edward Burns, and your sister in law phoned."

"Charlotte?" Jasper straightened in the bed, instantly awake.

"She wants to see you urgently and suggested meeting in York at the railway station. I have the message on my desk."

Jasper felt a shiver of apprehension cut through him. He had not spoken to Charlotte, other than a brief call to confirm Jennifer's death, and he sensed that they had unfinished business to cover. The prospect both excited and frightened him.

THIRTY TWO

The London to Edinburgh Flying Scotsman roared through Durham Station, creating a whirlwind on the platform that lifted papers and dried leaves into pirouetting spirals in its wake.

Jasper sat on a bench drinking hot coffee out of a paper cup, emitting a plume of steam into the cold air.

"You know, guv, I felt very uncomfortable doing this, as though I was snooping, not investigating," Lazlo said beside Jasper.

"You're an investigator, for Tommy Dodd's sake, you were investigating. Now, what did you find?"

Lazlo squirmed on the bench as he flipped through the curled pages of his bedraggled notepad.

"I've checked her phone records, I've checked her bank card statements you gave me, I've interviewed neighbours…"

"Yes, yes… did you find anything, Lazlo?" Jasper interrupted.

"No, guv. Nothing with any pattern, nothing… out of the ordinary."

Jasper sipped the hot coffee, his eyes fixed on the cold, steel rail tracks. On the platform beneath the Victorian wrought ironwork, adorned with Durham's deep blue and red crest, people continued to gather, standing alone or in huddles and waiting for the next departure. Everyone was wrapped up to fend off the biting cold wind that whipped through the station.

"What about her phonebook?"

Lazlo flicked over a few pages, licking his stubby index finger as he did so.

"Did you have onion for lunch?" Jasper asked, shooting a look of disapproval at Lazlo.

"Sorry, guv. Yep, I checked her personal phonebook and dialled all those numbers that were unaccounted for."

"And?"

"Well, Dr Giordano we know about," Lazlo made a ticking movement with his index finger on his pad as he worked down the list, "I don't think anyone else fits the profile of a… a…"

"A lover?"

"Yeah," Lazlo said, nodding, visibly embarrassed.

Jasper rubbed his chin thoughtfully. This should have been good news, reassuring news, but it did not help in any way to explain why Jennifer had so furtively sought contraception without his knowledge.

"But why, Lazlo, why did she need to see Dr Giordano?"

Lazlo was visibly uncomfortable at discussing his boss's personal dilemmas surrounding his dead wife, but he kept the notepad open and continued to stare at it.

"There is one number here, guv, that I cannot explain. Perhaps you can."

Jasper sat up straight.

"Did you call it?"

"Yep, it's in London. A clinic in Harley Street."

Lazlo flipped the notepad shut and shoved it deep within his brown leather jacket. He looked across at Jasper, whose coffee cup was trembling in his hand, his elbow flexing occasionally as it jerked away from the warmth of his lap.

"Jennifer had been to London many times to see... infertility specialists." Jasper's head bowed forward and he stared at the chewing gum splats on the platform. "That's what she told me, anyhow. To be honest, I never went with her."

Lazlo rapped his fingertips on the cold steel bench.

"Do you want me to check it out?"

Jasper stared at the tracks, then at the sea of brown and black coats on the platform; ordinary people going about their ordinary lives, just as he thought he and Jennifer had done.

"*The next train to arrive on platform two is the 14:21 to London Kings Cross, calling at Darlington, Northallerton, York, Peterborough, and London Kings Cross,*" said an announcement over the tannoy.

Everyone on the platform turned their heads to the right. Jasper stood up.

"If he's in Harley Street it's bound to be an infertility specialist."

"I don't know if it's a he," Lazlo said.

The train pulled in, the doors opened and people began to move around busily, like bees entering a hive. Jasper turned at the carriage door to see Lazlo standing up slowly, like a man older than his years.

"Lazlo!" Jasper shouted above the clamour. "I think you should check it out."

Though it was painful, Jasper wanted, in fact needed, to believe that there must have been someone secret in Jennifer's life, because the alternative was simply unthinkable.

THIRTY THREE

Dr Giordano was quite different towards Jasper this time. She was relaxed and smiled a great deal, revealing beautiful white teeth. She told him she was from a small, coastal village south of Naples called Positano, one of four daughters born to poor fishermen folk.

"The film *The Talented Mr Ripley* was made along the coast around Positano. It is beautiful there," Giordano said.

Jasper shook his head and shrugged his shoulders.

"Jude Law was in it," she prompted, raising her eyebrows hopefully.

Her informal approach was surely designed to make him feel at ease when the time came to ask him searching questions.

Jasper tried to relax, taking deep and slow breaths, aware of her alluring perfume, but his facial tic was omnipresent, always tugging, annoying, like a fly.

"Tell me about your childhood." she said, leaning back in her swivel chair.

Jasper folded his arms across his chest and forced himself to maintain eye contact.

"My parents are both deceased and I had a brother who lived in the east end of London, where I grew up."

She nodded.

"Were you a close family?"

Jasper hesitated.

"For a time I was close to my mother, but once I left London to study law in Durham we drifted apart. My father and I were not close," he bit on his lower lip, "regrettably."

"And your brother?"

Jasper sighed. He did not like discussing personal matters and felt as though he was on the couch, being emotionally eviscerated. But he also knew he had to persevere and tolerate the consequences.

"He fell in front of a train about... three years ago." Jasper said with downcast eyes before pausing. "Some said he was pushed by the surging crowd."

Giordano knitted her fingers together beneath her fine boned chin. She wore a simple gold wedding band and her short, unpainted fingernails completed elegant, olive-skinned fingers.

"Do you miss him?"

"He became very strange towards the end," Jasper shook his head and pulled his arms tighter around himself, "he was a doctor, and consequently despised what I did for a living."

Jasper could feel his shoulder muscles rippling beneath his clothing, threatening to distort his posture at any moment, and he knew he was powerless to stop it. As his neck twisted to one side he sensed Giordano's perceptive eyes studying him.

"How long have you been aware of these... movements, Mr Candle?"

Jasper's shoulders shrugged involuntarily and then his left arm writhed like a charmer's snake.

"Quite some time now."

She made brief notes on her desk with a stylish Mont Blanc pen.

"Are we talking months, years?"

Jasper rubbed his brow as it twitched under her scrutiny.

"At least a year, maybe two… but it wasn't this bad at the beginning."

"Have you ever had a convulsion?"

"No."

"Have you ever fallen or hurt yourself?"

"No."

She made notes.

"Which movements are most common?"

Jasper looked up as he considered this, his left eye twitching shut several times in the process.

"My left eye and the side of my face, my neck twists sometimes and my left shoulder does too."

"And the tremor?" she said, pointing the Mont Blanc at his hands as they lay quivering in his lap.

Jasper smiled – he could not hide anything from her.

"That's probably been there the longest, I have become very used to it."

She studied him reflectively and gently rubbed her upper lip to and fro with her flexed index finger.

"Have you noticed any memory lapses?"

Jasper paused.

"No."

"Concentration difficulties?"

He chuckled and ran his fingers through his hair.

"I'm a solicitor, Doctor, I was in court just last week winning a case on very flimsy evidence."

"So you must work pretty long hours?" she said.

"Oh yes," Jasper nodded, hiding a series of contortions of his neck.

"How much do you drink, Mr Candle?"

She didn't miss a thing, he thought. So, just how perceptive had she been when Jennifer came to see her? Had she penetrated through to the deeper motivation behind Jennifer's request for contraception? Did she indeed know what was behind it all?

"By your standards, Doctor, most likely too much."

She shrugged nonchalantly.

"How many units per week, would you say?"

Jasper chuckled and folded his arms once again.

"I don't do units, Doctor, but I go through a couple of bottles of Chivas a week, sometimes more."

"Do you drink when you're alone?"

"Yes."

"Do you drink during the day?"

"Yes."

He could see her eyebrows rise almost imperceptibly as she wrote a few words down.

"Do you think it's… a problem?" Jasper asked, inclining his head slightly to one side and ignoring the successive, tugging pouts around his mouth.

"Have you had a drink today, Mr Candle?"

Jasper felt his eyes wince and the tics betray his intentions as he maintained eye contact.

"No," he lied.

He couldn't tell whether she believed him, or whether she could detect the odour of alcohol on his breath. Giordano inhaled deeply and sat back in her chair.

"Yes, most certainly, Mr Candle, I will be honest with you and say that it is a problem. Have you tried therapy?"

"You mean AA?"

"That's one, yes," she said.

"I have. But it was before my wife... er... and it's been pretty damn hard since then."

Dr Giordano frowned and then put her pen down with a resounding clunk.

"I will need to examine you now, Mr Candle, then take some blood tests. Even before we get any results back, we do need to discuss a strategy for reducing your alcohol intake... before it's too late."

THIRTY FOUR

Lazlo sat motionless behind the steering wheel of his dirty white Ford van. His great hands rested on his knees and the only indication of a life beating within his bloated frame was the rise and fall of the binoculars that rested on his mighty belly.

In the background, Radio Five reverberated through tinny speakers. Lazlo reached absently for the remnants of a sugary doughnut amongst an untidy mess of empty food packets on the passenger seat, while glancing at his watch. This was usually the time that her shift finished on a Wednesday.

Lazlo was about to bite the lump of doughnut when he caught sight of her. His heart jumped and he hesitated a moment before pushing the quarter doughnut into his waiting mouth. Then he heaved himself out from behind the confines of the steering wheel, dripping sugar from his mouth, and slammed the door shut as he began to advance on his quarry.

She had exited the building on her own, still wearing her dark blue matron's uniform and carrying a floral motif book bag.

"Billie!" Lazlo called out, raising his right arm as if to hail her.

She saw him, lowered her head towards the pavement and carried on walking.

"Billie, wait up, please."

She stopped as Lazlo's waddling frame caught up with her.

"I know what you are, Lazlo," she said, stabbing her index finger at the binoculars hanging around his neck. "I know about Edward Burns and I don't want to talk to you."

She spoke in short, breathy bursts.

"Please, Billie, just listen for a minute."

Lazlo was also out of breath, his great stubbly cheeks flushed in the cold afternoon sunshine. A broad pewter ear ring danced about beneath an elongated ear lobe as he spoke.

"I trusted you, Lazlo, and now I…"

Lazlo stepped closer, raising his arm to touch Billie, but thought better of it.

"I'm sorry about how we met, but that's my job." He shrugged apologetically. "But it doesn't change anything that has developed between us, does it?"

"I'm scared of you now," Billie interrupted, looking at him with trepidation in her eyes. "You could ruin my life."

Lazlo shook his head in dismay and quickly re-established eye contact. He was bent over at the waist to accommodate her short stature.

"Look, I'll be honest with you, my guv'nor is progressing this case; Edward Burns' son is demanding action and I'm really concerned about you. I want to make sure that you're not implicated. You do not deserve to be in the firing line here."

Billie's eyes widened and she paled visibly.

"How can I trust you anymore?" she said in a faltering voice.

Lazlo's eyes searched around the pavement for something, then returned to Billie's face.

"Do you think my guv'nor would look kindly on me

speaking to you like this, discussing a case? These legal matters are… *sub judice*."

He wanted to sound authoritative with the legal jargon, but his delivery was less than convincing.

"What?"

Lazlo's forehead furrowed and he scratched at it with his sausage fingers.

"I don't know, secretive or something, certainly not for general discussion anyway. I want to help you, honest I do. Please, give me five minutes so I can tell you what I need."

"What more could you possibly need?" she said.

Lazlo grabbed her gently by the shoulders and pulled her round to face him squarely.

"I just found you, Billie, I want to keep you. So I need enough to help my guv'nor, but I want to protect you at the same time."

She nodded but he could tell her mind was in turmoil.

"Trust me, please. I really am your friend," Lazlo said, giving her shoulders another gentle shake with his meaty hands.

Billie's plump profile looked like a cranberry between Lazlo's huge arms as she stared deep into his eyes, trying to decide which way to leap, which instinct to trust.

"Five minutes?" she said, raising her eyebrows and sighing.

"Good girl, you will not regret this, I promise."

Lazlo's smile split his face from pierced earlobe to pierced earlobe. He looked immensely relieved.

THIRTY FIVE

Charlotte was waiting when Jasper's midday train pulled into York station, standing with her arms folded beneath the large black and gold Victorian clock. Jasper stepped onto the platform wearing a long, black greatcoat with the collar turned up to ward off the bitter north-easterly wind that was funnelled through the elongated red, brick building.

Charlotte was dressed in a long, red coat and calf length black boots, her tousled mass of blonde curls being blown asunder by the wind above a black cashmere scarf. They embraced with the minimum physical contact that was necessary.

"Lottie," Jasper said as he lightly kissed each of her powdered cheeks.

"Jasper," she said, giving his shoulders the slightest of fraternal squeezes.

They quickly shrank back from the cordial embrace. Jasper was immediately struck by how much she reminded him of Jennifer. The little features on her face that he had never paid much attention to before, the curl of her smile, the glint in her blue eyes, the delicacy of her nose: they were all Jennifer's.

"I'm so sorry, Lottie," he found himself saying, immediately questioning whose prerogative it should be to commiserate.

She smiled painfully, but did not reciprocate.

"Thank you for meeting me," Charlotte said, turning and walking off the busy platform. "Shall we do lunch?"

Jasper nodded, feeling the tug of his neck angling his head awkwardly to one side.

"Taxi?" he said.

"No, let's walk, York's apparently beautiful in the sunshine. Jennifer used to tell me about her shopping trips down here."

They crossed the River Ouse on Museum Street, heading straight for York Minster, its tall spires resplendent in the autumn sunshine. Outside the Minster a large group of rowdy school children on an outing ran around boisterously amongst the dried leaves on the grass. After a brief appreciation of the Minster's Gothic architecture, Jasper and Charlotte turned away from the noise and began to walk down the cobbles of High Petergate.

"Jennifer's greatest sadness was not having children." Charlotte said, her eyes taking in the quaint fudge and gift shops that lined the mediaeval street. "She was desperate to be pregnant. She told me that she would come to York for retail therapy after some of her failed fertility treatments."

Jasper masked his reaction to this and remained silent for several minutes, before pausing outside a golden sandstone church.

"This is the church of St Michael le Belfry, where Guy Fawkes was baptised. He was born right here in Petergate, you know."

Charlotte stared at Jasper in bewilderment.

"What are you talking about?" she said.

Jasper felt his facial composure eroding as a barrage of tics tore at his left eye.

"Do you know why she did it?" Jasper said, establishing eye

contact despite his twisting musculature.

Charlotte looked away. *God, she reminded him so much of Jennifer*, he thought, except for the mole on the left of her upper lip and a set of teeth crafted to perfection by expensive dentistry. They walked on slowly, Jasper clasping his hands behind his back.

"Not because she couldn't have children." Charlotte said, shrugging her shoulders before looking up at Jasper questioningly.

Jasper studied the cobbles beneath his black brogues, sucking his cheek as he pondered.

"Did you know that she was pregnant?"

Charlotte's face dropped, the beauty draining from it in an instant. She remained frozen like a mime artist for several seconds, until a passerby bumped into her. "Sorry."

"I didn't know either. The pathologist told me," Jasper said.

"What?" Charlotte said with a pained look on her face. "She didn't tell you?"

Jasper shrugged.

"Did she even know?" Charlotte said.

"The pregnancy was about twelve weeks, they say, so she should have been aware. But we'll never know."

"God, that's awful," Charlotte said, her face a deathly pale colour.

Hearing these words from Charlotte didn't in any way help to ease Jasper's pain, serving instead to underline the bizarre and unusual circumstances surrounding Jennifer's pregnancy.

They had reached a small square at the junction of Low Petergate and The Shambles, where a crowd was gathered around a group of street artists who were performing tricks with buckets of water atop ladders.

"This is very difficult for me, Lottie, and I want you to think really carefully now," Jasper said, turning to walk down The Shambles. The narrow mediaeval Butcher's Row with its overhanging wooden buildings and redundant meat hooks funnelled the pedestrians together, as Jasper and Charlotte were jostled constantly.

"I have reason to believe that Jennifer was seeing another man."

Charlotte stopped abruptly and a tall man in a tweed coat bumped into her from behind. Charlotte apologised and turned back to Jasper.

"No, not Jennifer. I don't… no, she would never."

"Lottie, we had been to so many specialists for fertility advice and they all told Jennifer the same thing – you will not be able to have children."

"Yes, but these things happen, all of a sudden one day… bingo!"

Jasper shook his head, feeling the contortions in his left shoulder beginning to ripple.

"She was seeing someone, she must have been."

"What a cruel thing to say about your recently deceased wife. She loved you, Jasper, despite your faults, she loved you," Charlotte said loudly, as people pushed between them and the quaint shop fronts.

Jasper continued to shake his head, trying to shut out her words.

"We hadn't spent much time together for months…"

"It only takes one… brief, indifferent, even forgettable, encounter…"

"Friar Tuck, Lottie, she was taking contraceptives!"

"What?"

Jasper drew a breath and sighed deeply, his eyes drifting down to the ancient, well-trodden cobbles. Charlotte's brow furrowed and she seemed lost for a moment.

"No, no she wouldn't have needed them. You're wrong."

"It's no mistake, she was on the pill and she had been for quite a while, probably for as long as we were having so-called fertility problems."

As he said this Jasper felt a rod of steel coring its way through him, filling him with renewed strength and resilience to face the corroding uncertainty surrounding Jennifer's pregnancy.

"Did you know?" Charlotte said.

"Of course I didn't know. She kept it secret from me. The question is why would she have hidden this from me, unless she had a..."

"Jennifer would not have cheated on you, Jasper, she loved you. That much I know. She was dying to have a family with you."

Jasper rubbed the left side of his face with the palm of his left hand, closing his eyes and burying his turbulent emotions. His hand trembled and his face writhed its wormlike ritual, all the while Charlotte stared at him.

"Are you all right, Jasper?" she said softly.

"No, I'm bloody well not all right," Jasper said from behind his hand. "I need to get to the bottom of this, Lottie. I must know why she... did it, and why else unless the child she was carrying... was not mine."

He lowered his hand and studied her face. She looked crestfallen, her beautifully made up eyes now bleary and smudged.

"Can you think of anything out of the ordinary, any

comments she may have made, any confidences? Who was she seeing in London, for instance? There's nothing much to go on in her phone records, or her diary. I need a trail to follow, any clue might be helpful."

Suddenly Charlotte shrank back from Jasper, her face transformed into one of revulsion.

"Listen to yourself, Jasper. You've turned Jennifer's death into an investigation, one of your cases. She was your wife, for God's sake. If you want a reason, look in the mirror. She was lonely, neglected, and sad…"

Charlotte began to sob, but as Jasper moved forward to comfort her she shook him off.

"What about the baby, Lottie?" Jasper said. "She didn't even leave me a note." He winced involuntarily, but it was not a tic, it was hurt.

"She's not even buried yet and you're snooping around her private affairs, accusing her of infidelity. This was not her fault. How dare you."

Charlotte turned and began to walk away, blowing her nose into a tissue. Soon, half a dozen people had occupied the space that had opened up between them.

"Lottie wait, I want to know more about Jennifer," Jasper said, stumbling after her through the crowd.

She turned and shot an icy stare in his direction.

"I used to wonder how you could be a compensation lawyer, how you could live with yourself and how my sister could live with you. But now I see exactly what makes you tick," she said.

"Please Lottie, I simply want to understand more about Jennifer; I want to know why this happened."

"It's too late now, Jasper, you had your opportunity when

you were married to her. Just let her rest in peace."

Jasper watched as she walked away. Seeing Jennifer's unsettling likeness in Charlotte had reopened the wounds and he tried in vain to remember when last he had seen Jennifer's warm, smiling face in front of his eyes, so close that he could have kissed it.

A violent spasm twisted his left arm and his neck, rhythmically, agonisingly. He noticed a small boy staring at him wide eyed, mesmerised, as though he had encountered a ghoulish apparition. Eventually, the boy's father tugged his arm to move him along.

Jasper suppressed an overwhelming urge to scream from within his tormented body, but as on so many occasions before he pushed it deep down, stifling the frustration.

THIRTY SIX

"Do you want to see what I've found, guv?" Lazlo said with a triumphant grin on his face, as he slumped his globular frame into the red leather chair in Jasper's office.

Jasper was sitting behind his desk, bright green and yellow striped braces cutting into a billowing white shirt, staring pensively into the glass tumbler of whisky that he was holding, tilting it this way and that to keep the ice cubes moving.

"Dr Giordano says I have to quit," Jasper said in a monotone whisper from behind the cut glass tumbler.

Lazlo nodded. "Good." Then he paused, his eyes tracking between Jasper's face and the whisky tumbler being fondled in his trembling left hand. "Are you going to?"

Jasper lifted the glass to his face and took a deep sniff.

"What do you want to show me, Lazlo?"

Lazlo pushed a newspaper onto the desk, twirling it around with his fingers so that it faced Jasper.

"Have you read today's *Guardian*?"

Jasper shook his head, took a quick gulp of whisky and then pushed the tumbler away in disgust.

"Page six, article on the winter vomiting bug, the norovirus," Lazlo said as his eyes danced energetically. He shuffled his copious buttocks forward to the edge of the creaking red leather chair in eager anticipation.

"What's the Frankie Dettori, Lazlo?"

Lazlo inhaled sharply and twiddled his pewter earring between his meaty thumb and index fingers.

"The story, guv, is about the impending winter outbreaks of gastroenteritis in hospitals."

"Ah, back to ol' tommy guns again."

"Precisely. The article describes how contagious the norovirus is, how it spreads easily in contained environments like hospitals, nursing homes, and schools, how to prevent spreading the infection, et cetera."

Lazlo sat back and rubbed his stubbly chin with satisfaction as he watched Jasper find the article and begin to scan it.

"Infection occurs primarily through person to person transmission," Jasper read from the paper, "and hand washing is an effective method of reducing spread."

Jasper smacked the paper with his hand and sat back with a smug grin on his face.

"No, guv, read on, the bit I want you to read is further down." Lazlo said as a look of concern creased his face.

Jasper's eyes returned to the paper and began to track the print.

"What am I looking for here, Lazlo? Give me a Scooby Doo."

"It says that sick patients must be segregated from other patients, especially those at risk, and that infected wards should be closed. Have you found it?"

Jasper read on in silence, then suddenly straightened and lifted the newspaper slightly off the desk.

"Interesting, very interesting."

"High risk patients should never come into contact with infected cases," Lazlo said.

"So, this is Department of Health policy?"

"It looks that way – I checked the website."

Jasper reached across to his phone and pressed the intercom button.

"Stacey, get Mr Ferret an appointment as soon as please."

"Yes, Mr C."

Jasper's attention returned to the article and he continued to read.

"Good work, Lazlo, reading the dailies while working," he said sarcastically without looking up.

Jasper reached for his whisky tumbler as he read and Lazlo cleared his throat loudly, even raising a hand to cover his great, big mouth. Jasper looked up at him and retracted his arm.

"I think we've got them, Lazlo, on all counts. It says here that a study in New York found that seven out of eleven norovirus outbreaks were by person to person transmission. They're... chicken plucked."

Lazlo sat back and lowered his gaze slightly, thoughtfully.

"Can I come to that meeting too, guv? I have new and more detailed information from... the matron."

Jasper looked up and stared at Lazlo, the tic around his left eye twisting and tugging almost relentlessly now, making him look angry, defensive and unapproachable.

Lazlo felt himself shift uncomfortably in the cramped chair.

"Yeah, sure." Jasper smiled.

Lazlo sighed in relief.

"Do you have anything for me on Jennifer?" Jasper said.

"Er," Lazlo mumbled, looking flustered and scratching in the pockets of his leather jacket. He extracted a crumpled piece of paper, like a magician pulling a rabbit out of a hat, and held it aloft.

"The unknown contact in Harley Street we found in her phonebook," Jasper prompted. "Who is he?"

"I'm still on it, guv. A foreigner."

"Is he an infertility specialist?" Jasper asked with raised eyebrows as he eyed his whisky tumbler.

Lazlo's saggy features betrayed his disapproval as he watched Jasper lift the tumbler to his mouth with a trembling hand.

"I'll find out, guv."

Jasper swallowed the soothing mellow malt.

"I'll bet he's our mystery man."

THIRTY SEVEN

Dr SP Whitehouse MB, PhD, FRCPath, LLM
Home Office Pathologist
Drury Lane
Durham

Dear Mr Candle,

Case 1167/53: Jennifer Mary Candle

I am now able to confirm the post mortem examination findings that will be forwarded to HM Coroner regarding the death of Jennifer Mary Candle. The decision to hold an inquest is then at the coroner's discretion. In the interim, however, we are able to formally release the body of Jennifer Mary Candle to enable funeral arrangements to be made.

DNA tests performed at your request and with your written consent have been completed. Please find attached the report from the Human Tissues Laboratory that undertook these tests. In essence I can summarise the results that confirm a match between the DNA sample supplied by you and that taken from the unborn foetus found at autopsy in the uterus of Jennifer Mary Candle. With greater than 98% certainty you are the biological father of the unborn foetus.

Please contact my office as soon as possible to arrange for transfer of the body of Jennifer Mary Candle to an undertaker of your choice. If you wish to discuss any of the above please make an appointment through my secretary.

Yours sincerely,

SP Whitehouse

Jasper let the letter slip from his fingers and it floated down to the desk with a levity that disguised the severity of its contents. He stared ahead through glazed eyes, for a few moments completely oblivious to the tics and contortions that racked his face and left arm, the tremble of his hands and the new onset of flickering in his thigh muscles. His thigh looked as though eels were writhing beneath the skin.

He could make no sense of this at all. Why would Jennifer withhold a pregnancy from him, especially when they had struggled for so many years to reach this seemingly unattainable point? Did she suspect the baby might be somebody else's? Was it simply a moment of blind panic that drove her to such despair? If only she had felt able to speak to him, to take him into her confidence. But perhaps she didn't know how he would react to such unwelcome confessions. He wasn't even sure now how he might have responded to such a disclosure.

Jasper's stomach churned and the smell of old whisky on his breath made him nauseous, to the point that he rose quickly and disappeared into the bathroom, retching loudly in between howls of anguish.

THIRTY EIGHT

Julian Ferret – oily hair, garlic breath, sloping shoulders reminiscent of the weak hind quarters of a hyena – sat on Lazlo's left in front of Jasper's desk. He was one of those unfortunate men whom Jasper had come to dislike without even getting to know him, not just because they were fierce legal adversaries. A black suit hung on his frame like a large coat draped over a coat stand.

Lazlo had removed his leather jacket and folded it over his chair, revealing a red, black and white checked shirt that was stretched across his belly, revealing patches of pale hairy skin at intervals between straining buttons.

"You intend to pursue this case?" Ferret asked, running his fingers through the shiny hair above his left ear.

"Unless you wish to settle? There is negligence in abundance," Jasper said with hands clasped together beneath his chin.

"You're fishing, counsel."

Jasper took a breath and leafed through some of the papers on his desk.

"There are DoH directives to keep patients infected with norovirus, or gastroenteritis, separate from convalescing and vulnerable patients. These were not followed."

Even Ferret's shiny skin seemed to exude garlic and Lazlo,

who himself emitted odours of his liver and onion lunch, found himself moving away from the man's unpleasant aura.

"Firstly, when the elderly woman, Mrs X, was admitted from the nursing home, it was not known that she was infected with norovirus," Ferret said, with his head buried in the case notes on his lap.

"She had the tommy guns," Jasper said, raising one eyebrow, which immediately began to twitch and burn.

"Secondly," Ferret continued, ignoring this remark, "it was a bank holiday weekend and the hospital was extremely full, therefore Mrs X was placed in an isolation bay some distance from the other patients."

"DoH policy was not followed."

"The NHS is an over burdened organisation with a moral obligation to treat all comers, Mr Candle. As strange as this may seem to your dubious profiteering ethics, it has to be adaptable and improvise from time to time, in the interests of society."

Jasper ran a finger beneath the tight-fitting peacock-blue braces that clamped over his white shirt.

"At what point do the interests of society take precedence over those of the individual?" Jasper said.

"I think you know what I mean, Mr Candle," Ferret said, without looking up.

"Perhaps you'd care to explain that to Edward Burns' grieving family."

Ferret shook his head and emitted a sigh of disapproval.

"No one intended any harm to come to Edward Burns. He was an unfortunate victim of unavoidable circumstances."

Jasper straightened and flipped over a page on the desk in front of him, before looking up at Ferret again.

"Unavoidable? NHS hand hygiene policy is clear and unambiguous, Mr Ferret, I quote: 'Hand washing is an effective method of preventing the spread of norovirus. Sanitising all surfaces is highly recommended. Such appropriate measures can reduce the transmission ratio seven fold'. "

"Reduce, yes, not eliminate. What is your point, Mr Candle?"

"Half a dozen people, staff and patients, contracted the virus from the infectious patient in the isolation bay, one of whom died. This demonstrates a clear failure to comply with the recommended hygiene policies."

Lazlo shifted uncomfortably in his chair as he sensed the heat coming closer to the nursing staff, and to Billie.

Ferret stared at Jasper quietly with a wry smile on his face. His dark eyes danced eagerly in his head as he relished the challenge of outwitting his arch nemesis.

"I will read out some medical facts that would be related in court." Ferret leafed through several sheets of paper in his lap. "As few as one or two norovirus particles are able to cause infection. No hand hygiene procedure in the world is able to guarantee one hundred percent eradication, meaning that even after a surgical scrub it might be possible for one or two virus particles to remain. Furthermore, patients are contagious even before the onset of symptoms and for up to a week or more after they appear to have recovered."

Ferret sat back with a satisfied look on his face. Jasper stared at him, his face writhing beneath a shower of tics.

"Why was Mrs X not moved out of the ward when it became evident that she posed a risk to other ward patients?" Jasper asked.

"Where would they move her, counsel, to another ward

and risk an epidemic throughout the hospital? Procedure is to lock down the ward, close it to both in and out going traffic to minimise the risk of a widespread outbreak."

Ferret leaned to one side and rested his chin on a balled hand. Jasper began to shift about in his seat, feeling his left shoulder writhing and twisting its familiar demonic dance. He desperately wanted a whisky, but he dared not, and Lazlo had made him promise.

"I would be prepared to take my chances with a jury and let them decide whether infecting half a dozen persons on an isolation ward during lockdown protocol is evidence enough of negligence on the part of the trained staff," Jasper said, twiddling an index finger across his lips.

Ferret remained silent, but Lazlo adjusted his great frame in the cramped chair. He looked uncomfortable, his face taut and his brow furrowed.

"I can show that procedure was not followed on the night of admission, and that there were alternative locations available to house… er… Mrs X," Lazlo said in a voice a little tighter and thinner than his usual relaxed self.

Ferret shot an icy look towards Lazlo and began to play with the shiny skin on his neck.

"How so?" Ferret said.

"Testimony of staff."

Ferret snorted dismissively.

"They'd be playing a dangerous game with their employer. I doubt they'd willingly do that when they fully understand the possible consequences."

Lazlo winced uncomfortably, feeling the pressure of the brinkmanship he was trying to pursue in deflecting culpability away from individuals on the ward. He sensed that he too was playing a dangerous game of poker, perhaps out of his league.

"We have two powerful allegations of negligence against the hospital. One, the decision to place Mrs X on that ward and expose vulnerable patients like Edward Burns to potential serious harm. Two, that better standards of hygiene on the ward by staff would have prevented the spread of the norovirus to others, like Edward Burns," Jasper said.

"We will contest both allegations," Ferret said, pursing his lips and closing the papers in a document wallet in his lap, before standing up and walking to the door.

"I have great faith in the common sense of our jury system, Mr Ferret."

Ferret paused and turned to face both Jasper and Lazlo.

"So do I, counsel. Good day to you both."

THIRTY NINE

"Thank you for stopping by," Debra said. "Shall we walk?"

She was wearing faded, loose denim jeans and a padded white ski jacket, her hair was neatly combed and her face tidily arranged.

Jasper walked silently beside her as they picked their way across the uneven cobbles of Bow Lane, heading past Hatfield College down to Kingsgate Bridge.

"You are a Durham alumnus, aren't you?" she said as they passed the imposing wrought iron gate with its freshly painted forged crest of Hatfield College.

"Yes, University College."

"But you wouldn't have encountered my Harry."

"Not unless he was a lecturer in criminal law."

Debra chuckled. The uplifting sound of the cathedral bells ringing in cyclical descending cadences echoed across Durham's mediaeval skyline.

"English classics, they were Harry's passion – Brontë, Lawrence, Eliot." She paused and Jasper found himself staring at her fragile features, fine cheek bones and delicately sculpted lips, through which the warmth of her breath steamed in the cold air. "He was quite a bit older than me, but he knew how to sweep a woman off her feet."

Jasper pushed his hands deeper into his black coat pockets,

defying the biting chill while simultaneously hiding the trembling and twisting.

"Did you meet your wife at Durham University?" she asked, turning and looking at him with her blazing emerald eyes.

Suddenly, she stopped and placed an arm on his.

"I'm sorry, do you mind me asking about her?"

"Yes, I mean no," Jasper fumbled. "I met Jennifer in York when I was completing my articles. We literally bumped into each other one day... over... some rope." His voice trailed off.

"Rope?"

Jasper tried to banish the immediate memories from his mind.

"The Yorkshire Show – a tug of war contest."

Once they had descended the steps beside the elevated and contemporary architecture of Kingsgate pedestrian bridge, Jasper and Debra turned to walk downstream along the river bank. Through a camouflage of autumn shades they watched rowers in white vests glide by with powerful elegance as they walked, their footsteps crunching on the fresh, white powder of an early frost.

At the top of the steep, ivy clad riverbank and just discernible through the ebbing foliage stood the aged and imposing university buildings of St Chad's and St John's Colleges.

"Are we any closer to legal proceedings, Jasper?"

"I have taken advice on the strength of our case, which would be one of manslaughter by gross negligence. It's ambitious but there is a lot going for it." Jasper said as they resumed their walk beneath the canopy of golden chestnut leaves.

"Gross negligence?"

"Yes, the assertion that every member of society has a duty of care not to jeopardize the safety of others by reckless or careless behaviour, like not drinking and driving for example. Vaccinations such as MMR are in place to protect society as a whole, just as much as the individual."

"So they broke the law by not having their children vaccinated?" Debra said.

"That's one of the problems," Jasper said, pausing, "they have not broken any laws. However, that is not to say that they have not, by refusing to follow the widely recommended and accepted MMR vaccination, unreasonably put at risk the lives of others."

Debra's face was creased with concern and the worry lines etched into her pale complexion did not flatter her.

"You sound awfully... uncertain."

They had stopped outside the Count's House, a diminutive stone dwelling of peculiarly ostentatious architectural design.

"Do you know the story about this little stone house and the dwarf?" Jasper asked, digging his fingernails into the palms of his writhing hands, in the hope that inflicting pain might prevail where sheer willpower had failed in diminishing the insolent movements.

"Do you mean Count Joseph Boruwlaski, the Polish dwarf who fell in love with Durham in the eighteenth century? You forget who I married."

Jasper nodded and felt his mouth pout several times as his neck twisted to the left in a slow and agonising cramp.

"I'll be honest with you, Debra, this is one of my most challenging cases ever. There are no precedents in this section of law, there have not been for about a hundred years. I have to convince a jury that the Mallorys owed a duty of care to society by ensuring that their children were vaccinated. I have to show that by refusing the MMR they breached this duty and that this breach of duty caused Ollie's… death."

"Isn't it obvious?"

Jasper pulled a face and shrugged slightly.

"To you and me, perhaps, but in law we have to convince a jury that gross negligence has been perpetrated. Without precedents, that is never simple."

Debra's eyes began to fill with tears and her creased chin wobbled with emotion. She sniffed away her embarrassment and wiped her eyes with a balled up tissue.

"Can you win this case?" Debra asked with a thick voice.

Jasper paused, turning to face her despite the display of tics and spasms engulfing his body.

"There is a powerful lobby of support for this amongst many influential medical professionals who see compulsory vaccinations as the only solution. With the spectre of political backing in the wings, anything is possible."

"It sounds like such a long shot, Ollie deserves more than that," Debra said with a blocked nose and a shuddering chest.

Prebends Bridge appeared around the corner of the river, through branches languishing just above the surface of the water. Jasper stopped and held Debra firmly by her shoulders.

"I agree with you, but we do have a good case. Now think of it this way, Debra, Ollie could be immortalised. There is a measles epidemic spreading across Britain; if as a result of our case laws are changed to ensure the safety of millions of children out there, what a laudable outcome that would be."

"You mean his death would not be for nothing, if we won?"

Jasper nodded. "Just imagine – Ollie's Law."

Debra managed a cautious glimmer of a smile as they walked in silence past Prebends Bridge and then on towards Fulling Mill.

"Can I ask a favour of you, Debra?"

"Of course," she replied without hesitation.

He walked in silence a little longer, trying to organise his thoughts into words.

"I am hopeful that the coroner will release Jennifer's body in the next day or so and I have arranged the funeral for Friday."

Debra nodded as she dabbed at her eyes with a tissue.

"I feel that... that you... understand what has taken place," Jasper said, as tics ripped apart his dignified countenance.

He cast his eyes downwards, slightly embarrassed and self conscious, apprehensive at revealing his vulnerability.

"Would you please come to the funeral... for me?" he asked, looking up briefly into her green eyes before averting his gaze to the cascade of white water over the Fulling Mill weir.

FORTY

It was a beautiful bright day, the sun shining low in an unbroken powder-blue sky as the little huddle of mourners stood in lengthening November shadows. The frosty ground had thawed wherever the pale sunlight warmed it, leaving shrinking icy patches visible only in north facing shadows.

Even Lazlo was wearing a black suit as he stood beside Jasper. Charlotte was the only person wearing a hat, an ostentatious creation with a black veil that, were it not for the colour, might not have looked out of place at Ascot. She stood next to Jasper, but more than an arm's length away, protectively embracing her two young boys, Jack and Charlie, whose tear streaked faces required constant wiping on their sleeves.

A little distance behind Jasper stood Debra, maintaining a discrete presence, biting her cheek and lips continuously as she reflected on her own recent and still painful losses. Her fingers twisted around each other as she sought physical outlets for her inner torment.

Jasper could not help himself from scanning the faces of all the male mourners not known to him, searching for something, a facial sadness, a clue, a sixth sense even, that they may have been more to Jennifer than merely friends. Then a pang of guilt would leave him reeling from a wave of nausea, as he realised that no other man had been responsible for impregnating his wife, that no other man could be held accountable for a pregnancy that, for reasons yet unknown to him, drove her to the ultimate depths of despair.

He alone could fill those shoes, yet he still had no idea why such an elusive and joyous event should have lead to him standing beside an open hole in the frosty ground, bidding farewell to the only woman he had ever loved.

The turmoil in his soul seemed to be rising and closing around his throat. How could he methodically seek out and find the culpable party responsible for his wife's untimely death, when with every advancing step all fingers seemed to point back at him?

Were all the mourners staring at him, regarding him as responsible for Jennifer's death? He was in no doubt, not only from his recent encounter in York, but also from her reproachful glare, that Charlotte most certainly did.

Jasper spoke only twice. Once to thank Debra for being there, recognising the personal difficulty she must have experienced being at another funeral so soon, and once to Lazlo as the mourners began to disperse.

"The Swan, Lazlo? I have never needed a gay and frisky so badly."

Lazlo nodded his great head sombrely.

FORTY ONE

Three years previously

Evelyn Candle struggled to keep her eyes open as she lay struggling for breath beneath the starched, white sheets. Her shrivelled mouth remained slightly open, unable to shut even momentarily between desperate gasps for air.

"Has she gone?" Evelyn asked, with an urgency that she appeared incapable of mustering.

Jennifer sat down on the bed beside her mother-in-law and took hold of her skeletal hand, purple from bruises and with barely a morsel of flesh covering the protruding bones. The pale blue hospice room decorated in floral decals smelled pleasantly of lavender. *It was not a bad choice for one's last breath,* Jennifer thought.

"Yes, mum. The nurse has gone out for a coffee break, she said to call her if your pain returns."

Jennifer looked sad, her normally sparkling eyes dark and subdued, like a grey sky.

"Where's Jasper?" Evelyn asked, casting her wide, anxious eyes around the room.

"He's in court today, mum, but he said he would be here as soon as he could. He is on the late afternoon train."

Evelyn thought for a moment, as her little chest heaved up

and down ineffectually beneath the thin bed sheets.

"He's definitely… not here?" she asked, pausing for breath.

Jennifer shook her head in puzzlement.

"No, but he will be soon, he promised."

"I haven't long, Jennifer," Evelyn said and then stopped to catch her breath. "My time is near."

Jennifer squeezed her bony hand comfortingly. There was nothing to say, it was not a statement that she could refute.

"Have you and Jasper… ever thought… about children?" Evelyn said, looking intently into Jennifer's face through watery eyes that were sunken into her bony skull.

Jennifer managed a sad smile and nodded her head with some enthusiasm.

"Oh yes, mum, we are very keen to have children, probably quite soon I should think, I can't wait forever."

Evelyn did not return the smile and appeared to become more agitated, shaking her head from side to side.

"There's a letter… top drawer… for you," she said between sharp intakes of breath, inclining her head towards the bedside cabinet.

"For me?" Jennifer repeated, frowning and holding the palm of one hand across her chest.

"Please get it… before Jasper…"

Evelyn lifted her stick like arm and gestured for Jennifer to retrieve the letter. On the bedside cabinet a clear glass vase of mixed summer blooms, bright yellows, pinks, reds and violets, tried their best to cheer the atmosphere.

"This one?" Jennifer said holding a white envelope in her right hand and reading from it. "Private and Confidential. For Jennifer Candle only. To be opened immediately after my death. Evelyn Candle."

Evelyn nodded and licked her lips in agitation as she patted the space beside her where Jennifer had been sitting.

"Are you sure… Jasper's not here?" Evelyn said, her edgy eyes darting about the room.

Jennifer frowned, still distracted by the cryptic wording on the envelope.

"He's not, mum, but I'm sure he will be soon, don't worry."

Evelyn shook her head and patted the bed for Jennifer to sit down. Then she grabbed Jennifer's hand in both of her bony claws and looked at her intently.

"Listen, please Jennifer."

Jennifer frowned and felt her heart beginning to beat faster.

"I am so sorry… I never had the… courage…" Evelyn had to pause.

"Please, mum, don't make yourself so out of breath. You should rest."

"No!" she said with as much tenacity as she could muster in her failing little voice. "Listen, it's… very important."

Jennifer sat quietly, unable to take her eyes off her mother-in-law's desperate face.

"Are you pregnant yet?"

Jennifer was taken by surprise and looked away.

"Are you?" Evelyn repeated.

"No, no mum."

"Good."

Jennifer frowned. Evelyn nodded her head and breathed deeply several times, licking her dry, cracked lips with a tongue that looked as rough as pumice.

Jennifer was both stunned and puzzled by her response. Was it the medication perhaps? She was after all on morphine. Was she getting confused as her body and mind inevitably began to wane?

"I failed as a mother," Evelyn breathed heavily, "Failed. I could not… tell Jasper… could not… tell you. The letter… you must read…"

"I will, mum, I will," Jennifer said, her face deeply furrowed with incomprehension.

"Not until I die… promise me."

"I promise, mum."

Jennifer stared at the envelope in her right hand, and at Evelyn's spidery handwriting in HB pencil. The envelope wasn't excessively thick and contained perhaps two or three pages at most.

"Put it away," Evelyn said, gesturing with her emaciated arms, "and promise me…"

"I promise, mum, I will wait," Jennifer said, tucking the envelope into her black, leather clutch bag.

"Promise me… you won't ever… tell Jasper."

Jennifer's composure began to melt and she felt sobs breaking through her anxious, confused tension.

"What is going on, mum, you're scaring me?"

Evelyn slumped back on the pillows and closed her eyes, exhausted.

"Read the letter… I'm so… so sorry."

Jennifer began to sob. She was frightened. She was alone, and she had just promised to keep it that way.

"Won't it help you to talk about it, mum?" she said, with desperation in her faltering voice.

Evelyn did not open her eyes and as she spoke she barely moved a muscle.

"Call the nurse… I need morphine… please dear…"

Jennifer stared at the shrivelled old lady, feeling pity, confusion, a sense of unease. What a bizarre and unexpected few minutes with her mother-in-law. She was about to leave the room and call a nurse when she heard a soft whisper escape from Evelyn's inert face.

"Forgive me."

Justice is a temporary thing that must at last come to an end;
but the conscience is eternal and will never die.

Martin Luther

FORTY TWO

It was not a wake in the traditional sense, but this did not seem to bother either Lazlo or Jasper. They sat side by side at the bar on padded high wooden stools, because their usual brass table at the window overlooking the tranquillity of the River Wear was occupied by a couple who seemed unable to keep their passionate hands off each other.

Jasper had stopped glancing in their direction. Watching the hunger and mutual appreciation in their eyes only intensified his guilt and remorse for opportunities lost, for permitting the banality of his prosaic marriage to become entrenched.

"I can't even remember it happening," Jasper said as he tilted his tumbler this way and that, clinking the three ice cubes against the glass.

Lazlo finished a deep gulp of Black Sheep ale, before flicking a subtle glance in Jasper's direction.

"What happening?"

Jasper sighed with irritation.

"She was pregnant, Lazlo, with *my* baby," Jasper accentuated the word 'my'.

Lazlo nodded thoughtfully.

"Why would she kill my baby? Why would she do such a thing?"

Lazlo turned his bloated head towards Jasper's downcast frame and tried to make eye contact.

"You don't know that she was thinking of killing the baby, guv."

Jasper snorted and took a warming mouthful of amber Chivas.

"I'll never know that she wasn't. I wanted a child just as much as I thought she did."

"Why would she want to kill your unborn child and herself, guv? It makes no sense. She could not have known that she was pregnant."

Jasper stabbed the bar counter with an extended index finger.

"Exactly, Lazlo, it makes no sense. She must have thought the baby wasn't mine. Perhaps the fear of all that inevitable shame and indignity was just too much?"

Barely audible above the jovial murmurings of The Swan's clientele, Louis Armstrong croaked his way through the timeless melodies in 'What a Wonderful World'.

"Mrs Candle was a good wife, guv, an honourable and faithful partner to your good self. As much as I have loathed digging into her private affairs for you, I have found nothing to indicate otherwise."

Jasper's eyes drifted down to the floor, focusing between his polished brogues on the peanuts and crushed crisps scattered on the rich, red pile carpet.

"In the early years Jennifer and I... we were very close. But with time, as everything became stale and no family was forthcoming... well... it was like she became more of a bread knife to me, you know, than a hugs and kisses. I had my clients, the demands of my work, but if Jennifer was lonely who is to say that she didn't find herself an artful dodger?"

"But, guv, I haven't found a shred of evidence that there was anybody else in her life."

Jasper dropped several peanuts into his mouth before pulling a small notepad from the pocket of his starched, white shirt.

"Let me show you something, Lazlo. Do you know how many unaccompanied men were at the funeral today?"

Jasper flicked through the notepad pages as Lazlo looked at him with a furrow in his brow. He studied his boss's flickering eyelids, the twitches, the distortions, the uncontrolled roll of his left shoulder about once every minute, the occasional spasmodic pout of his lips, and he felt a deep stirring of sympathy.

"I looked into each of their faces as they stood, assembled around the coffin, and counted them – thirteen, excluding you, the vicar and me."

Lazlo looked down dolefully into his glass of Black Sheep.

"Your missus played the cello in a chamber group, guv," Lazlo suppressed the urge to say 'remember'. "Most of the musicians are men. I checked."

Jasper shook his head defiantly.

"But think of it, Lazlo, does a chamber group of men not provide opportunity?"

"But she didn't have motive, did she, guv?"

Lazlo regretted this remark as soon as the words were cold on his lips and he saw the hurt on Jasper's tormented face.

"You're wrong, Lazlo, I just know it. There has to have been someone. If not one of the chamber group then what about all those secretive journeys down to London?"

"The infertility specialists?" Lazlo said making a face.

Jasper twirled a hand in the air as he shook his head.

"No, not them, the other recent visits. Did you find out who she went to see?"

Behind them a salacious giggle pierced the pub's background noise and both Jasper and Lazlo turned around instinctively on their stools to trace the libidinous emission. The young woman, bursting out of a dress several sizes too small, was now draped across the young man's lap. Their faces said it all as they cavorted suggestively. Lazlo groaned.

"There was only one," Lazlo said as he turned around again, exchanging a look of disapproval with Jasper.

"One?" Jasper looked disappointed. Then his brain moved on sluggishly through the malted euphoria and he asked the only question that seemed important in his quest. "How long ago? Did she see this person around two, maybe three months back?"

Lazlo paused and sought solace in his Black Sheep. He could not bring himself to meet his boss's searching eyes, the eyes that pinched and squeezed like a puppet on a maniac's string.

"Two days before she died, guv."

FORTY THREE

Dr Majid Eldabe's secretary was plump and middle aged. Her knitted mauve dress moulded into the grooves and crevices that formed around her midriff as she sat down in front of his desk. Eldabe was reading and she waited patiently, holding a sheet of A4 paper in her hand, glancing down occasionally at it and pressing her lips together to smooth the freshly applied dark plum lipstick.

"Yes, Mrs Caruthers?" he said, in a deep and strongly Arabic inflection, without looking up.

Eldabe was in his late fifties, with greying temples and eyebrows, a deep walnut complexion and aristocratic brown eyes.

Mrs Caruthers cleared her throat, perhaps from the overpowering scent of musk that emanated from him, and lifted the sheet of paper, hesitating as her eyes flicked between it and Eldabe's face which was still very much focused on the papers he was reading. He was aware of her dilemma but failed to look up, merely raising the fingers of his right hand that had been busily twirling his pencil thin moustache.

"What is it?"

She cleared her throat again.

"A private investigator has been calling."

Eldabe licked a finger to turn a page, then used that finger to twirl his moustache as he continued to read.

"And?"

"He was asking about a patient you saw recently."

"Well, it is none of his business. Tell him that." Eldabe said dismissively and turned another page on his desk.

"I did, Dr Eldabe, several times, but he keeps calling. He says this patient committed suicide two days after seeing you."

Eldabe's eyebrows lifted slightly and his eyes appeared to lose their point of focus.

"Who does he work for?"

Mrs Caruthers fumbled with the sheet of paper and squinted at it.

"He works for the patient's husband, who is a compensation lawyer."

Eldabe turned suddenly and fixed his deep, brown eyes on his secretary.

"Is that what they want?"

"I don't know, sir. He said the husband is trying to understand why his wife committed suicide."

Eldabe returned to his reading, appearing to have dismissed the importance of the issue.

"My consultations with patients are a confidential matter all the same. He is not entitled to know anything."

She stood up to leave, perhaps accustomed to his mannerisms and knowing when a conversation was over.

"He did say that if we couldn't co-operate he thought the husband would make an appointment to see you himself," Mrs Caruthers said hesitantly.

Eldabe shrugged his narrow shoulders beneath an immaculately tailored platinum silk suit.

"Let him, I cannot tell him anything either."

She began to open the door quietly to exit.

"Mrs Caruthers?" he said, looking up.

"Yes?"

"What is the name of the patient they are interested in?"

She looked down at the sheet of paper she held.

"Jennifer Candle."

He nodded silently and pursed his lips, twirling his moustache as he pondered, hoping to recall the patient and trying to decide on a course of action.

"Bring me her file, please."

FORTY FOUR

Jasper concentrated on the little white ball, willing and hoping that his arms would not jerk the club awkwardly as the moment of impact approached. He swung the club slowly above his shoulders, trying to focus his every fibre on just that one small, white spot. Then the club began its forward acceleration, smoothly, controlled, until suddenly the muscles of his left shoulder contorted. The shaft of the club sliced across the ball sending it skidding unsuccessfully across the manicured lawn at a discomfiting angle.

"Bad luck, old boy," Merrill Bradshaw said jovially.

"Brad Pitt!" Jasper cursed under his breath.

Merrill was wearing black and white checked plus fours, long black socks and shiny white golf shoes, all topped with a bright orange golf shirt. But for the noble belly, his appearance was reminiscent of Payne Stewart's extrovert style of dress.

"Try keeping your left arm straight during follow through, like this."

Merrill addressed his ball and executed a short and stiff swing which, despite its awkwardness, connected more effectively with the little ball and propelled it into the air surprisingly well.

"Thank you for seeing me, Merrill," Jasper said as he placed another ball on the driving mat.

In stark and distinctive contrast, Jasper was wearing his work clothes, pin stripe charcoal trousers, billowing white shirt tamed by peacock-blue braces and black brogues.

Stretching to the left and right of them in a gentle semi-circle were dozens of small cubicles occupied by an energetic mosaic of aspiring golfers, all practising their addictive hobby.

"Glad you could join me at the club. You should come over more often."

Merrill swung again and thumped the ball impatiently into the abyss beyond the semi-circle. In the distance, visible above the thinning golden foliage, was the outline of Brancepeth Castle's sandstone battlements.

Jasper leaned on his club, reticent to make another attempt at hitting the evasive little ball given his additional impediment of unpredictable muscular spasms.

"I wanted to discuss the Ollie Kowalski case with you," Jasper said.

"Shoot old boy."

Merrill paused momentarily as he lined up his club and ball.

"Was this the one involving the boy who contracted measles from someone at school – allegedly?"

Jasper nodded.

"You told me that I should consider carefully the reasons why the parents did not have their child vaccinated."

"I did," Merrill said nodding, before swinging successfully once again. "*Mens rea* is a powerful argument in any reasonable legal defence, as you well know."

Jasper licked his lips excitedly and shifted weight from one leg to another as he sensed the spasms invading his thigh.

"In 1998 some research was published suggesting a link between MMR and autism. It became a public media storm when the newspapers went into a fit and spasm over it."

"Claiming what?"

"That MMR vaccination caused autism in children."

Merrill lifted his eyes away from the golf ball and looked at Jasper with interest.

"And does it?"

"Apparently not," Jasper said, "but you would certainly think otherwise if you read the newspapers."

Merrill shrugged.

"Good old sensationalist British journalism – headlines to sell papers."

"The research was quickly discredited; its author vilified, censured, and struck off the GMC."

"… but the damage to public confidence in MMR was already done." Merrill finished, resting his elbow on the top of his golf club in contemplation.

Jasper addressed the ball before him, grinding his teeth with determination to control the trembling and twitching in his arms. He swung as a spasm in his thigh twisted his posture monstrously, and the club missed the ball completely.

"Bad luck, old boy. It'll come," Merrill said with a chuckle.

Jasper wished for his rotund friend to mishit the ball, even only once, to boost his flagging spirits.

"How many parents have taken similar actions in shunning the MMR for fear of autism?" Merrill asked.

Jasper leaned his weight on to his club and raised his eyebrows.

"Thousands, perhaps tens of thousands," he said with a shrug of his shoulders.

Merrill drew breath through clenched teeth.

"Many casualties?"

"Lots of them, plus a few deaths. Ollie Kowalski was by no means the only one."

Merrill leant on his golf club with crossed forearms, a posture that pushed his globular belly closer to the Astroturf driving mat. He looked into Jasper's face with his head inclined slightly to one side.

"What is your argument in this case, counsel?"

Jasper took a deep breath and squared up to Merrill as spasms racked his left arm and shoulder.

"Gross negligence," Jasper said as his left eye twitched violently, "a failure to conform to accepted vaccination policy, a failure to heed medical and DoH advice thereby posing an imminent danger to other members of society."

"You can prove that?"

"There can be little doubt that Ollie Kowalski contracted measles solely because Seamus Mallory was not vaccinated and consequently brought measles into the school."

Merrill nodded slowly, swaying back and forth, using the golf club as a fulcrum as he pondered Jasper's statement.

"If I were your opposing counsel, my defence would be," he paused, "that the medically uninformed and emotively vulnerable in society would likely be influenced by the media storm, brainwashed, if you like, into a genuine fear for the safety of their children. Their state of mind might be such that they denied their children the MMR with the very best of intentions for their personal safety."

"But they were so terribly wrong."

Merrill gripped his club in both gloved hands once more and aimed it at the little white ball.

"That they were, but *mens rea* is established and provides a reasonable defence."

Jasper felt his frustration mounting. He tried to address the ball and expunge some of his irritation by sending it flying into the early autumn evening sky, but the worsening tremor in his hands and the rolling contortions of his shoulder made him realise that he would achieve only greater humiliation by further attempts at punishing the ball.

"The courts will over rule the decisions of parents who unreasonably deny their children medical treatment, like blood transfusions. Surely denying them the MMR is no different? In addition to which the endangerment posed by this act extends beyond the immediate legal jurisdiction of their children and threatens the wider public, does it not?"

Merrill nodded slowly as he processed this.

"Compelling argument, Jasper, I'll give you that. But entirely without precedent; don't forget that parents are free in the eyes of the law to make reasonable decisions relating to the welfare of their children."

"Denying Seamus Mallory the MMR resulted in the death of Ollie Kowalski. That is hardly reasonable."

"But their state of mind in reaching that decision could be argued as being reasonable, could it not? They were, along with thousands, influenced by the reporting in the media. *Mens rea*, Jasper, *mens rea*."

Merrill could sound so sanctimonious at times, Jasper thought as he glared at him. Merrill looked down at the golf ball and swung again, sending it flying once more with monotonous predictability.

"You could say the authors of that flawed research have blood on their hands," Merrill said.

"Not to mention the newspapers," Jasper added.

"Well you can't very well file a class action against the entire newspaper establishment, old boy, as lucrative as that may sound," Merrill mused with a throaty chuckle. "Candle versus Fleet Street." He painted a slogan in the air with the sweep of his hand.

Jasper did not miss the intentional jibe and replaced the golf club into its bag.

"You all right, old boy, you haven't hit many balls today?" Merrill said.

Jasper turned away to rub his deforming face and pouting lips.

"I'm absolutely bloody Rolls Royce, thank you for asking."

Jasper's voice reverberated thickly in his ears, as though it was not his own. He walked away somewhat unsteadily, watched by a curious and mystified Merrill Bradshaw who shook his head briefly before punishing another ball.

FORTY FIVE

The carriage doors closed with a muted hydraulic sigh and in an instant the interminable drone of station noise almost vanished, but for the footsteps of disembarking passengers leaving the platform. Jasper leaned against a pillar, his hands pushed deep into the warm pockets of his black cashmere coat.

"Jasper!" said a familiar voice.

Jasper turned and found himself staring into the broadly grinning face of Magnus Burns. He was wearing a camel greatcoat with a long, burgundy woollen scarf tied ostentatiously around his neck and held in one hand a dark brown violin case with a big red 'fragile' sticker on it.

"Magnus, what a surprise," Jasper said.

They shook hands energetically as soft puffs of vapour formed in front of their faces in the cold air. Magnus smelled of expensive *eau de homme.*

"In town for a concert?" Jasper said.

Magnus shook his head.

"Just passing through, on my way to a concert in Edinburgh tonight. How are things with the case?"

Jasper returned his trembling hands to the obscurity of his coat pockets.

"Going well, Magnus. We're in discussion with the trust solicitors about our intentions."

Magnus looked pleased.

"Does this mean court soon? Have you found a guilty party?"

"I am still hopeful that the trust will offer a settlement because there are so many individuals in the frame for culpability."

"Settlement?" Magnus frowned deeply as his shoulders dropped slightly.

"That's often the outcome of a negligence suit."

"I don't understand. Are you not finding anybody responsible for my father's death?"

Jasper shifted weight as his thigh muscles began to ripple beneath the charcoal pinstripe trousers, managing to time the move such that he disguised a spasmodic roll of his left shoulder.

"Do you know how many people work on a hospital ward?"

"Yes, but somebody must have been responsible. What about the patient who brought the gastroenteritis on to the ward in the first place?" Magnus said, slightly sharply.

Jasper frowned.

"She died."

Magnus hesitated and looked around before returning his gaze to Jasper's face.

"But how did the infection get from her to my father?"

Jasper nodded animatedly.

"That's what we're focusing on. That and why the patient with tommy guns was admitted to your father's ward in the first instance."

"Tommy guns?"

"Sorry, gastroenteritis."

Magnus nodded thoughtfully, changing the violin case from one hand to another.

"So you may never be able to blame anyone for my father's death?"

"That depends on how much they contest our allegations. It's quite a complicated case, Magnus, with so many people potentially culpable along the way. We feel negligence is evident, but finding a specific person to blame may... well... be difficult."

Magnus appeared deflated and moved to sit down on a nearby open bench.

"I never thought that all I would get from this was money. I wanted justice, I wanted..."

"An eye for an eye?" Jasper offered, taking the seat beside him and rubbing away several violent pouts that corrupted his lip and cheek muscles with the flat of his hand.

Magnus did not notice as he stared emptily at the platform.

"I don't really know."

"I can offer you closure, Magnus. Whatever form the outcome of legal proceedings assumes, what it will hopefully bring to you is closure of a painful chapter in your life."

Magnus looked up at Jasper with big, imploring eyes.

"And what about the guilt, Jasper, is it not the act of someone saying 'sorry' that helps me to overcome my guilt?"

Jasper remained silent as his mind turned to his own turmoil, his own gnawing guilt. Who could he hope to get an apology from for Jennifer's death? How would he achieve a sense of closure in his own grievous personal loss?

"I can't fix everything, Magnus, but I am doing my best to ensure that they do not get away without some apportionment of blame, so that your father did not die unnecessarily and without any restitution."

Magnus placed the violin case squarely across his lap and

rested his arms on top of it. His left leg bounced rhythmically and he began to tap his fingers on the case as he stared over the rail tracks.

"Tonight I'm playing Mendelsohn's violin concerto. I think I am in the right frame of mind to perform it well."

"How so?" Jasper said

"It is filled with reflective melancholy."

The two men sat in silence for a moment, deep in thought. Between them they possessed enough regret and misery to fill the entire Usher Hall in Edinburgh without playing a single note of Mendelsohn.

"*The next train to arrive at platform two is the 13.20 to Edinburgh calling at Newcastle, Berwick upon Tweed, and Edinburgh Waverley,*" the muffled tannoy speakers blurted.

Magnus stood up and brushed his coat.

"That's my train."

Jasper stood and extended his right hand.

"Good luck."

Magnus gripped Jasper's hand and looked straight into his eyes.

"No, good luck to you. I'm counting on you, Jasper."

Magnus boarded the train and Jasper sat down with a thump and a sigh. His shoulder rolled, his neck twisted to the left and his thigh rippled. What next, he wondered, staring at the trembling hands in his lap? He felt a vibration from within his coat and pulled out the iPhone.

"*This is a redirected call from… 0-1-9-1-3-8-7-6-5-3-2.*"

Jasper had had all incoming calls to his home redirected to his mobile number.

"Jasper, yes?"

"*This is Framwellgate Dry Cleaners calling. Jennifer Candle brought in a red coat for dry cleaning and has still not collected it. It's been here over three weeks now. Could you please ask her to call for it."*

Jasper felt his heart sink as he was reminded again that not everyone in the world knew of his loss, that not everyone shared his grief. Two days earlier he had taken a call from Jennifer's dentist, protesting at the fact that she had missed her appointment without the common courtesy of cancelling it. Jasper tightened his lips as he was again reminded that the world continued to revolve and function as normal for everyone else around him.

"I'm sorry, I'll have it collected," Jasper said in a monotone voice and disconnected the call.

FORTY SIX

Jasper's walk through the centre of Northallerton was slow and pensive, each leaden footstep thudding as he gradually approached the formidable Salvation Army signpost, his landmark for locating the surgery. *Blood and Fire:* the words of the Salvation Army motto resonated in Jasper's head as he contemplated where he might be destined to end up.

The waiting room was more cheerful, with brightly dressed mothers and their children, smiling pensioners, everyone nursing some form of ailment, but seemingly none the worse for it.

"Mr Candle," Dr Giordano called to him in her mellifluous Neapolitan voice, rescuing him from a little girl who was going around the waiting room offering jelly beans to all the doting pensioners.

Jasper unbuttoned his thick cashmere coat before sitting down in her consulting room, quickly regretting this decision. His arms disobeyed, his neck contorted and his waist twisted twice, most of which would have been largely obscured beneath the thick folds of his coat. He felt self conscious, embarrassed and under scrutiny.

"How have you been?" she said with a concerned smile, tapping at the keyboard on her desk to bring up his details.

He shrugged.

"I'm keeping busy, I'm coping, I think."

"Have you been to see Dr Montgolfier yet?"

She glanced across at him.

"No," he said quickly and looked down.

Giordano nodded but the smile faded slightly.

"He's very good, you know."

"I have made an effort to cut back. It's been difficult though… Jennifer's funeral was only… on Friday."

"Good," she said and oozed positive appreciation. "You will need to, Mr Candle, your liver tests are quite worrying."

"I will, I promise. I mean, I know I have to do it."

Giordano swung around in her swivel chair to face Jasper. He felt uncomfortable as the full concentration of her educated eyes took in his corrupted features. Every twitch, every spasm of his shoulder and arm suddenly seemed enormously amplified to him under her perceptive gaze, like an owl – she missing nothing.

"I must tell you, Mr Candle, that I cannot fully explain some of these movements that you have."

"You mean it's not the whisky?"

She frowned, eyes searching the room.

"The trembling could be, the occasional unsteadiness could be too…"

Jasper sighed. It was time to face up to the mounting severity of his physical problems. There was no point in denying them any longer. But deep within his tormented soul he was suddenly afraid, afraid of losing control, afraid of what he did not know and understand.

"They're getting worse, Doctor. First it was my eye, and my face, then my neck and then my shoulder. Now my legs are affected as well."

Giordano made a brief note with her Mont Blanc pen, but said nothing.

"What's happening to me? I've assumed, perhaps hoped, that it was all due to stress and… perhaps the whisky…"

She paused.

"I'll be honest, Mr Candle. The whisky has certainly not helped, but I don't fully understand what is going on."

Jasper lowered his head and studied his hands as he intertwined his fingers nervously. This was the moment he had been so afraid of confronting.

"Would you consider seeing a specialist?" Giordano said.

That word had so many connotations and associations for Jasper that he could not help but recoil from it.

"What sort of specialist?"

"A neurologist."

"Why a neurologist? Surely I just need to see someone like Dr Montgolfier to help me with the drinking?"

He nodded and clasped his hands together tightly, squeezing them until the knuckles blanched. Yet still they trembled and twitched like those of a possessed man.

"I think we should make sure that there is nothing else going on with you."

Jasper breathed deeply. He just didn't want to accept what his problem was – he was afraid.

"I suppose I don't have much choice."

"And you must stop drinking, Mr Candle. No question about it."

Suddenly he heard himself blurt out: "You don't think I might have something like a brain tumour, do you?"

Giordano put down her pen and sat straight up as she addressed him.

"I really do not know at this stage."

Jasper tried to swallow, but his mouth was too dry. He had just one thought in his mind – how much he wanted a whisky.

FORTY SEVEN

Lazlo stepped forward cheerfully and held out a cup of steaming coffee as Jasper descended the station steps. It was a bitterly cold day and Lazlo had covered his head with a woollen hat in combat green, the worn collar of his favourite leather jacket turned up against the cold.

"They've launched their seasonal varieties, so I got each of us a gingerbread latte, guv," Lazlo said before sipping from his own paper cup.

"I hate ginger."

"Sorry, guv. Want to change it?"

"No," Jasper grunted, "I want to put Chivas in it."

Lazlo nodded and shrugged his shoulders as the pair walked down the roadway, away from the station and across the arched pedestrian bridge leading to the town centre. The bridge was damp with trampled, rotting leaves, from which emanated a smell reminiscent of shaded woodland.

"How did it go, guv?" Lazlo asked.

"Well, I cannot put Chivas in my coffee, even if I had some."

"Oh."

They walked down the hill, past Highgate, towards the distant, elevated stone walls of the central markets.

"I have managed to find out that there were more than just the seven staff members affected by the gastroenteritis outbreak on Edward Burns' ward," Lazlo said through the clouds of steamy vapour around his face.

Jasper looked up as he drank some of the latte.

"Actually, this is not bad, Lazlo, even without scotch."

"Two catering staff also got it, one of the floor cleaners and a family visiting someone in Edward Burns' cubicle. There is some doubt as to whether this family were already symptomatic with it at the time of the old woman's admission."

"Oh that's just chicken plucking great, that is."

Lazlo stopped at the pedestrian crossing and pressed the button. Jasper drew up beside him.

"I don't know if I can get all their names, guv." Lazlo said, with an apprehensive grimace on his face.

"Your sweetheart getting nervous, is she?"

Jasper sighed and dropped his unfinished coffee cup into a dustbin on the railing.

"I don't think it matters that much, Lazlo. I was talking to Magnus Burns and I think he might be getting used to the idea of a more general claim of negligence, rather than specifically blaming individuals. There are just too many permutations in this case."

They began to cross the road and walk over Framwellgate Bridge, with its impressive backdrop of Durham Castle's elevated battlements above nearly naked, wintry trees.

"I need some time to reconsider our strategy in this case, Lazlo," Jasper said, sucking air in through his teeth.

Lazlo frowned. He had never known Jasper to take his boot off the other man's throat when he was floored. The guv'nor that he knew did not abide by the Queensbury Rules. His success was not borne out of meakness, or gentlemanly consideration.

They walked up Silver Street and paused beneath the newly refurbished statue of the Marquis of Londonderry upon his steed.

"I contacted that specialist in London, guv," Lazlo said.

Jasper's eyes brightened up despite the nagging tics and twitches distorting his face.

"Uh-huh."

"Dr Majid Eldabe. He wouldn't speak to me, but his secretary told me his patient consultations are confidential."

Jasper nodded and looked down as he scraped the granite paving stones with the toe of his brogue.

"They always say that."

"I told him you would be in touch."

"Is this the doctor Jennifer saw two days before... er?" Jasper said.

"Yes, guv."

Jasper hesitated as he tried to imagine what could have affected Jennifer so significantly in those two days to drive her beyond the limits of desperation.

"What kind of specialist is he?" Jasper asked quietly, without looking at Lazlo.

Lazlo fumbled in the pocket of his leather jacket and extracted a crumpled pad. He flipped through the pages, habitually licking the tip of his index finger as he did so.

"He's a... neurologist, guv."

Jasper felt his heart skip a beat, then his neck twisted demonically to the left and his arm jerked against his ribs several times.

"Cheese and rice."

"You okay, guv?"

Jasper stared past Lazlo blankly with his mouth slightly

agape. The only visible signs of neural activity were the tics and contortions of his ashen face.

"No, I'm bloody well not."

Lazlo creased his brow as he studied his guvnor's tormented face.

"Isn't it time to go home again, guv? You can't keep living in your office."

Jasper glanced at Lazlo and then looked across the market square, watching people sitting on benches around the statue eating sandwiches, or pasties.

"No time for sentimentality, Lazlo, I have to go to London. Give me the number for that neurologist so Stacey can make an appointment for me."

FORTY EIGHT

Jasper used to walk wherever he went in London. He loved feeling the gritty pace of the city at close quarters, hearing the little conversations and smelling the cafés and bars as he passed them. But he had been forced underground, travelling blindfolded and isolated from the vibrant activity of the streets way above the tunnels. The crippling contortions and increasing stiffness of his legs simply could not carry him from Kings Cross Station and along Euston Road to Harley Street, a journey he would, in the past, have walked with ease.

He exited Regent's Park underground station, squinting in the bright light, then walked the short distance along Marylebone Road until he reached Harley Street.

Jasper felt as though he was being watched by the ghostly presence of Jennifer, who must have trodden these very same steps in her final days. What was it that had brought her to Harley Street? More importantly, what was it that had driven her from Harley Street to that makeshift noose in their entrance hall?

He passed Devonshire Street and hobbled further on to Weymouth Street, pausing at times to rest his cramping thighs.

The address he sought turned out to be a stylish, end terraced property built out of elegant, pinkish sandstone, rather like rosé. He pushed through the heavy black door and followed the signs to Dr Eldabe's reception.

It felt eerie to retrace Jennifer's ill-fated footsteps and he was overcome slightly by the mysterious irony of unfolding events.

"Please take a seat, Mr Candle. Dr Eldabe will only be a few minutes," said Mrs Caruthers, sat behind a computer and typing with professional dexterity.

She wore a peach coloured suit with a large dragonfly broach on the lapel. The waiting room smelled strongly of exotic spices, though Jasper was unable to identify them.

Jasper sat and stretched his stiff, aching legs, his quadriceps rippling rebelliously and constantly. He was alarmed at how much stamina his once sturdy legs had lost on the failed attempt at walking from Kings Cross. Jasper rubbed his trembling hands and noticed that the receptionist took no notice of his twisting neck or disobedient arm movements. She was no doubt accustomed to all manner of neurological peculiarities in this waiting room.

"Mr Candle, please," Dr Eldabe ushered Jasper into his office with a smile and flourish of his arm as he held the door ajar with the other.

The office was richly furnished with turned wooden side tables, chairs and a collection of elegant smoking hookahs: one made out of burnished brass and adorned with plush red satin; the second crafted from flecked Carrera marble, the third out of cut crystal decorated with filigree gold. Hanging on the walls, rich tapestries featured horsemen riding in the desert.

"What can I do for you, Mr Candle?" Eldabe asked from behind his wide desk, twirling his pencil thin moustache between two fingers.

His eyes never left Jasper's face, studying the muscles that worked away beneath the skin, never resting, ever mutinous.

"I've come about my wife, Jennifer."

Eldabe nodded slowly.

"You've journeyed a long way for nothing, as I told you, sir."

Jasper took a deep breath.

"Doctor, my wife hanged herself two days after sitting in this very same chair I am in now."

"I am deeply sorry to hear that," Eldabe said with sincerity.

"I am struggling to understand why she would do such a thing. I need to know."

Eldabe sat forward and placed both elbows on the desk, resting his chin on clasped hands.

"What do you expect me to be able to tell you?"

"Why she came to see you? What you told her? We think her visit to you could be crucial to understanding her suicidal motivation."

"We?" Eldabe frowned.

"My associate and I; he is my investigator."

"Ah yes, you are a compensation lawyer, are you not, specialising in medical negligence? You have an impressive website, for clients that is, not doctors."

Eldabe sat back and folded his arms tightly, lifting one hand to twirl the moustache again.

"I'm not here as a lawyer. I'm here as a grieving husband... a widower."

"Even so, Mr Candle, your wife's medical details are protected by a code of confidentiality that I cannot break."

Jasper's twitching eyes became imploring.

"Please think back, can you not remember her state of

mind when you saw her? Was she upset, depressed, irrational?"

Eldabe hesitated.

"Not to diminish your wife's memory in any way, sir, but I see a lot of patients every day, and I cannot recall Mrs Candle that clearly."

Jasper looked deflated and his brow creased as his lips pouted several times.

"But you must keep notes?"

Eldabe nodded.

"I have reviewed them in anticipation of your visit and despite now being refreshed about the discussions that took place, I cannot specifically recall Mrs Candle."

"What?"

"This may of course be taken positively because she did not make so memorable an impression on me, either because of her behaviour or demeanour, that I would remember. She was just… another patient."

"Please, Doctor, I need your help. Tell me why my wife came to see you down here in London. We live 350 miles up country. Why you? Why a neurologist? She was not to my knowledge in poor health of any sort."

Eldabe shook his head slowly and maintained his eye contact with Jasper.

"I understand how you feel, but I'm sorry, sir, I cannot."

Jasper breathed deeply, his eyes wandering the room as he searched the recesses of his deepest emotions. Everywhere that he had searched for answers had drawn a blank and Dr Eldabe seemed to represent his last opportunity to understand the desperation that drove Jennifer to her death.

"You understand nothing. Jennifer and I were declared infertile after years of tests, broken hearted and unable to have children, yet upon her death I found out not only that she was taking contraceptives, but from the post mortem examination that she was pregnant, with my baby inside her. How am I supposed to feel, Doctor?"

Eldabe pursed his lips and twiddled his moustache but said nothing, the small skin creases around his eyes tightening and relaxing as he searched the depths of his compassion.

"I've had my investigator spying on the ghosts of my wife's past, looking for clues that would point me in the right direction, to help me unravel this tragedy. How do you think that makes me feel, looking for evidence that my wife of fifteen years was unfaithful?"

Jasper stared at Eldabe, his eyes strained, his mouth drawn, then extracted a brown envelope from his coat pocket.

"I have brought a copy of my marriage certificate to Jennifer, a copy of my passport as well as Jennifer's and I have her death certificate here as well. You cannot harm her by helping me, Doctor, you cannot disgrace her or embarrass her. I ask you to examine your conscience, your sense of benevolence. What did you discuss with her... please?"

Eldabe stood up and walked across to the row of hookahs on a polished wooden mantelpiece. He ran a sentimental finger along the elegant, curved lines of the Carrera marble hookah, perhaps his favourite.

"I've been practising here for twenty five years now and in the past, before all these ridiculous health and safety laws, I used to sit down every day and enjoy a relaxing smoke on one of my hookahs. It helped me to see things clearly, muddle over dilemmas and calm myself from the distress of my patients' often tragic circumstances."

Jasper's eyes remained downcast in his lap, staring at his

trembling fingers, his twitching arm occasionally rolling to one side as his shoulder lifted.

"But the law is the law, and as much as I detest and despise it, I too have to abide by it. Now my hookahs are merely ornamental. You are a lawyer, I'm sure you understand this, Mr Candle."

Jasper stood up unsteadily and picked up the envelope. He pulled his black coat straight and walked to the door, past Eldabe without uttering a word. He felt deflated and empty, overcome by a despondency he had not known since the days when his father would berate him and criticise his failures, realising that he might now never know why his life had taken such a tragically bitter turn.

"Mr Candle."

Jasper paused at the door, his outstretched palm pressing down on the brass door handle.

"I cannot reveal to you the contents of my consultation with your wife, but I can tell you that she was deeply concerned about you, concerned for your welfare."

Eldabe stared at Jasper, whose twitching eyes were riveted to the door.

"I gave her a typed letter summarising the key points of our discussion."

Jasper looked sharply across at Eldabe, into his confident gaze.

"She took it with her," Eldabe said quietly.

Jasper's heart jumped. The search was not over.

FORTY NINE

His house was cold and Jasper went straight to the kitchen and activated the central heating. It smelled dank and stale. All the house plants had died, little flying insects lay strewn in the kitchen sink, fruit in a bowl on the table had rotted, the apples a mushy caramel-brown colour, the shrivelled oranges had turned a mildewy-white and were tinged with greenish mould.

"What are we looking for, guv?"

"A letter, perhaps in an envelope, perhaps not. It may be in a dustbin, she may have hidden it, it might even be torn into pieces… I don't know."

"Do you have a loft, guv?"

Jasper nodded.

"Cellar?"

"No."

They began to search; opening drawers, looking under magazines and in between books, amongst the groceries, even methodically emptying the dustbins.

Lazlo opened the freezer and sifted through the frozen food.

"It won't be in there!" Jasper said shaking his head.

"I hide valuables in my freezer. It's a good place, guv."

After nearly an hour they had scoured all the downstairs reception rooms.

"You take the garage, don't forget Jennifer's car, I'll start in the bedrooms," Jasper said at the foot of the stairs.

Jasper returned to the bathroom where he had made that awful discovery in the cabinet just weeks back. There was nothing new to find. In the chill of the garage, Lazlo opened the boot of Jennifer's silver Audi TT, searched the glove compartment and even lifted the floor mats. The garage was neatly packed and tidy, what one might expect from someone obsessed with order. Stacked in one corner were several boxes, each marked with a different year and securely sealed with packing tape.

Probably client files from work, Lazlo thought, as he left the garage and headed back upstairs.

Jasper sat on the bed in his bedroom and scratched his forehead, having just turned over the mattress in desperation. As his thigh muscles rippled, making his leg bounce slightly, and his left arm writhed like a charmer's snake, his eyes wandered around the bedroom, trying to imagine where Jennifer might have placed a letter. Had she hidden it, intending for him not to find it? Did she destroy it? But why would she do such a thing? What could Dr Eldabe have told her that would have such a devastating effect on her? Might it have been something that she did not want him to know? His brain hurt from poring over the almost endless possibilities.

Jasper pulled out his iPhone and dialled. It was answered after five rings.

"Charlotte, it's Jasper here. Can we talk, please?"

His face was solemn and only his eyes moved.

"Please listen, I just want to ask you one thing, please."

A pause.

"Yes, it is about Jennifer, but believe me it is vitally important."

He waited.

"Please, Charlotte, just listen and you decide."

"Thank you. I have traced Jennifer's movements to a neurologist on Harley Street, two days before she…"

"Yes, a neurologist… I don't know why either. I can't understand it."

"Uh-huh. Look, Charlotte, I think that her consultation with this neurologist, a Dr Eldabe, may well have had something to do with her… er… decision to… you know…"

"Yes, of course I've been down to see him, but he wouldn't tell me anything."

Pause.

"His medical oath of confidentiality."

"Absolutely ridiculous, tell me about it."

"This is what I want to ask you. He says he gave Jennifer a letter when she left his rooms."

"Yes, apparently."

Jasper listened, frowning.

"He told me that the letter contained a summary of their discussion."

He took a deep breath and rubbed his forehead.

"The thing is we can't find it anywhere."

"Lazlo and I."

"Yes, she may have… but did she perhaps send anything to you for… er… safekeeping?"

"Nothing at all?"

Jasper hesitated, rubbing his writhing and pouting lips with trembling fingers.

"Are you quite sure?"

"No, definitely not a letter from Dr Eldabe?"

"Okay, thank you, Charlotte."

"Yes, I'll let you know if I discover anything. Bye."

Jasper looked towards the doorway as he heard Lazlo's footsteps approaching. Lazlo peered sheepishly around the corner of the bedroom door as though he was intruding.

"Found anything?" Lazlo asked.

"Not a Friar Tucking thing."

"Who is going up in the loft, guv?" Lazlo said, pointing up with an index finger.

"Will you fit through the hatch, Lazlo?"

Lazlo mouthed an expletive back to Jasper and continued to lean against the door frame with his left leg bent at the knee.

"Have you checked through the pockets of her clothes, guv?" Lazlo asked casually.

Jasper shot straight up, swayed slightly to the left, steadied himself, and raised a finger straight in the air.

"Bloody good idea, Lazlo. You're not my investigator for nothing."

Jasper began to slide open the large, oak panelled wardrobe door, revealing an expansive rail of colourful clothing. Lazlo squirmed awkwardly at the sight of his guvnor's wife's clothes.

"Loft hatch is on the landing. Call me if you get stuck," Jasper said.

There was no other way around it; Jasper started at one end, hunting through the clothes for pockets and then pushing his trembling fingers deep into each one. Smells reminiscent of Jennifer oozed out of every dress, some of her golden hairs still visible and curled on the fabric. Jasper found it emotionally traumatising to invade the sanctity and intimacy of her clothing, items that had enjoyed the luxury of caressing her warm, living skin not long ago. In a strangely absurd way he envied them. Gritting his teeth, he continued mechanically.

After much groaning and grunting, Lazlo re-emerged from the landing, his clothing dishevelled and dusty, his shirt hanging out of his trousers as though he had been pulled through a barbed wire fence backwards. In the bedroom he found Jasper two thirds down the clothing rail with a small pile of tissues and till receipts forming on the carpeted floor behind him.

"Anything?" Lazlo asked, slightly out of breath.

Jasper shook his head in silence, his features again succumbing to an overshadowing look of despondency. Lazlo stood with his meaty hands on his broad waist and studied his guvnor's twisting, writhing limb and neck movements. It was something about which they had never spoken, but Lazlo realised the enormity of their failed initiative to engage in Montgolfier's AA group therapy.

Once he'd reached the end of the rail Jasper turned around and surveyed the small pile of rubbish on the floor with disdain. The only items of value recovered were a tube of lipstick and a ten pound note.

"Brad Pitt!" Jasper muttered under his breath.

Lazlo knelt down with a groan of effort and sifted through the pile of tissues and receipts methodically. Investigative work demanded even the most menial task be undertaken with due diligence. Suddenly, one receipt caught his eye.

"Framwellgate Dry Cleaners." he said, picking up the crumpled receipt in his fat fingers and squinting at it.

Jasper turned his face from its resting place in the palm of his right hand towards Lazlo. Something had stirred in his memory banks.

"Cheese and rice, Lazlo, that's it!"

FIFTY

Debra stood beneath the naked boughs of the giant oak tree on College Square at a safe distance away from the children. A bright pink scarf was wound around her neck and head like a babushka and both arms clung disconsolately to her tiny body in a closed embrace. She stood without moving a muscle, the only sign of life being the misting of her breath in the cold air.

The rising sounds of childhood enthusiasm pierced the air, as parents standing about in an informal semi circle welcomed their little darlings back into their embraces. The end of the school day – something she would probably never experience again on a personal level, Debra realised.

She watched as Seamus Mallory ran across the cobbles to his waiting mother. He was a scruffy boy, socks down around his ankles, grubby knees, tousled black hair somewhat longer than Debra would have tolerated, and longer than most of the other boys.

Debra felt her pulse quicken as she stared at Mrs Mallory, first name unknown, but unmistakeably the person towards whom Debra felt the greatest possible sense of resentful anger.

Mrs Mallory looked ordinary enough: knitted knee-length grey coat, long black boots, scarf, laughing with friends. She crouched down low and hugged Seamus, who kissed her on the cheek as he flung both arms briefly around her neck.

Debra swallowed hard.

Why had she done it, why had she taken such an irresponsible risk not only with her own child, but with others too? What kind of a mother was she? What kind of a human being was she?

Debra wanted to run across, grab her by the shoulders and shake some sense into her, feeling that if she shook long and hard enough she might even turn back the cruel hands of time.

Yes, turn back time and erase all this unnecessary heartache and tragedy. She began to sob, turned and walked away. It was no longer clear to her why she had gone to the school.

Wiping her eyes and nose with a tissue, she pulled out her phone and dialled.

"Jasper? It's me, Debra." She said with a thick voice and a blocked nose.

"I've done a silly thing and I need to see you, please."

She closed her eyes and squeezed out tears that ran down her bright red cheeks.

"OK, I understand. Call me when you can. Please."

Her shoulders shuddered and the flood gates opened as misery poured from her soul.

FIFTY ONE

The black Audi TT drew up outside Framwellgate Cleaners and Jasper shut the engine off. Both men released their seatbelts simultaneously, but Jasper placed a hand on Lazlo's arm.

"I need to do this alone, please."

Lazlo met Jasper's pleading eyes and his great, shaved head nodded. Then he sat and watched as his guv'nor walked towards the door of the shop, lurching ever so slightly to one side just before he reached it. There it was again, the snakelike writhing of his left arm, then the twisting neck. Lazlo stared with a deep frown on his face. The investigator missed nothing.

Inside the shop Jasper was met by a middle aged woman behind the counter, wearing a pale green uniform with her hair tied up in a bun on top of her head. The place reeked of chemicals and benzene, but the woman smelled even more strongly of tobacco smoke.

"Can I help you?" she said in a husky voice and without a smile.

"I've come to collect an item for Jennifer Candle. You called me a few days ago."

"Do you have a receipt?"

Jasper fumbled in his pocket with trembling fingers.

"I have this, but it may be an old one. Same name and address, though."

He handed the crumpled receipt to the woman, who turned it around and studied it without moving a facial muscle.

"This is from last year, love. Where's the receipt?"

Jasper shrugged.

"I don't know. Look, the coat has been here for several weeks now and you called me…"

Suddenly the woman became animated as if someone had flipped a switch on her back.

"Oh yes, I remember!" She said excitedly, before bursting into a salvo of mucus-laden coughs.

She disappeared in between rows of clothing hanging in plastic bags, emerging after a few moments with a red coat covered in plastic and held aloft like a victory salute.

"Here it is!"

She draped it over the counter, pulled the paper ticket off it and tapped on the till.

"That's nineteen quid please, love."

Jasper stared at the coat disconsolately. Anything left in the pockets would be gone now.

"Something wrong, pet?"

"Was anything found in the coat?" Jasper said, handing the woman a twenty pound note.

"If there was anything in the pockets, love, other than tissues and rubbish," she gave a sudden throaty laugh, "it will be stapled to the inside of the bag."

She handed him one pound in change and a till receipt.

Jasper left the shop, holding in his hand what he believed might well have been one of Jennifer's final deeds. Was it an act of routine domesticity that simply became a forgotten victim of the malignant change in her mind, or was it an act of deliberate and calculated deception?

The whole tragic business had an air of surrealism about it. Jennifer had been his wife for fifteen years, yet he was beginning to wonder just how well he had known her, or rather just how much about her he didn't know.

Jasper opened the small TT boot and laid the red coat in it. Lazlo was listening to Barry White and nodding his great head rhythmically to the music. Jasper hesitated, rubbing his fingertips together nervously, then peeled back the plastic and turned the coat over. There it was, stapled to the back of the bag, an envelope. His heart skipped a beat.

"Did you find it?" Lazlo asked, as Jasper returned to the driver's seat.

Jasper nodded, feeling the envelope crinkle against his shirt in the breast pocket of his jacket.

"Aren't you going to read it?"

"Not here. Let's go to The Swan."

FIFTY TWO

The two men stood side by side at the bar, leaning on their elbows like a comedy double act about to commence their routine. It was mid afternoon and The Swan was relatively quiet, ironically a time when service was often slowest.

Lazlo licked his lips in anticipation, glancing across at Jasper, who simply stared straight ahead as the rather youthful looking barman eventually approached.

"I'll have a Perrier, please," Jasper said in a flat voice.

Lazlo turned to look at Jasper as surprise creased his great, butternut shaped face.

"Er," he mumbled, "I'll have a… a bitter lemon, lots of ice."

They sat at their favourite brass table and stared out of the window as they sipped their alien drinks tentatively.

"I don't think I can do it, Lazlo," Jasper said as tics convulsed around his left eye.

"Do you want me to leave you alone, guv?"

Jasper sat without replying, staring at the bubbles rising out of his Perrier water.

"No, I want you to stay, Lazlo. I'm just thinking what a day I picked to give up drinking."

They sat in silence, Jasper with trembling knuckles pressed against his lips, Lazlo staring patiently out of the window at the rowers on the calm river below. Jasper had never known fear and apprehension like this. Suddenly he didn't want to know what secret Jennifer had carried back from London with her, or whether she had tried to bury it at the dry cleaners. He shuddered to think what her motivation might have been, but deep down he realised that he was past the point of repudiation and that it was too late to try and airbrush over the glaring wrinkles in his life.

Chris de Burgh began to sing 'Lady in Red' in the background.

"Friar Tuck!" Jasper said tersely and pulled the envelope out of his jacket pocket.

He opened the envelope with trembling fingers and spread the letter out on his lap, covering the rippling muscles of his left thigh, then sat up straight as he narrowed his eyes to read the small print. Lazlo adjusted his posture awkwardly, wishing he had a Black Sheep in his hand to ease his tension and discomfort.

Dr Majid Omar Eldabe MB (Cairo) FRCP (London) PhD (Camb)
Consultant Neurologist
67 Harley Street
London
W1G 8PP

Mrs Jennifer Candle

Confidential summary of discussion

Source: self referral for genetic counselling regarding unborn foetus, estimated gestation ten weeks.

As explained to you in consultation today I am

somewhat limited in the scope of my responses, both by the extent and depth of information you have presented to me, as well as my need to protect prior patient confidences.

What I can confirm with certainty is that Huntington's disease, about which you enquire, is a very rare disease that is most likely to develop as a consequence of inheritance from affected parents. It is passed on from one generation to the next by autosomal dominant inheritance. This means that one copy of the HTT gene is all that is required to produce Huntington's disease in an individual.

Therefore if one parent has Huntington's disease, the chances of each child inheriting the disease are one in two, which is like flipping a coin.

I cannot tell you with absolute certainty whether your unborn foetus is carrying the HTT gene for Huntington's disease, but from what you have told me and from what I already know confidentially, I will go so far as to say that there is good reason for you to be very concerned about this possibility.

If you wish to be referred to a gynaecologist to discuss terminating the pregnancy, I would certainly be able to arrange this for you.

I am sorry I cannot be more helpful.

MO Eldabe FRCP PhD

(dictated not signed)

Jasper stared at the letter in his lap, his face denuded of expression but for the tics around his left eye and the corner of his mouth.

"What does it say, guv?" Lazlo said, casting a discrete glance in Jasper's direction.

"I need to read it again."

Jasper read in silence, his mouth opening slightly.

"Cheese and rice," Jasper said, turning his head to look out of the window and covering his mouth with one hand.

"What, guv?"

"Read it." Jasper passed the letter to Lazlo, who applied a pair of gold framed reading glasses to his broad face.

Lazlo's great head moved from side to side as he scanned the sentences, his lips moving ever so slightly as he read in silence.

"Jennifer couldn't face terminating the pregnancy, so she took both of their lives," Jasper said quietly, almost as if thinking out loud.

Lazlo removed the reading glasses and looked up at Jasper.

"What is Huntington's disease?"

"Haven't the foggiest idea," Jasper said, gesturing into the air with the hand covering his mouth and then returning it.

Lazlo replaced the spectacles and passed the letter to Jasper, who looked at it with disdain.

"What the hell does 'prior patient confidences' imply?" Jasper said.

Lazlo leaned back and took a deep breath, rubbing his unshaven chin back and forth with a spade-like hand.

"I think it means that he knows more than he is letting on," Lazlo said.

Jasper nodded thoughtfully.

"What I do know is that if my unborn baby does not have the HTT gene, then Dr Eldabe is going to be held accountable for Jennifer's death."

FIFTY THREE

Jasper stared at the jars containing human tissues and organs, wondering if amongst them, somewhere on one of these dusty shelves, a piece of Jennifer, or perhaps a piece of his unborn child, might be floating in formaldehyde. A chill ran down his spine. He was sitting patiently in the worn office chair, his legs crossed at the knee and his elevated foot tapping the air to a repetitive and anxious beat.

Suddenly the door opened and Sally Whitehouse burst into the office wearing green surgical scrubs and a green paper theatre hat.

"This is an unexpected surprise, Mr Candle."

He uncrossed his legs, but before he could even straighten to stand up she had flopped into the swivel chair in front of a desk strewn untidily with folders, papers and unopened mail.

"Thank you for seeing me so…"

"You said it was urgent. What is it?" she said, slightly out of breath.

She shook her rebellious copper hair out of the theatre cap and fluffed it with her hands as it burst into life.

"Do you still have the foetus you found in my wife?"

She frowned and pursed her lips.

"Why would you think that?"

"Do you still have it?" Jasper said somewhat sharply.

Whitehouse straightened in her seat.

"No, of course not. Human remains have to be destroyed or appropriately buried, Human Tissues Act 2004."

Jasper's eyes wandered across the multitudes of jars on shelves as his face was ravaged by tics.

"I want the foetus to be tested for the HTT gene."

Whitehouse sat forward and pulled out a pad from the top drawer of her desk. Picking up a pencil, chewed on one end, she began to write.

"What is this about, Mr Candle?"

Jasper pulled Eldabe's letter out from within his charcoal jacket and offered it to her. The letter shook in his trembling hand.

"Jennifer saw this doctor, a neurologist, who told her that the baby would very likely have something called... Huntington's disease. He urged her to consider an abortion."

"Oh my God," Whitehouse said, taking the letter and reading it.

"I think he was responsible for Jennifer's decision to er... you know..."

She lowered the letter when she had finished reading it and met his eyes.

"And you want the baby tested for the HTT gene?"

Jasper hesitated. His tongue felt thick and stupid in his mouth, disobedient, insolent. He tried to form words but they wouldn't come out of his throat.

"I need to know... if he was wrong," he managed to say, slowly.

Whitehouse sat back, and ran fingers through her copper hair.

"The foetus is buried along with Jennifer Candle."

"Don't you have any of its tissues left in the lab?"

She shook her head emphatically.

"We need to exhume the body then," Jasper said with a casual shrug of his contorting shoulders. The words began to flow more easily again.

"Mr Candle, the law in this country protects human remains buried in consecrated ground. You cannot just go exhuming them on a whim."

"This is hardly a whim, Doctor."

"You need to make application for a petition, the local authorities have to consent and the Home Office has to issue a licence."

"A petition?" Jasper said pulling a face.

"You will need a compelling reason to desecrate a human grave. Exhumation licences are not granted lightly."

Jasper paused for a moment and rubbed his chin; the muscles in his left leg were rippling and his left shoulder rolled spasmodically inside his jacket.

"Is a foetus of ten weeks technically a human being yet?" Jasper asked, fixing Whitehouse with an intent stare.

She hesitated, mouth slightly open, looking away.

"I forget you are a lawyer, Mr Candle, for whom the perspective of being human rests on an article of law. Strictly speaking, a foetus of less than twenty four weeks' gestation does not require a licence for exhumation, you are correct."

Jasper separated and then clapped his hands together in mock adulation.

"Well then, there we go."

"It's not so simple, Mr Candle. The foetus is inside your wife's grave and it would be her remains that have to be exhumed."

Jasper leaned forward.

"A technicality, surely. You must know the coroner very well, Doctor. Let's get the process started then."

Whitehouse studied Jasper with a look of perplexed intrigue.

"There is no guarantee your application will be granted."

"Oh, I think it will," Jasper said.

Whitehouse frowned and sighed deeply.

"Do you really want to go through with this, Mr Candle? She has only been buried, what, a week? Think of her family, think of her memory, think of yourself."

Jasper's eyes never left hers, fixed with a steely determination to prevail.

"I am thinking of myself, Doctor, and I am determined to find out who put my wife in that grave and exactly why."

FIFTY FOUR

"Charlotte, it's Jasper," he said into his iPhone, shielding it from the breeze.

"Fine thank you, and you?"

"Yes, we found the letter."

Jasper was crossing Prebends Bridge en route to his office. The late afternoon light was fading fast and autumnal gloom accentuated icy patches of unthawed frost on leeward ground.

"Uh-huh. Jennifer definitely knew she was pregnant, Charlotte, that's why she went to see Eldabe."

A red bicycle with a wicker basket on the handlebars brushed past Jasper, pedalled by a student with his girlfriend sat astride the bar.

"She was asking about Huntington's disease, apparently runs in the family. Do you know anything about this?"

"Are you sure?"

"Well, Eldabe told her that the baby might very well have inherited it. That's why I think she…"

He waited.

"No, he did mention an abortion, but I don't think Jennifer could go through with that."

Suddenly Jasper's right arm writhed violently and the iPhone fell from his grasp and clattered to the flagstones on the bridge.

"Brad Pitt!" he cursed loudly. "You tomtit, bottomless pit."

He bent down, red in the face, to retrieve the phone and took a deep breath to calm down.

"Sorry, Charlotte, I dropped the phone."

He rubbed his nose and turned to face the parapet.

"Did Jennifer ever mention this disease to you? Do you know anyone in your family who had it?"

He listened.

"Uh-huh. What next, you say?"

Jasper rubbed his chin thoughtfully, suddenly conscious of voicing his unpleasant intentions.

"I have discussed how to have the foetus tested for this HTT gene."

"Why? Well if the baby was not affected, then Eldabe was wrong to push Jennifer past the edge of despondency, of course."

He listened, rubbing his forehead. The right arm convulsed spasmodically and two passersby stared briefly in Jasper's direction.

"No, there are no samples left. It would necessitate a formal… er… exhumation…"

"Yes, that's what I said."

"Oh come on Charlotte, please don't say that."

Jasper's face hardened.

"Please, whatever you do don't formally object."

"Charlotte, I'm just trying to figure this whole… bloody tragedy… out. Don't you want to know what happened?"

"Charlotte?"

"Charlotte!" he shouted.

Jasper took the iPhone from his ear and stared at it, his eyes burning, shaking his head in disbelief that she would hang up.

His face twitched, his arm rolled and writhed and three times his trunk twisted first to one side and then the other, as if he had an insatiable itch beneath his skin.

In a sudden fit of silent and deeply frustrated rage, Jasper flexed his arm like a cricketer and hurled the phone off the bridge into the dark waters down below. The tiny splash was virtually inaudible.

He wanted to scream. He wanted to scream at the top of his voice and expunge the demons that were suffocating his life. But, conscious of the wary stares of a few passing people, he closed his eyes, took several slow breaths and pushed his trembling hands deep into his coat pockets, hiding them from the watching world.

Beneath an early evening crescent moon rising just above the trees, he began to walk somewhat unsteadily off the bridge.

FIFTY FIVE

It was well past six o'clock when Jasper finally reached his office, where he was surprised to find Stacey still sitting at her desk. Looking particularly Gothic with deep eye shadow softening the fringes of freshly dyed midnight black hair, she was tapping her short black fingernails on the neatly kept desk. Her bright purple coat was a welcome distraction from the sombre stygian shades, but did not soften her sullen mood.

"I've been waiting for you, Mr C."

"You didn't need to," Jasper said quickly.

"I've been calling you. Didn't you get my messages?"

Jasper hesitated and inclined his head slightly to one side, just in time to disguise a twisting roll of his neck and shoulder.

"I… er… lost my phone."

Stacey shrugged.

"Mrs K has been sitting in your office since four o'clock. She is extremely upset and won't leave until she sees you." Stacey inclined her head towards the door to Jasper's office and pulled a face.

Jasper closed his eyes and rubbed his forehead; this was the last thing he needed. It had been a long, emotionally draining day and, to rub salt into the wound, one during which he had denied himself even a drop of Chivas to pass his desperate lips. He was beginning to feel as irritable as a caffeine addict.

"I'm sorry, Stacey. Get yourself home."

Stacey stood up and walked past Jasper to the door, pausing as she realised the depth of dispiritedness written across his face. She half turned and studied him from behind, observing the subtle writhing of his shoulder muscles beneath his camel great coat.

"Do you need anything, Mr C?"

He was silent for a moment, not turning around to face her.

"No."

"Are you going home tonight?"

Silence.

"Coffee and croissant in the morning?" Stacey said.

"Make it a bacon roll."

"Sure."

He turned his head just enough to make brief eye contact with Stacey.

"Thanks."

*

Debra Kowalski spun around to face the door as Jasper entered. Her face was puffy, her eyes red and swollen as she dabbed at them with a tissue balled in her claw-like fist. She looked more upset than when he had first met her.

"I'm sorry Debra, I didn't know you were waiting for me," Jasper said, walking straight to his swivel chair behind the desk.

She sniffed and blew her nose into the tissue.

"You promised me justice for Ollie. You said we had a strong case," she said with a thick and emotionally charged voice.

Jasper frowned and placed his elbows on the desk, clasping his errant hands together tightly.

"Yes, I did."

"Why did you lie to me?" Her face contorted as she suppressed a strong urge to cry.

Jasper's gaze faltered and he blinked several times.

"I don't understand."

"Ten thousand pounds! Is that all Ollie is worth?"

Jasper unclasped his hands and leaned forward, his eyebrows knitted and almost meeting in the midline.

"Where did you get that from?"

Debra lowered the crumpled tissue from her face and fixed Jasper with an intense stare.

"Is it true? A dead child is worth ten thousand pounds in compensation?"

Jasper rubbed his forehead, trying to maintain Debra's fearless eyes.

"It's not just about the money, Debra, I told you that."

"Is it true?" she said, angrily as tears rolled down her cheeks and dripped into her lap, staining the light green skirt like droplets of blood.

Jasper slumped back in his swivel chair with a vanquished sigh and covered his eyes with a trembling hand in an attempt to assuage the tics ripping into his face.

"More or less, yes."

Debra emitted a noise that sounded like a sob and a gasp combined, the moan of a wounded and hurting animal.

"Ten thousand pounds, for the life of a healthy, perfect little boy, with everything in this world ahead of him."

Jasper nodded sadly.

"It was increased in 2002, it used to be even less."

It was a statement of fact, but he regretted saying it the moment the words left his mouth. Debra emitted a muted scream.

"I trusted you, I believed you when you told me this was a big moment, a possible landmark case, that Ollie's death would not be in vain."

Jasper sat forward suddenly and erupted.

"I did not lie to you. It is a big case and it's about the verdict, the apportionment of blame, not the ten thousand pounds."

Debra's mouth fell open as she shrivelled under his stern tone.

"A child death is worth less than an adult death in compensation terms because adults have earning capacity and responsibilities, that is how the actuaries calculate compensation multiplicands. The highest awards go to severely injured children needing lifelong care with medical costs. That's just… how it is."

Jasper's frustration boiled over, but in the end his voice softened and tailed off in silent recognition of her evident suffering. Debra burst into tears, bowing her head and sobbing into her lap. Jasper lowered his head and rubbed his tired, rippling face.

"I'm sorry, Debra, I didn't mean to… I've had a pretty bad day myself," he said quietly.

His head turned to the drinks cabinet in the corner and he stared longingly at the bottle of Chivas. God, he needed a drink so badly, today of all days, he thought.

"Would you like a drink?" he said, breaking the silence.

Without looking up, she nodded, as the sobbing gradually subsided. Jasper walked to the drinks cabinet and poured the whisky.

"Ice?"

"Please."

He returned with a glass and offered it to her before sitting down again. Debra took an immediate sip, the tumbler shaking in her lily white hand. Jasper's gaze was fixed on the golden amber liquid as he imagined it lingering on the back of her tongue, warming, soothing, easing those rough edges.

"Remember what I said, Debra. It is closure that you need and you will only get it once you've been through the entire process. Don't feel denigrated by the compensation value. It is not a reflection of Ollie's worth as a human being. It is not a reflection of the extent of the love you felt for him, or the depth of your loss. It is merely an actuarial calculation, a cold, heartless figure, nothing more."

"You're not drinking?" she observed.

He paused and rubbed his trembling hands together as his left knee banged against the side of the cherry wood desk.

"I've given up."

FIFTY SIX

Stacey found Jasper sound asleep in the corner bed in his office when she arrived in the morning. Beside his bed an empty bottle of Chivas lay next to an upturned photograph of Jennifer and the tumbler beside his bed still contained a little whisky. The room smelled sour and she made a discreet exit.

Half an hour later he emerged from the small en suite bathroom having showered, shaved and dressed in fresh clothing from the small wardrobe he kept in the office. Stacey knocked and entered the room to find Jasper staring at the tall, Mexican cactus, inclining his head this way and that as he studied the prickly plant.

"When last did you water the cactus, Stacey?" he said, without turning.

She stopped, pressing her lips together as her eyes scanned the room in contemplation.

"All the plants in our... my house... have died. It's a good thing that cactuses don't need much care, don't you think?" Jasper said.

She shrugged.

"The perfect plant for me to look after."

Jasper turned round to face Stacey, who was wearing a slate grey, double breasted blouse and black slacks.

"Here is your bacon roll and coffee, Mr C."

She placed a brown paper bag on the desk.

"You're not drowning in black today, Stacey," Jasper observed, taking a sip from the coffee cup.

"I thought you needed some cheering up, Mr C." She forced a smile and produced a small square of paper. "Two messages, a new client has an appointment this morning and someone called wanting to meet you in Wharton Park at noon."

Jasper frowned.

"Wharton Park? Who?"

"She wouldn't leave her name. Just said she was a friend of your wife and has something very important to tell you."

Jasper's heart leapt as he felt his stomach churn with nervous apprehension. He rubbed his chin with a trembling hand, regretting his surrender to the lure of the calming Chivas the night before.

"Cancel the new client, Stacey."

"I can't, Mr C, he's due…" she studied her large, masculine wristwatch "… in about ten minutes."

"Brad Pitt!"

Jasper's mind was nowhere near prepared for the exacting demands of evaluating a new client's case and he briefly contemplated making himself unavailable with some or other feeble excuse. Then suddenly the client was there, in his office, a fresh expectant face, deeply etched with sadness and something else, something hard and cold, looking to him for some form of redemption.

Dugal Tavistock, from Grasmere in Cumbria, soberly dressed in faded non proprietary denim and a worn yellow mountain jacket, stood six feet tall with a white cane in one hand and the lead for a golden retriever, who sat beside him obediently, in the other.

"You come highly recommended, Mr Candle," said Tavistock, looking vaguely in Jasper's direction through sunken, milky eyes.

Jasper guided him into the office and to the chair. The retriever lay down quietly on the carpet beside Tavistock and appreciatively received a friendly rub behind his ears.

Jasper sat behind his desk, hands clasped in front of his chin, bright yellow braces cutting into the generous folds of his starched white shirt.

"What can I do for you?"

Tavistock folded the thin, white cane up into quarters and clutched it in his lap.

"Ten years ago I was skydiving in Snowdonia when my parachute failed to open properly. My fault I know, I packed it. I was pretty badly injured – broken bones everywhere – but they patched me together again."

Jasper managed an encouraging smile wondering whether it would be noticed.

"You're a fortunate man, Mr Tavistock."

"I am most certainly not. I should have died that day. Is it fortunate to be blind, having lost my wife, my profession, my dignity?"

There was an icy edge to Tavistock's voice, a result of ten years of simmering bitterness and resentment. Jasper frowned and adjusted his posture in the chair, his mind drifting to Wharton Park, wondering who would be meeting him, whether he would recognise her, or perhaps even know her? Then the inevitable thought – what did she want to tell him?

"I am only fifty two and I don't want to live out my days as a blind dependant man, Mr Candle," Tavistock said.

"What do you want me to do?"

"A month ago I fell down a flight of stairs and broke my hip – occupational hazard of being blind. I had to have it operated on and I told the doctors that if something untoward happened then I did not want to be resuscitated. I completed a living will, a declaration of my wishes which was signed and witnessed."

Tavistock leaned over and passed a small biscuit snack to the dog, who licked it out of his hand, thumping his tail on the carpet.

"The surgery was quite bloody, apparently, and when the bone cement was introduced, I had a cardiac arrest."

Silence for a few moments.

"Obviously they disregarded my express wishes."

Jasper sat back in the leather, high back swivel chair and rubbed his chin between thumb and index fingers.

"I'm sorry, I don't understand."

Tavistock sat forward and narrowed his cloudy eyes.

"I should be dead Mr Candle, free from my misery, liberated from this living hell. They had no right to take that away from me."

Jasper sighed.

"They saved your life, Mr Tavistock. Twice now, I believe."

"I didn't invite it, in fact quite the opposite."

Jasper glanced at his watch, unable to focus, his mind wandering continuously to the mysterious caller he was to meet and what it might herald. How long still to wait?

"Do you have a life threatening illness?" Jasper said.

"No, but I can barely see you, Mr Candle. I can just make out your shape and see when you glance impatiently at your watch, but no details, no colours. I am dying slowly, every minute of every day."

"So you want me to sue the doctors who fought to save your life?" Jasper was startled by the irritable indifference in his voice, surprised by the inescapable prejudice that was already taking shape in his mind.

"Life is not always worthy of preservation, you know. Doctors value every life regardless, not considering that it might be a life like mine: not worth living. It was my right to die, it was my time."

Eldabe did not value life above reason, Jasper thought to himself, having urged Jennifer unambiguously to consider an abortion – the spectre of another case of Huntingtons disease clearly an intolerable alternative. Did he have remorse for causing two deaths?

Jasper glanced down at the dog by Tavistock's side, panting contentedly as it looked around his office. He contemplated Tavistock's words – 'it was my right to die'.

Had Jennifer felt that way, that it was her right to die? Had she chosen it freely in the expectation of being liberated from her own living hell, whatever it was? Would she have resented him if he had bothered to go home and check on her sooner and perhaps caught her in time to cut her down and save her life? Was it reasonable for Dugal Tavistock to feel legally dispossessed of this right by eager doctors? Or was he simply demanding euthanasia?

"Mr Candle?" Tavistock said sharply, startling Jasper from his thoughts.

Jasper sat forward, clasping his trembling hands beneath his chin as his left shoulder and neck began to twist to the discordant rhythm of his demon.

"I don't know if I can help you, Mr Tavistock."

"What?"

Jasper paused, unclasping his hands briefly.

"I need to think about this. I'm not sure I could convince a jury that you have been wronged to such an extent by having your life saved."

Tavistock sat back with an astonished look on his face.

"I signed a legal document empowering doctors not to resuscitate me, a contract, and they disregarded it. That's breaking the law, isn't it?" Tavistock spoke bitterly, his tone such that the retriever's ears flattened slightly against its head.

Jasper breathed in deeply.

"Did they not breach their contract with me, Mr Candle?"

"As I said, I need to give this some thought," he lied, lowering his head and burying his face in his hands.

What was going on? What was happening to him? Was he losing his self belief, his will to win, his edge? He would have jumped at a case like this in the past. He had won the most feeble of arguments on innumerable occasions before. But this time it felt different. Was it because of Jennifer? Was he developing a conscience?

"I don't believe this. What now?" Tavistock said, shaking his head in disbelief.

"I don't know. Leave your details with Stacey and I'll think it over."

"Think it over? Mr Candle, that's insulting, look at me, just look at me!"

"You're alive, Mr Tavistock, that is what I see. You're a survivor. Be thankful and enjoy your life."

FIFTY SEVEN

Wharton Park, elevated above the small city of Durham, was deserted at noon. Children were still at school and it was too cold for picnickers. The brightly coloured swings and roundabouts stood silent, covered in the undisturbed frosty icing of another cold night.

Jasper walked about slowly, leaving footprints on the milky grass, wishing he had put gloves on his hands. Visible through the naked branches of trees, the distant twin towers of Durham Cathedral glowed in the weak winter sunshine. His arms and legs shook but he could not tell if it was his usual affliction, the one he presumed was caused by his whisky habit, or if it was due to the heartless cold.

"Jasper?" a nervous voice called out from behind him.

Jasper turned sharply, almost losing his balance and awkwardly having to assume an undignified posture to right himself.

"Jasper Candle?"

"Yes?"

The woman was middle aged, dark haired beneath a fluffy grey and white Russian hat, wearing an elegant black coat and scarf. She stared at him with grey eyes wide open; she looked terrified. Jasper did not recognise her at first glance.

"I'm sorry to bring you out here like this. I was a good friend of Jennifer's."

Jasper smiled, trying to suppress the immense apprehension he harboured.

"I'm sorry, I don't think we've met," Jasper said with an open gesture of his cold, bluish hands, inviting an introduction.

"That's not important. I saw you last night on Prebends Bridge."

Jasper groaned inwardly, recalling his frustrated behaviour, the swearing, the petulant phone toss and the stares he had drawn from passersby.

"I need to tell you something, something that I was reminded of when I saw you last night." The woman's eyes looked pained, as though she was struggling with a conflict. They kept darting to the frosty ground that separated them, but when she met his eyes they were confident, assured.

Jasper was too nervous to say anything. He could feel his heart beating.

"Jennifer was deeply troubled by something that she just couldn't talk about, not even to her friends. She made me promise."

"Promise what?"

"She really loved you, Jasper. This whole thing broke her heart and she didn't know how to cope with it. I just wish I could have helped her, but she was so loyal."

Jasper felt a huge lump forming in his throat and moisture welling up in his eyes. He kept looking at the mystery woman, at the struggle within her. Once or twice he feared that she might be about to lose her bottle and walk away.

"Loyal to whom?" Jasper said.

"This is so hard, I promised her and Jennifer was one person who always kept her promises."

Jasper could see that she was on the verge of tears.

"What is it?"

"Jennifer sent some secret letters away for safe keeping."

"Letters?"

The woman nodded as vapour enveloped her face.

"What sort of letters?"

"I've no idea, she would never say. But I gathered enough to know that they had turned her life upside down."

"Do you know where they are?" Jasper said.

The woman remained silent, biting the corner of her lower lip as her eyes flicked about Jasper's face. Eventually he could take it no more.

"Who has them, please?"

The woman hesitated just long enough for Jasper to begin doubting whether she would reveal any more.

"Her sister."

Jasper frowned and his eyes widened.

"Charlotte?"

The woman nodded and her steady gaze faltered and dropped to the ground. Jasper was stunned. Charlotte had denied knowledge of any documents, even in the face of direct questioning.

"I don't know anymore. I think Jennifer regretted telling me, but she so badly needed a friendly shoulder to cry on."

They stood in silence for a moment, looking into each other's pained eyes. Jasper did not know if the implication was that he had not been around enough to offer Jennifer that much needed shoulder, or if Jennifer was intent on keeping this matter secret from him at all costs. But what was she keeping secret?

"Thank you," Jasper said. "I don't even know your name."

The woman looked flustered, her eyes welling up with tears as she began to squirm in her coat.

"I am so sorry, I really miss Jennifer."

With that she turned and walked away briskly, embarrassed at her rising emotions, leaving footprints on the crisp, icy grass as she went. Jasper watched her, his mind ruminating over her revelations. Did Charlotte know what the secret was that she had been keeping from him all this time? If so, did she know what it was that had pushed Jennifer to her desperate end? Why was he being kept in the dark? It was beginning to look as though he had been deliberately shielded from something, something significant enough to take Jennifer's life.

The word 'conspiracy' crossed his mind. *Don't be ridiculous*, he told himself.

FIFTY EIGHT

Jasper Candle
Court Lane
Old Elvet
Durham

Mr Derek Swinter
HM Coroner
Quarryheads Lane
Durham

Dear Mr Swinter,

I am writing to you about the forthcoming inquest into the death of my wife, Jennifer Candle. You will by now have received the post mortem report from Dr SP Whitehouse and you may also know that Jennifer's body was released for burial two weeks ago.

I would like you to postpone the inquest until further tests have been carried out on the exhumed remains of Jennifer and the unborn child she was carrying. Information has come to light indicating that the foetus may have been carrying an inherited disease which Jennifer became aware of, and which may well have been a contributory factor in her decision to end her life.

I have discussed the matter with Dr Whitehouse and urged her to support an exhumation for further pathological tests. The reasons are twofold.

Firstly, Dr Majid Eldabe, the medical specialist who told Jennifer that she was very likely to be carrying a genetically tainted foetus, is now invoking patient confidentiality and will not provide any further information on the matter. His actions need to be considered in the context of Jennifer's death.

Secondly, if the foetus is carrying the genes to which he refers, then the inheritance pattern needs to be identified and delineated, for the benefit of those remaining family members who may be affected by it.

Please discuss this with Dr Whitehouse and give the matter your utmost consideration. I implore you.

This is a deeply unpleasant circumstance for me and I do not make this request lightly.

Yours sincerely,

Jasper Candle

FIFTY NINE

Jasper sat at the desk in his office, massaging his temples rhythmically as he stared ahead thoughtfully. Beside him on the desk a half eaten salad from the Italian deli around the corner exuded fragrant odours of garlic and coriander. A small pesto stain had ingratiated itself on his white cotton shirt.

Jasper turned his head slightly and looked apprehensively at the telephone. He had been doing this for half an hour, frightened of making the call to Charlotte for fear of the extent of the deceit he might uncover.

Suddenly there was a loud knock at the door that disturbed Jasper's unproductive inertia.

"Come," he said.

Lazlo burst in, out of breath, and manoeuvred his pear-like body over to the chair in front of Jasper's desk. He sank his bulky frame into it, loosened the front zip on his leather jacket and cupped his hands before blowing through them.

"It's freezing out there today. Where've you been, guv?" Lazlo said, rubbing his chapped hands together.

Jasper shrugged.

"Your phone doesn't ring – goes straight to voicemail," Lazlo said.

Jasper lifted the fingers off his temples languidly and twirled them in the air.

"Yeah, I… er… lost it. Stacey's getting me another one."

Jasper hadn't yet made eye contact with Lazlo and he felt self conscious displaying his mutinous tics – the pouting mouth, the flickering eyelid, the rolling shoulder, and the trembling fingers – all in full view of his investigator's studious gaze.

"Ah," Lazlo nodded, but frowned simultaneously. "You all right, guv? You look…"

Jasper emitted a snorting sound.

"Dishevelled?" he said with a wry grin as he sat back in his padded swivel chair, interlocking his hands behind his head.

He sighed deeply.

"Lazlo, my china plate, I'll tell you how I feel. I've applied to have Jennifer exhumed and re-examined."

Lazlo's face twisted. "What?"

"Charlotte won't speak to me and the key to what the Friar Tuck is going on has been in her secret possession for years, it would appear."

"What?" Lazlo said even louder, shifting his considerable weight to the front of his creaking chair.

Jasper nodded as his neck twisted demonically to one side. He watched as Lazlo's intrigued eyes tried to look away discreetly.

"How did you find out?"

"I got an anonymous tip, one of Jennifer's friends who knew about it. She saw me on Prebends Bridge last night, where I lost my phone, and she… er… I don't know… suddenly felt moved to come forward."

Jasper shrugged and made a face as he maintained eye contact with Lazlo.

"So, what does Charlotte have?" Lazlo said.

"I haven't a Scooby-Doo, but I'm presuming letters, documents or something. I cannot understand, Lazlo, why Charlotte didn't tell me?"

Lazlo rubbed his stubby chin with a big, fleshy hand.

"Why the exhumation, guv?"

"Because of the letter."

"Eldabe?"

Jasper nodded. "I have to find out whether the foetus was carrying that gene. I have to know if Jennifer died for..."

As Jasper's left arm writhed he buried his face in cupped hands, before peering over the tips of his fingers at Lazlo.

"Have you seen a doctor, guv?"

Jasper chuckled.

"Too many."

"Seriously, guv."

Jasper nodded.

"I have been told to stop drinking, Lazlo. The whisky is doing me no good, worse still, it may even be bad for me..."

He attempted a little smile, but Lazlo did not reciprocate.

"Can I do anything for you, guv?" Lazlo said, raising his eyebrows.

Jasper leaned forwards and placed both elbows on the desk.

"Persuade Charlotte to send me Jennifer's secrets."

Lazlo leaned back and the chair he was sitting in groaned.

"I think you should go and see her, guv, face to face. Don't phone. I'll come along, if you like."

SIXTY

Jasper's journey to meet Charlotte was arduous and tiring. First there was the three hour train journey to Kings Cross Station, then the Victoria Line to Oxford Street, followed by the Bakerloo Line to Waterloo and then a rattling train that smelled of old motorcar down to Esher Station.

He sat in silence all the way, staring out of the carriage window, deeply absorbed in his thoughts. Although he had a new iPhone he had not yet synchronised any music onto it, not that he had felt in the frame of mind for listening to anything other than the reassuring rush of his own heartbeat in his ears – the one constant in his life.

From the station Jasper caught a taxi to Charlotte's home close to Sandown Park, an ostentatious house that she shared with her city banker husband. Jasper arrived as Charlotte was walking to a burgundy Range Rover in the driveway, keys in hand and brown leather hold-all slung over her shoulder.

"What on earth do you want?" she said in astonishment as Jasper paid the taxi and turned to face her.

"We need to talk, Charlotte."

Jasper's face twisted and he tried hard to subdue the writhing of his left shoulder. She narrowed her eyes as she took it all in. Then, suddenly, she dismissed him with a wave and moved to open the car door.

"I haven't time. You should have called."

"Wait, this is extremely important. Please give me just five minutes, that's all I ask."

She stared at him, her hand still holding the car door open.

"Five minutes?" he begged, inclining his head to one side.

"I have to fetch the boys from school," she said, looking at her wrist watch.

"I'll come with you, we can talk in the car."

She hesitated, her eyes breaking from his.

"OK."

They pulled off sharply before Jasper had even fastened his seatbelt and he noticed that Charlotte had failed to secure hers. Was she always so careless, or was she flustered?

"What do you want? Is this about the exhumation again?"

Her tone was sharp and uncompromising.

Jasper sat and studied his trembling hands, the constant writhing and twisting of his limbs now virtually impossible to conceal. Every now and then his mouth and cheek would pout and contort in such a way that the sound of his speech would be altered.

"This is extremely difficult for me, Charlotte, but I believe Jennifer took a massive secret to her grave, a secret with potential implications for all of us."

Charlotte shot a piercing look at him. She had cut her hair short since he had last seen her in York and it had not in any way softened her face. Her glare was menacing.

"You mean, for you?" she said.

"Yes," he said, nodding, "and perhaps your family too. I believe Jennifer knew a lot more than she let on and it now seems almost irrefutable that this knowledge, this secret, was the reason for her death."

Charlotte was quiet, biting her lip and driving the car hard.

"Jennifer's visit to Dr Eldabe pushed her over the edge and I need to know what it was that took her so close to the edge in the first place."

"Perhaps she didn't tell you because she didn't want you to know," Charlotte said.

Jasper nodded slowly as a twist of his neck corrupted this ponderous movement.

"Charlotte, Jennifer may have taken our baby's life because of incorrect assumptions. She believed there was something wrong with the baby and Eldabe did nothing to dispel her fear. In fact, he fuelled her apprehension. What if he was wrong, what if Jennifer was wrong?"

Charlotte shook her head and pursed her lips as she pulled up at a traffic light. She turned to Jasper with argumentative eyes.

"What if she was right?" She sat back, sighed and shook her head. "Does it really matter now anyway, she's gone, and nothing can bring her back."

Jasper lowered his gaze and stared at his increasingly errant hands, the hands of someone who drank too much, the hands of a diseased person, someone with an affliction. The hands he was looking at did not seem to belong to him.

"She left behind her others who might still be affected."

The car behind them hooted and Charlotte, realising suddenly that the lights had changed, pulled away abruptly.

"What are you saying?"

"Eldabe was talking about a genetic condition which Jennifer's baby may have inherited. It had to come from somewhere, Charlotte, either from Jennifer's side of the family, or from mine."

He could see that she was frozen in her seat, her facial muscles afraid to move, her fingers clenched around the cream leather steering wheel, knuckles blanched.

Jasper broke the silence.

"I know that you have letters from Jennifer. I don't know when she sent them to you, or exactly why, but I am certain that they hold the key to understanding this tragedy."

Charlotte pulled up under a large, leafless oak tree behind a row of similar Chelsea tractors. They had arrived outside Charlie and Jack's handsome sandstone school buildings. She kept her hands firmly on the steering wheel, staring ahead. Jasper's neck twisted and his left eye jumped wildly, distorting the entire side of his face.

"What genetic condition?" Charlotte said without looking at Jasper.

"It's called Huntington's disease – a degenerative disease of the nervous system that only manifests in mid-adult life."

"I've never heard of it," Charlotte said glancing at him dismissively.

Jasper paused, drawing on the well-honed skills he used in the court room, manipulating witnesses, outwitting opposition counsel.

"Consider for a minute that this condition might run in your side of the family. Imagine if Jack, or Charlie, have inherited it."

Jasper watched as Charlotte stared ahead at nothing, chewing with increasing fervour on the inside of her cheek. Her hands still gripped the steering wheel and seemed reluctant to let go. He could see the tiny muscles around her eyes flinching nervously.

"Wouldn't you want to know?"

Charlotte bowed her head and sighed deeply.

"A friend of Jennifer's told me that you have her letters, Charlotte. I need them, please. I have to know why Jennifer did this and what it means for the rest of us."

"What about the exhumation?"

Jasper hesitated, rubbing his face hard, willing the demons away.

"It will help us to know if the foetus, our baby, was affected or not, and also… whether Jennifer was…"

Charlotte looked at him, the sparkle gone from her usually vivacious blue eyes.

"What if Jennifer did have this condition?" Charlotte asked, her voice tinged with uncertainty.

"Then… you need to think about the boys…" Jasper said softly.

"And if not you can sue Dr Eldabe?" she countered, with an edge to her voice.

Jasper knew that this was what bothered Charlotte most, her perception that he was only motivated by apportioning culpability, by pursuing his professional ambitions. Perhaps it was a perception that he deserved.

"I don't want to blame, I want to understand."

He became aware of her eyes studying his erratic and demonic movements, his restless limbs and face occupied by an alien force.

"Are you all right, Jasper? You seem… agitated."

Her voice seemed a little softer and she began to relax her grip on the steering wheel.

"I don't know," Jasper replied as his voice undulated uncontrollably and his mouth pouted. "I've been seeing a doctor."

Charlotte let go of the steering wheel and buried her face in her hands.

"God, this is a mess."

Jasper looked at her, a small part of him feeling that he should place a comforting hand on her shoulder, after all, she was his sister-in-law. But another part of him recognised that she may have been complicit in Jennifer's lengthy deceit, excluding and isolating him.

"That's why I need those letters, Charlotte."

The sounds of young voices laughing and shouting drew closer, as young school children wearing yellow and red striped ties and grey blazers emerged from the Georgian school buildings. Like inmates freed from prison, they ran to the line of waiting cars in which Jasper and Charlotte were parked.

"This is all we wanted, you know," Jasper said quietly, gesticulating towards the mêlée of small people around them. "Children, a normal family life. For some reason we were denied this, all of this. I think Jennifer knew why and she was prepared to die for it."

Charlotte straightened.

"Oh God, here come the boys. I don't want them to see you like this, Jasper, it will frighten them."

"Like what?" Jasper protested.

"You know what I mean."

"I won't do anything."

"No, please go."

Jasper felt hurt, scorned for his obvious imperfections, not good enough to be seen by his own nephews.

"What about the letters?" he said.

"I'll send them to you, I promise."

Jasper nodded and sighed. She did have them.

"Thank you."

Silence.

"I have not read them and Jennifer never said anything to me about them," she paused, perhaps a moment of regret, "I gave her my word, you understand."

It seemed incredible to Jasper that Charlotte could have been unaware of Jennifer's secret. As sisters they had been close, spending many weekends in each other's company. It now seemed evident that Jennifer had deceived her husband, so why not her close family as well? What on earth was she hiding? He shuddered.

"They're almost here. Please go."

Jasper clambered awkwardly out of the high vehicle, almost losing his precarious balance, and disappeared surreptitiously before Jack and Charlie could catch sight of him. He did wonder if they would even have recognised him and he then imagined how Charlotte might have described him to the boys – wicked Uncle Jasper, the family ambulance chaser, devoid of ethics or morals, the Fagin of modern times.

Surely Aunt Jennifer would have described him in a more favourable light, wouldn't she?

SIXTY ONE

Jasper was unsettled after leaving London. His meeting with Charlotte had left him deeply troubled with a nagging anxiety of vulnerability, even though he had achieved what he so desperately wanted: the secret cache of letters. There had been no apology, no comfort; right down to the last frantic moment when he was prevented from seeing his nephews because of his peculiar affliction he had been made to feel like an intruder, an unwelcome outsider.

"Drinks, sandwiches, hot and cold," said the steward, pushing a trolley laden with refreshments up the narrow aisle.

Jasper did not move. He sat with his chin resting on a clenched hand, his head turned slightly so that he could stare out of the window at the blur of gliding shadows created by the northbound train pushing ahead in the gathering gloom.

The carriage was filled with the sounds of people discussing the events of their day and their plans for the evening. Many were making phone calls to spouses, arranging the time that they would reach home. The smells of bacon sandwiches, warm Cornish pasties and salt and vinegar chips wafted through the cabin as passengers snacked their way through the end of a long day.

It all swirled together and amplified Jasper's sense of isolation and abandonment. He now realised that this process of exclusion had begun long before Jennifer's tragic death. Even Charlotte had admitted complicity, to some degree. The question now was simply how far back this deception would extend. Worse still was the growing apprehension of what he personally had to fear from the secretly hidden letters.

Only a few months back, despite a less than fulfilling marriage, Jasper's life had seemed pretty normal. Now, as he stared emptily into the darkness that threatened to engulf him, that life seemed a world away from the predicament and uncertainty of his present reality.

Jasper was overcome with a growing need to lose himself.

SIXTY TWO

The Swan and Three Cygnets was busy that evening, packed with students, many of them from the rowing club and wearing clothing bearing the crossed oar logo. A small number of suited people, freshly released from their daily toil, mingled amongst them in small groups.

Jasper pushed his way unsteadily through the noisy throng. His throat thirsted for the smack of a strong Chivas and his mind longed for the welcome release and the afterglow. He saw Lazlo seated at their usual brass table.

"Lazlo!" he called out excitedly, raising an arm that almost immediately began to twist and spiral like that of a classical Indian dancer performing *mudras*.

"Hello, guv. Care to join us?"

Us? Jasper did a double take until he realised that Lazlo had company – a woman of similar pear drop build to Lazlo, topped with a short bob of black hair and full rosy cheeks. She was sitting where he usually sat, opposite Lazlo.

"This is Billie, guv," Lazlo said with a cautious smile.

Billie smiled but could not mask her sudden nervousness.

"You must be Mr Candle?" She had a sweet, small voice that did not seem matched to her generous physique.

Jasper forced a grin and extended his hand, only to withdraw it awkwardly when he realised it was trembling and the arm that supported it was less than steady. It was an embarrassing moment for both he and Billie.

"Success in London, guv?" Lazlo asked, raising his eyebrows in a boyishly furtive way.

Jasper, seemingly frozen to the spot, turned his eyes away from Billie's face abruptly and stared at Lazlo.

"Er... in a way... er... yes."

"Please join us, guv," Lazlo said, perhaps sensing Jasper's awkwardness.

"I need a drink first."

"I thought you had..." Lazlo began.

"Cheese and rice, Lazlo, give me a break."

Jasper approached the bar and Billie leaned forward to whisper to Lazlo.

"I should go, don't you think?" she said, making a face.

Lazlo shook his head.

"No, I think you should stay. Consider it an opportunity."

She hesitated, her eyes betraying her anxiety, her face tense and unconvinced.

"Are you sure?"

Lazlo nodded slowly, rubbing his stubbly chin with meaty fingers.

"I think the timing is right."

Jasper sat down next to Lazlo with what appeared to be a double Chivas and three ice cubes. Lazlo stared at the drink but said nothing. Jasper raised his glass.

"Bottoms up."

Silence engulfed the table as Jasper sank into the Chivas like a hungry pup. Then he sighed deeply, savouring the warming promise of the malt as it slid down into his troubled soul.

"What do you do, Billie?" Jasper said, turning slightly to face her.

She exchanged apprehensive glances with Lazlo who urged her on.

"I'm the matron in charge of several surgical wards at the local hospital.

Jasper felt himself stiffen slightly, as though he had walked into an ambush.

"Oh, a matron," he said, looking at Lazlo for a sign.

Lazlo nodded.

Jasper drank more Chivas, cradling the thick glass in both hands, appreciating the contrast of the icy cold glass on his palms with the warmth of the liquid in his throat. He was beginning to relax.

"So you know about Edward Burns then?"

Again Billie and Lazlo exchanged glances. Lazlo nodded encouragingly.

"Yes."

Jasper paused without eye contact.

"You know I am investigating the case on behalf of his family?"

She nodded and drank nervously from her beer. Jasper sighed.

"Do you think his death was avoidable?"

"Yes," she said without hesitation.

Her answer surprised Jasper, who straightened and glanced at her.

"As a health professional I regard almost every death in my wards as avoidable. You have to in our job, our responsibility is to preserve life wherever possible."

Lazlo surveyed the proceedings cautiously, sipping from

his Black Sheep and crunching nervously through crisps.

"So what would you have done differently to avoid his death?"

"If it were up to me?" she said, pointing her index finger at her chest.

"Uh-huh."

"I would provide better isolation facilities on wards for barrier nursing of contagious patients. Also, I would have more staff on the ward to deal with routine and infected patients, and more hospital beds."

"So why doesn't the hospital do that?"

"Because there is limited space; our hospital is an old building with inherent limitations and, as ever, there is insufficient funding."

"Has this been drawn to the attention of management?"

Billie sighed.

"It's the same everywhere in my hospital, Mr Candle. The hospital is cash strapped, we never have enough nurses, we never have enough beds. It's nothing new."

"But isn't that the whole point – it's not good enough?"

Billie shrugged her rounded shoulders ineffectually around her short, fat neck.

"We do the best we can in an imperfect system. I have to run wards with two qualified nurses and three health care workers for thirty patients, Mr Candle. It's frantic."

"No time to wash hands?" Jasper said sarcastically.

Billie's eyes betrayed a hint of resentment.

"Of course we do, it's an integral part of our responsibility. But there are so many surfaces that may still convey infective organisms from one person to another. Computer keyboards, case notes, pens, desks, doors, equipment, visitors. It is physically impossible to control everything, we simply can only try our best."

Jasper nodded thoughtfully as he returned to his Chivas and emptied the glass into his mouth. He felt no regret, no guilt; he had savoured every molecule of the whisky.

"If it had been your decision would you have admitted the patient with tommy guns onto a surgical ward?"

Billie made a face.

"Gastroenteritis," Lazlo said, nodding so that his large pewter ear ring wobbled.

"Yes."

"But she killed Edward Burns, who was well on his way to a full recovery and should right now be walking amongst us."

Billie flushed slightly and turned towards Jasper.

"That's a bit strong, Mr Candle. She was a frail old lady who was very ill and needed a hospital bed."

"Imagine Edward Burns was your father. Would you have wanted an infected patient admitted to his ward, posing a genuine threat to his life?"

"Had the old lady been your mother, Mr Candle, would you have been happy if we had denied her a hospital bed, leaving her to lie for hours on a hard gurney in casualty without proper nursing and medical care?"

"Where do you draw the distinction?" Jasper said.

"Exactly," she said. "Where do you draw it? I work in a hospital that treats sick people. We aim to help everyone and in my world you cannot have it one way one day, and another the next."

Lazlo pulled his bulky frame into a standing position.

"I'm getting another, anyone else?"

Both Jasper and Billie nodded.

The silence between them was broken by a sudden outburst of raucous laughter from a group of women in the corner.

"You know, Mr Candle, every death in our care is treated as a failure, no matter the cause or circumstances. Some are old and have lived their lives, some are young and have not, some seem destined to recover and others look certain to die. With experience and hindsight one realises that we alone do not control the destiny of our patients, though we may try as hard as possible under testing conditions to do so."

"What is your point?" Jasper said, as his head twisted to one side and his eyelids fluttered erratically.

He felt Billie's eyes upon him, studying him.

"This week one of our nurses died from a blood clot on her lung. She was recovering from spinal surgery for a back injury sustained when she helped a patient who had collapsed in the toilet. Who's fault is that?"

Jasper gratefully accepted another double Chivas from Lazlo, who creaked into his seat with a Black Sheep for both himself and Billie. Jasper surrendered without hesitation to the golden liquid as the muscles in his left thigh began to ripple and dance.

"Was it the surgeon who did the surgery, the nursing care afterwards, was it the patient who collapsed and caused the injury in the first place, or was it her own fault for being a smoker on the contraceptive pill thereby increasing her risk of thrombosis?"

Jasper was silent.

"Is it anybody's fault?" Billie said.

"Yet tragedies do need to be prevented from recurring," Jasper said sitting forward and wagging his index finger.

"People must learn from their mistakes and sometimes to achieve that proportional culpability is appropriate," Jasper said ponderously, to no-one in particular, his voice becoming thick as he slurred his way through the words.

Billie drank from her beer, leaving a frothy moustache on her upper lip. Lazlo leaned forward with a smile and wiped it clean with a napkin.

"Are you going to sue my staff, Mr Candle?" Billie said.

Though his eyes were openly pleading for help, there was no reply from Jasper. He had slipped from his chair and was on the floor, his arms and legs jerking spasmodically, the empty whisky glass still clutched in his hand and three ice cubes spilt on the carpet beside him. Lazlo jumped to his feet and knocked his Black Sheep over, spilling beer all over the table and Billie's legs.

"Jesus! Ambulance! Somebody call an ambulance!" he shouted.

SIXTY THREE

Jasper opened his eyes and immediately recoiled from the smell that had terrified him since childhood – hospital antiseptics. The room was starkly white, almost too white, except for three blurry splashes of colour beyond the foot of his bed. As these slowly sharpened into focus, one turned out to be a large colourful bouquet of flowers and the second was Stacey, in muted shades of black that were lifted by the swirl of an ample purple scarf around her neck. The largest splash of colour turned out to be Lazlo.

"Hello, guv. You OK?" he heard Lazlo say, as if he was speaking from the bottom of a barrel.

Jasper tried to lick his lips, dry and crusted, but even his tongue was like a piece of sandpaper. He looked down at his arms with wide eyes and followed the narrow clear tubing from the cannula in his skin up to an infusion pump beside his neatly made bed.

"You're on a bit of medication, don't worry guv," Lazlo said.

"What day is it?" Jasper said with a parched mouth.

"Friday."

He managed to focus on Stacey's worried face.

"Thank you for the flowers, Stacey," Jasper said slowly.

"They're actually from Mrs K. I brought you chocolates, Mr C."

She stepped forward and placed a box covered with a red bow on the table beside his bed. Neither she nor Lazlo could hide the concern etched on their drawn faces. Jasper's skin had a sallow colour and his eyes were as yellow as Sicilian lemons.

"What happened?" Jasper said, struggling to separate his tongue from his palate.

Lazlo stepped closer, rubbing his chin as he usually did.

"They don't know yet, guv, but they've done lots of tests, scans, you know."

Jasper widened his eyes and tried to sit forward.

"I need to get up, I've got work to do."

But as Lazlo moved quickly to calm him, Jasper faltered and fell back on the pillows, his body strangely weak and unresponsive.

"You should rest, guv. There's no need to go anywhere."

Jasper tried to make sense of his situation, but his mind was too foggy, *perhaps it was the medication*, he thought.

"Billie sent these to you, guv. I told her that you like marzipan."

Jasper nodded as Lazlo placed a small foil bag beside the chocolates. The door opened and a thin, freckled nurse wearing a light blue tunic walked in.

"I'm afraid visiting is over, Mr Candle needs his rest," she said in a strong Glaswegian accent, presented with a business like smile.

Stacey and Lazlo edged obediently towards the door, waving to Jasper like school children.

"Oh, I've put your mail in the bedside table for when you feel up to it, Mr C," Stacey said.

But Jasper's eyes were closed and it appeared that he was already nodding off into a medicated sleep.

SIXTY FOUR

Charlotte waited until she had dropped the boys off at school and the house was empty. She made a cup of red bush tea, which was all she ever drank. Her husband kept important documents and papers in a safe bolted to the utility room wall and Charlotte used it for her jewellery. Her slender fingers worked the rotary dial with practised smoothness and soon the door popped open. She sorted through the envelopes, plastic flip files and loose papers until she found what she was looking for, retrieved it, locked the door and went through to the sitting room with her cup of tea.

In the background Mozart harmoniously soothed the airwaves with a flute and harp and Charlotte sat on the heavy cream fabric sofa, staring at the A4 envelope in her lap. It was simply marked in Jennifer's neat, block-type script – "CONFIDENTIAL, PLEASE DO NOT OPEN – JENNIFER CANDLE, PERSONAL."

She wondered why her dear sister had never confided in her. Charlotte had always believed that they had shared everything, like the time when she confessed her brief and foolish adulterous interlude to Jennifer. The fact that such a mounting depth of deception was withheld not only from Jasper but also from her hurt Charlotte to the core.

Charlotte sighed and then stood up, walked to the Bose

Music Centre and turned off Mozart. She returned to the envelope and again stared at it impotently, this time in silence. Finally she slid a Fleur de Lys-styled letter opener down one side and pulled out several folded and some crumpled sheets of yellowed paper. They smelled mouldy and stale.

She could feel her heart beating and her inner voice instinctively cursed Jasper. *But then*, she thought to herself, *was it really his fault after all?* Was he not merely caught up in this peculiar business as was she?

Charlotte began to read, taking the letters in chronological order, the first one dated over thirty years ago. Beside her the forgotten cup of red bush tea grew cold.

SIXTY FIVE

"You're making good progress, Jasper," said Dr Giordano as she sat beside his bed on a firm hospital chair.

She had slipped into a white coat worn over her tailored olive green dress suit, on which a large, yellow lapel badge declared her as 'Visiting Doctor'. In her lap she cradled a violet coloured folder and though she never used it she played with her Mont Blanc pen between her fingers.

Jasper was sitting up straighter in bed, the intravenous line now discontinued, leaving only a small, white, square dressing on his forearm where it had been. Thankfully, due to her taste in expensive perfume, Dr Giordano was the only thing Jasper could smell in the usually blandly antiseptic room.

"When can I go home?"

Jasper stared at his arms, where the trembling was lessened but still visible.

"Home?" Giordano smiled teasingly and raised an eyebrow. "Your associates tell me you've been living in your office."

Jasper made a false smile and opened his arms in a placatory gesture.

"What's the diagnosis, Doctor?" Jasper asked meekly, placing the fingertips of each hand together.

"Acute alcohol intoxication: your liver was beginning to

decompensate, but hopefully there is no permanent neurological damage."

Jasper nodded in a way that suggested acceptance of his self inflicted pathology.

"Treatable?"

"If you stop drinking, completely," Giordano said firmly.

"When can I leave hospital?"

"Probably in the next day or two, but only on certain strict conditions."

"I can't wait." He rolled his yellowed eyes.

"You have been signed up into Dr Montgolfier's counselling sessions for alcoholics and you are being put on a daily dose of disulfiram, Antabuse, to discourage even your slightest urges."

Jasper nodded as he stared at the neatly ironed creases in the hospital bedding.

"Did they do any other tests, Doctor?"

"What other tests?"

Giordano shuffled in her seat and adjusted her skirt self consciously.

"I thought they might have done other tests?"

She hesitated.

"Did you ask them about tests?"

"I can't quite remember," Jasper fumbled, though now he was beginning to feel that perhaps he should have chosen to continue in the blissful ignorance of denial.

"Ah," Giordano said softly, "I honestly don't know, but I will find out for you."

A short silence ensued as Jasper sat, deep in thought. Suddenly the door creaked open after a gentle, tapping knock. It was Debra Kowalski.

"Howdi, partner," she said cheerfully in mock western style.

Jasper was surprised and a little embarrassed to see her.

"Clients are not supposed to see their solicitors in backless hospital garments," Jasper said with simulated horror on his face.

The two ladies' eyes met and locked briefly.

"Dr Giordano, my doctor, and Debra Kowalski, one of my clients," Jasper said, gesturing with an outstretched arm which was trembling but no longer writhing.

The two women exchanged pleasantries and Giordano rose to leave.

"I will see you before you are discharged, Jasper, and I will find out about the tests for you," Giordano said, smiling warmly and leaving discreetly.

"My God, what happened to you?" Debra said with a look of deep concern written across her attractive face.

She smelled like a meadow of spring flowers and looked nothing like the grieving widow he remembered previously. Jasper unclasped his hands, widened his eyes and made a face of exaggerated surprise, then clasped his hands together again.

"Too much work, too much stress, and too much…" he paused, "Chivas. There, I said it."

Somehow his face did not convey the conviction of levity that his voice did, as though it knew the story was incomplete.

"Nothing that can't be fixed, I hope?" she said, shrugging her shoulders.

"Look at you, you look fantastic, Debra. Thank you for the flowers, very thoughtful."

She smiled and blushed slightly, hiding her sparkling grey blue eyes.

"I brought you some chocolates. Doctor's orders," she laughed.

The bedside table was full up with books, boxes, glasses of water, and a charging iPhone.

"Thank you, can you put it in the cabinet for me?"

Debra bent forward and opened the small cabinet door, upon which several envelopes slid out on to the floor. She retrieved them.

"You have unopened mail here, did you know?"

Jasper frowned.

"No, I didn't. I'll read them later."

She placed the small pile on the bed beside him and he gathered them together, glancing briefly over them.

"I'm sorry I have not been able to do much about your case in the past week or so. There has been… er… a lot going on regarding Jennifer," Jasper said, "even before I was admitted."

Debra shook her head.

"I understand, please don't worry yourself. It has given me opportunity to think things through as well."

"So much has happened to me recently."

"It's OK, nothing has changed," Debra said reassuringly, with a warm smile. "We can pick up the pieces when you're better."

Deep down Jasper knew, however, that this was not true. He just did not yet know why, or how. But everything was about to change forever, of that he was certain.

Suddenly he looked straight into her penetrating eyes.

"Have you ever had a moment in your life when you begin to consider that things will never be the same again?"

Debra nodded without taking her eyes off his, the smile gone from her face.

"Oh yes," she said, "More than once. It's like being in a Minnesota blizzard, you never know how bad it's going to be, how long it will last, or how much it might affect you."

SIXTY SIX

Stacey looked up from her desk where she was puzzling over a Sudoku, gripping a pencil in a most unorthodox way in between the black painted nails of her third and fourth fingers.

It was the corpulent figure of Merrill Bradshaw standing before her, wearing a camel cashmere great coat over his shoulders without his arms through the sleeves.

"Oh God I hate those things," he said pinching his face in disapproval as he glanced at the Sudoku.

"Can I help?" Stacey said cautiously.

"I am Merrill Bradshaw, here to see Jasper Candle."

She frowned, revealing the intensity of the deep purple eye shadow behind her upper eyelids.

"Do you have an appointment?"

"Oh, we're old friends, we go back years Jasper and I," Merrill said with a dismissive sweep of his hand, before adjusting his red on white spotted bowtie.

Stacey hesitated, trying to evaluate the strange rotund man with rosy cheeks standing before her. Merrill sensed her intransigence and produced a card from his breast pocket.

"I'm from the Crown Prosecution Service, my dear. Jasper has been consulting me about a case and I have some news that he will find most interesting."

Stacey studied the card with her mouth slightly ajar.

"Er, Mr C is in hospital, sir."

Merrill's face fell.

"Good God, child. What happened?"

"Mmmmmh, he… er… collapsed," she said warily. "He's getting better now."

"Oh dear, oh dear, I must go and see him."

"He's expecting to be discharged very soon, actually. Do you want to make an appointment and see him here rather?"

Merrill hesitated.

"Let's do it properly then. I think he will be more than a little surprised by what I have to tell him."

Merrill could not hide his boyish ebullience, as though he had just been made captain of the rugby team.

SIXTY SEVEN

Jasper picked his way through the postal items, flicking most to one side on his hospital bed with disinterest. He singled out two envelopes, turning each over in turn to examine them front and back.

One was from Dr Whitehouse at the mortuary, the second was postmarked in Walton on Thames without a return address. Jasper felt his heart skip a beat as he realised it might be from Charlotte. He froze momentarily, afraid to proceed, contemplating the potentially catapulting consequences that he might unleash by breaking the protective seal on Jennifer's past. Jasper feared it might be like releasing a snowball down a steep slope, unable to control its gathering speed or check its increasing size and powerless to prevent its inevitable impact.

Jasper decided on the less mysterious envelope first and with a sweep of his index finger opened the letter from Dr Whitehouse.

Dr SP Whitehouse MB, PhD, FRCPath, LLM
Home Office Pathologist
Drury Lane
Durham

Dear Mr Candle,

With reference to your enquiry about an exhumation order

for the remains of Jennifer Candle, I wish to announce that I have given my support to this application which now rests with Mr Swinter, HM Coroner Durham.

I believe there are compelling medical reasons for an exhumation in view of the likely history of Huntingtons disease in the family. Had we been privy to this information prior to burial, we would certainly have conducted these tests at post mortem examination.

These applications can take time and I cannot give you a time scale for a Home Office decision at this early stage.

Yours sincerely,

SP Whitehouse

Jasper was pleased with Dr Whitehouse's letter and carefully reinserted it into the envelope. He hoped he had done enough to convince Charlotte not to object to the exhumation. Despite his excitement, intermingled with nauseating apprehension, he felt a sudden pang of guilt.

"Please forgive me, Jennifer," he said softly, as he placed Whitehouse's envelope to one side, his eyes staring at it as though it represented his disrespect for the consecration of Jennifer's final resting place.

He stared at the second envelope held in his trembling fingers, frightened and aware of the dryness in his mouth. He cautiously opened the envelope, revealing several sheets of yellowed paper that emitted a musty smell as they were unfolded. He sat in stunned silence as his alert eyes darted from one sheet to another, picking out numerous bombshells that exploded behind his pained expression: a letter from Dr Majid Eldabe written thirty years ago; mention of the names of his father Freddie, his brother Baz, and his wife Jennifer. But the biggest shock was recognising his mother's untidy spidery handwriting.

As his mouth dried out even more and the colour drained from his face, Jasper continued to read. The only movement discernible was the rhythmic tremble of the paper in his grasp and the return of a nagging tic around his left eye.

Dr Majid Omar Eldabe MB (Cairo) FRCP (London) PhD (Camb)
Consultant Neurologist
St Thomas' Hospital
Westminster Bridge Road
London
SE1 7EH

Mr Freddie Candle
17 Scratham Close
Stepney

8 July 1979

Dear Mr Candle,

This letter serves to confirm in writing the details of our last meeting in Neurology Out Patients at St Thomas' Hospital.

You were referred to me with intermittent jerky movements of your arms and legs, trembling in your hands and contractions and tics of your facial muscles. You told me that your father had been similarly affected in his later life and you recalled being told that he 'had gone mad'.

I believe the phrase you said that your mother used was 'madness runs in your family' and that several of your uncles and cousins had suffered from similar conditions.

On enquiry, you stated that your abnormal movements had been noticeable for at least a year and were getting steadily worse. That would time their onset with approximately your forty third birthday.

When I examined you I was able to confirm significant choreo-athetoid movement disorders, ataxia, dysphasia and also the beginnings of early dementia. The CT scan we performed last month showed atrophy (degeneration) in certain areas of your brain.

Together all of this information unfortunately adds up convincingly to a diagnosis of Huntingtons disease, which almost certainly runs in your family. There is as yet no absolutely infallible test for Huntingtons disease, but I am very confident that this is the diagnosis in your case.

Huntingtons disease is in most people an inherited condition that is progressive and relentless. Unfortunately there is as yet no cure and the disease is inevitably fatal within ten to twenty years, by which time you will be dependent on full time nursing care.

One very important matter to consider and discuss is genetic counselling, by which I mean family planning. There is a 50% chance that each of your children will inherit Huntingtons disease from you. If you have not had children yet then I would urge you to enter into formal genetic counselling, as the risks of transmitting this are significant.

As ever, I am available to discuss any matter that you may wish to raise. I have enclosed literature on Huntingtons disease: what to expect, where to find help, how to join Huntingtons support groups, etc.

I am very sorry to have to be the bearer of such devastating news.

At the end of next month I will be leaving St Thomas' Hospital and setting up full time consulting rooms at 67

Harley Street. I will be more than happy to continue seeing you there, or if you prefer I can refer you to one of my esteemed colleagues here at St Thomas'.

Yours sincerely,
MO Eldabe

Jasper's heart was racing and his hands were trembling more than they had for several days, making the paper flutter in his grasp. He tried to lick his lips but they were as dry as leather. He felt as if he'd been kicked in the abdomen. On his bedside table the iPhone registered an incoming message, but Jasper either did not hear it or totally ignored it. Apprehensively, he turned to the next letter, handwritten in his mother's distinctively blotchy and untidy scrawl and began to read. He could taste his own nausea and his eyes were burning from a sustained lack of blinking.

My dearest Jennifer,
    I have regarded you more as a daughter than a daughter-in-law and you in turn have always been very kind to me. This doesn't make it any easier for me to say what I have to and I cannot apologise enough for being such a coward. I am ashamed that I never had the courage as a mother to face Jasper and be honest with him.
    Jasper was never that close to his father and I felt that when he died Jasper held against me the fact that I never stood up for him more at home. Jasper's father jumped off Westminster Bridge and drowned himself in The Thames on the way home from work one day in 1979. It was a complete shock to everyone who knew him, including Jasper and his brother Baz.
    Where I failed was in not telling them why their father

could no longer live with himself. I had been a peace monger and a coward in my marriage; I remained so as a widow and as a mother.

Freddie, Jasper's father, told me one night that 'madness ran in his side of the family' and that, in addition to his father, several of his aunts and uncles had also been afflicted before they died. We knew nothing of the nature of this terrible disease and Freddie thought, by the time he reached mid adult life, that he might have cheated it and was in the clear. Soon after he began to develop peculiar jerky movements in his arms and legs, even his hands and his face twitched constantly near the end.

He had particularly vivid memories of his Uncle Arden, who had been a father figure to him during the war. Arden apparently ended up being restrained, incontinent, unable to communicate and care for himself. Freddie was terrified of ending up like this.

He eventually took medical advice and was referred to a neurologist at St Thomas' Hospital. They were very interested in the family tree and the history of who had been affected in the past. Though they did a brain scan, I recall that there were no specific tests that they undertook on him to reach a diagnosis in those days. However, they were pretty confident that he had Huntingtons disease, which they said he had inherited from his father. I have enclosed the letter from the neurologist that I found amongst his possessions after he died. Freddie never said a word to me about any of this.

Knowing that he was facing a dreadful deterioration in independence, bodily function and dignity, I don't think Freddie could face life anymore and ended it within a week of the diagnosis. What he failed to deal with, however, was the issue of his own two children and what might happen to them. That impossibly difficult task he left to me and, unfortunately, I shrank from the responsibility, until now.

Jasper was only eighteen and his brother Baz twenty three when their father died. Huntingtons usually only strikes people in their forties or fifties apparently, so I gambled that it would be many years before they would be affected, if they were affected at all, as there was always the possibility that they might not have inherited the disease from Freddie. I never thought for a moment about grandchildren.

Baz was a qualified doctor and I think he connected the dots a little sooner once his symptoms began to develop. He seemed prepared for it and had tests done immediately. By that time genetic testing was already available and they confirmed that he had Huntingtons disease.

He asked me one day if I had known all along that his father had been diagnosed with Huntingtons and all I could do was cry, covering my shameful failure in tears. I realised that my nightmare was becoming a reality. He stormed out and died at Lambeth Underground station in the rush hour. The newspapers said the crowd of passengers was exceptional that evening, raising the question of whether it surged and pushed him over the edge into the path of the oncoming train. But I knew instantly what had happened and I began to fear that I might lose Jasper, my last remaining son, in a similarly tragic fashion. Two suicides in one family was more than enough for any mother to have to deal with. I was determined to prevent this happening to Jasper as well.

It was then that you confided in me about wanting to start a family and I realised my time to act was running out. Though I could not bring myself to tell Jasper about the terrible fate that quite possibly awaited him, I knew that an even greater tragedy and injustice would be to bring another generation into this world carrying that terrible gene.

So, my darling Jennifer, contrary to the natural and strong mothering urges that now drive you to raise your own children, I must ask you to deny yourself the most precious gift that a mother can give to this world – children. This is especially vital if you begin to notice any strange symptoms in Jasper, the signs of early onset Huntingtons disease. As these may be delayed, you cannot necessarily take normality for granted and the safest course of action is undoubtedly not to have any children with Jasper.

Both his father and Baz started with trembling and jerking of their limbs, strange facial tics, mood swings, loss of focus and concentration, even forgetfulness.

Doctors can now do genetic tests to diagnose the condition and Jasper may, of course, not even have it. But if he has begun to develop any of these signs, then it is probably too late.

If there is even the slightest possibility that Jasper may have Huntingtons, you must, please, my dear Jennifer, not fall pregnant and potentiate this curse into another generation of Candles.

It's a lot to ask I know, especially in such a cowardly fashion, but I beg you to heed my words. Doctors cannot treat this disease, but you can stop it from developing further in our family.

I am so sorry that I wasn't a stronger person and able to deal with this horrendous family tragedy better. You will always be in my thoughts, Jennifer. I am forever in debt to you for assuming this great burden.

Thank you.

Love
Evie Candle

SIXTY EIGHT

It was Lazlo who discovered that Jasper had absconded from hospital and was missing. Walking into Jasper's room with his swaggering waddle, he found the bed sheets peeled back, partially covering a small pile of yellowed papers.

Following a gentle knock at the door, Dr Montgolfier walked in and seemed surprised to find Lazlo standing in the room. He frowned and rubbed his fuzzy beard with one hand, half turning as if to check that he had entered the correct room.

"I'm looking for Jasper Candle," Montgolfier said uncertainly, folding his arms and revealing brown leather elbow patches on his green tweed jacket.

"So am I," Lazlo said, his eyes surveying Montgolfier from head to foot. They came to rest on the array of pens in the breast pocket of the country gentleman's jacket.

"Are you his doctor?"

Montgolfier extended his hand.

"Dr Montgolfier. Where is Mr Candle?"

Lazlo's eyes wandered down to the floor beside the bed where a discarded set of crumpled hospital pyjamas lay in a heap. The iPhone beside the bed was gone, the small wardrobe in the corner open with empty hangers visible on the rail.

"I think he's done a runner, Doc."

Concern creased Montgolfier's face and he again folded his arms.

"Why on earth would he do that?"

Lazlo's gaze settled on the partially hidden yellowed papers beneath the bedding. He surreptitiously drew the sheets across to obscure the letters.

"I'm a little worried about Mr Candle, Doc. He's not been himself lately."

"I beg your pardon, I didn't catch your name..." Montgolfier said, leaning forward slightly.

"Lazlo, I work for Mr Candle."

Montgolfier nodded and thoughtfully stroked his beard.

"I agree with you, I am concerned about where he might be and what state of mind he may be in. Any idea where he could have gone, Mr Lazlo?"

Lazlo shrugged, his eyes furtively flicking to the hidden letters.

"Doctor Montgolfier, a call for you," said a nurse, popping her head around the door.

Montgolfier excused himself and followed the nurse. Lazlo quickly snatched the letters and stuffed them inside his leather jacket, before hastily leaving the room.

He could not explain what investigative instinct had driven him to look on Prebends Bridge, especially as his very first thought had been that he would find Jasper in The Swan and Three Cygnets, halfway through a bottle of whisky. Perhaps it was the content of the letters on Jasper's bed that had sparked a subconscious connection in his brain as he read through them quickly.

"Jesus!" Lazlo muttered, shaking his head, his brow creased and his astonished eyes darting from one letter to the next.

Lazlo stepped off the cobbles on North Bailey and stopped beneath the stone gateway on the cathedral side of the river bank, observing Jasper carefully before approaching. Lazlo had been rushing about and the welcome pause gave him opportunity to catch his breath as he studied his quarry.

Jasper was leaning against the stone parapet, his breath visible in short rapid plumes of vapour around his face as he stared down into the icy December waters.

"Guv?" Lazlo said as he gradually drew closer.

A ghostly mist clung to the water, gathering in thicker clouds in some places. A few people walked the riverbank pathways, but the bridge was deserted.

"You all right, guv?"

Jasper sighed but did not turn to acknowledge Lazlo. He would never know that just weeks earlier Jennifer had stood, in a similarly forlorn state of mind, staring into the Serpentine in Hyde Park, mesmerised by the allure of the tranquil waters.

"You must be cold, guv," Lazlo said, removing his brown leather jacket and draping it around Jasper's shoulders. Jasper was wearing only a creased white shirt beneath peacock blue braces that had become twisted as they were hurriedly attached to his pin stripe trousers.

The square white dressing covering his intravenous site was visible over his left wrist.

"Everyone's been so worried about you, guv. Why did you leave the hospital?"

Lazlo glanced at Jasper's trembling fingers, tinged blue from the cold. The iPhone Jasper held rolled rhythmically between his thumb and index fingers.

"I don't know what to do, Lazlo," Jasper said softly.

"What's happened, guv?"

Lazlo's face was creased with concern as he eased forward slowly and placed his elbows on the parapet beside Jasper, making sure he did not crowd him.

"All my life I have helped people through their tragedies by finding a guilty party to blame."

Lazlo nodded, the large pewter ear ring bouncing against his cheek.

"You've helped many people, guv."

Jasper looked upwards at the leaden sky, the tics around his left eye visible but not as corrupting as they had been. Lazlo noticed that even Jasper's arms seemed to be writhing less.

"In my experience there is always somebody to blame, even if it means having to dig a little deeper. You know all this, Lazlo, how long have we worked together?"

"I know, guv."

A silence descended from the chilly, damp air and hung between the two men.

"I've always believed that closure is achieved through the process of understanding cause, which usually means blaming someone."

"That's what we do, guv." Lazlo nodded.

"But now I am the one needing closure and it doesn't look that simple from where I'm standing."

Lazlo rubbed his great hand across his rough chin several times.

"I don't know how to help myself, Lazlo. I'm lost. Searching through my family's well kept secrets, I cannot easily find anyone to blame for this… this… bottomless pit of a tragedy."

Lazlo wondered how long he could feasibly continue pretending that he had not read Jasper's private letters. He maintained a discrete silence and listened.

"I cannot blame my father for inheriting this awful disease and passing it on to all of us. I can no longer blame Jennifer, God rest her poor soul, for finding herself caught in an impossible situation with no apparent escape. It was not of her making."

Lazlo turned his head slightly to watch a group of school children running across the bridge ahead of their parents as they made their way home at the end of the school day.

"If only Mrs Candle had been able to tell you what was on her mind, guv."

Jasper glanced at Lazlo and frowned ever so slightly.

"Is it my fault, Lazlo? Was I unapproachable, unavailable? Is that why she…?"

Lazlo shrugged, feeling that perhaps he had over reached himself.

"I had to read the letters, guv, I found them on your bed and I needed to know what had happened and where to look for you." He paused, looking like a remorseful schoolboy. "I'm sorry."

This revelation seemed to act as a catalyst to Jasper, whose shoulders began to shudder beneath Lazlo's giant leather jacket.

"Every chicken pluckin' member of my family has deceived me. I initially thought it was just Jennifer, but there was also Charlotte, my father, cheese and rice Lazlo, even my own mother!" Jasper's voice rose in intensity as he spoke.

Lazlo's mind raced as he tried to figure out how to handle this situation. He was not trained in negotiation or crisis management and he was worried that one wrong move could ignite Jasper's volatile vulnerability.

"It's freezing out here, guv, shouldn't we go inside?"

Jasper turned to face Lazlo, revealing his bloodshot and moist eyes, the tics pulling at his eyelids.

"My mother, Lazlo, cheese and rice, my own mother knew about this… this curse… for thirty years she knew… and didn't even tell me…"

Jasper lowered his head and stared down at the mist swirling gently across the calm waters, disturbed only by the occasional swoop of a hungry bird seeking food.

"All those times I visited her, the conversations… all a complete sham, a charade of normality. I feel betrayed by her… no… violated." Jasper shook his bowed head.

Lazlo frowned as the silence engulfed them and he was left without a notion of how to handle his grief stricken guv'nor.

"Is *anyone* to blame, guv?" Lazlo said cautiously.

"I don't know how to deal with this unless there is."

Jasper stared straight ahead. Far below a crew of four intrepid rowers in white T-shirts braved the cold, as their oars made clean cuts in the virginal surface of the water, powering their boat forwards as the bow sliced through the mist.

"It has suddenly been revealed to me at the age of forty seven that I'm going to die from this horrible disease, Lazlo, I could easily blame my father for that, though it is hardly his fault. But…"

Jasper hesitated for a moment as he tried to order his rabid thoughts, bloodshot eyes darting about in a tormented face as the ideas gelled and he began to nod.

"But… Jennifer and my unborn baby, they both died quite unnecessarily, tragically. The only person I can blame for that… is my mother."

"Come on, guv."

"No, Lazlo, I mean it. If she had only broken her silence thirty years ago, Brad Pitt, even one year ago, Jennifer would still be alive today."

Down below on the river, the distant voice of the rowing coach echoed through the swirling mist as the rowers rested their oars on the surface of the water and listened.

"It's as though she didn't care about me, Lazlo. My mother didn't tell me because she didn't care what happened to me. Did I mean that little to Jennifer as well?"

"Perhaps, guv, they couldn't face telling you because they cared too much. Sometimes love motivates us to adopt courses of action that... don't always work out."

Jasper shot a look at Lazlo, his face twisted in confusion.

"What are you saying?"

Lazlo sighed and looked up at the towering spires of Durham Cathedral for inspiration.

"I don't think your mother or your wife... what's the word... deliberately plotted to hurt you, guv. It must have been very hard for them, keeping such terrible secrets."

Jasper snorted in disapproval and shook his head sharply.

"Then why did they do it? It makes no sense."

Jasper clenched his jaw, making the muscles ripple around his temples. Lazlo looked down at the rowers who were turning their boat in the centre of the river and readying it for the return slog to Elvet Bridge.

"Perhaps, guv, they did it out of love?" Lazlo said softly.

Jasper pinched his eyes shut and squeezed them, but as the tics humiliated his face a tear of bitter regret managed to escape and drip on to the ancient sandstone parapet.

"I saw a client recently, he wanted me to sue the hospital for ignoring his explicit wishes and not allowing him to die. I listened to him and... legally it's probably an open and shut case... but I just could not see myself doing it. It seemed so... pointless, so wrong. For the first time, Lazlo, I questioned myself about whether he would gain any closure from it."

Jasper turned to Lazlo and their eyes met. The pain and torment in Jasper's eyes leapt out and moved Lazlo, who had never seen his guv'nor like this before.

"What is happening to me, Lazlo?"

SIXTY NINE

Jasper was in his office packing clothes and personal items into a leather holdall when Debra arrived unexpectedly. She was wearing blue denim jeans with a heavily padded black jacket and a bright rainbow scarf tied around her neck.

"Hello, Jasper, it's good to see you out of hospital," she said.

Jasper looked up at her and managed a thin smile. Debra looked around the room and watched him packing. She smelled of spring flowers, bringing a welcome freshness into the stale office.

"Are you going somewhere?"

He sighed.

"I'm moving back home."

He hoped she wouldn't ask him about Ollie's case as he just could not bring himself to think logically, let alone legally.

"If there's anything I can do to help, please ask."

He stopped packing and looked up slowly, his face pained and drawn.

"Thank you."

She bit her lip and folded her arms tightly across her chest.

"I know what it's like to feel… lost…"

A silence followed but it did not feel awkward, both parties perhaps aware that words alone could not describe every moment of significance.

Stacey popped her head and shoulders around the door into the office without warning, black lipstick, black mascara, black nail polish and a jet black blouse.

"There's a Dr Montgolfier here, Mr C, he says it's very urgent that he speaks to you."

Jasper's eyes met Debra's as he felt a rise of embarrassment wash over him. The moment of shared silence had suddenly become awkward.

"I'll go," Debra said turning quickly to leave. "If you want to talk anytime, please call me."

Montgolfier was shown in by Stacey and looked slightly ill at ease. His hands were restless, clasping and releasing constantly over the handle of his small, brown briefcase.

"Mr Candle, you may remember me – Dr Montgolfier."

He extended his hand which Jasper shook firmly with a small nod of acknowledgement.

"We were very concerned about you, Mr Candle, absconding from hospital and all that, highly irregular."

"I'm sorry," Jasper said in a monotone voice without looking up.

"I have been assigned to oversee your rehabilitation program – I believe Dr Giordano explained some of that to you?" Montgolfier's voice rose towards the end, emphasizing the question.

Jasper sighed and stared into the leather holdall.

"I just don't see the point, Doctor, I mean I've not got much time left and I have no reason to…"

Montgolfier frowned, stroking his beard.

"Not long left, what do you mean?"

"I've got Huntingtons disease, it runs in my family. It's incurable, isn't it?"

Jasper stopped packing and looked up at Montgolfier, holding his gaze, a few subtle tics tugged at his face and his thumb and index finger rolled rhythmically over the shampoo bottle that he held in his hand.

Montgolfier stepped forward and placed the briefcase across the corner of Jasper's desk, beside his leather holdall.

"May I?" he said politely, opening the case and extracting a violet coloured folder before sitting down in the chair.

Montgolfier scanned the pages, pulled the spectacles off his face and began to suck the curved end.

"Mr Candle, your affliction is due to alcoholism, that's one of the fundamental precepts we must accept before we can move forward at all."

Jasper nodded without looking up.

"Yes, I love my gay and frisky too much, I accept that. But I also have Huntingtons disease, it's just been diagnosed."

Montgolfier replaced the spectacles on his face and flicked through the notes, his brow creased in the centre. Jasper moved over to the cactus and retrieved a framed black and white photograph of Jennifer from the carpet beside it.

"You underwent an MRI scan of your brain and also genetic testing for Huntington's." Montgolfier said, as though thinking aloud, as his index finger traced his progress through the notes.

Jasper shrugged as he moved across to the desk, holding the photograph in a trembling hand.

Montgolfier pulled the spectacles off his face again and chewed on the end as he turned over the final pages in the folder.

"The tests are negative, Mr Candle."

Jasper dropped the photograph. It clipped the edge of the

desk, shattering the glass before falling silently onto the thick pile of the deep blue carpet.

"Negative?"

"You do *not* have Huntington's disease."

Jasper lifted his hands and turned them over in front of his face methodically as he studied them with disdain – the rhythmic rolling of his thumb and index finger and fine continuous tremor. His left eye twitched. He felt nauseous.

"What's all this from then, Doctor?"

Montgolfier looked up at Jasper and closed the folder in his lap.

"You have Parkinsons, Mr Candle. Medication was commenced in hospital and you've made remarkable improvement. Now all we have to do is beat the alcohol and you have everything to live for."

Jasper felt his knees weaken and a loud buzzing sound develop in his head, as a snowstorm of spots invaded his field of vision. The last thing he remembered was that he was going to vomit.

SEVENTY

Drifting in and out of wakefulness, seeing blurred faces around him, aware of strange smells that had no firm origin; Jasper's days merged into one long and surreal hallucination.

He recalled muffled voices that now swirled about in his head like smoke in a blender, a cacophony of subliminal and persuasive sound bytes manipulating his guilty conscience.

"It is not your fault that this has happened."

"You are not to blame for your wife taking her life."

"Don't torture yourself about events over which you had no control."

"Not everything in life is rational and easy to understand."

"Human actions do not necessarily follow a logical thought process."

"You are not to blame for your wife's decision making."

"You could not have prevented this."

In spells of prolonged wakefulness he found himself staring at his hands, at the fine but ever present tremor, remembering how it had ridiculed him from the outset and how it had now made a mockery of his life, fooling everyone dear to him. He wanted to hate the tremor, to blame it for everything that had happened, but then a lucid spark would remind him that this was absurd.

Gradually, the days got longer and he remembered more.

After a while he was able to recognise Montgolfier's voice even with his eyes shut and he could predict what he would say next. He liked Montgolfier.

He hoped Debra had not visited. Fortunately, he thought, even if she had he had no recollection of her being in his room.

He knew Lazlo had been there and that pleased him.

One day he woke up and found himself in a neatly made white hospital bed, bright flowers on the table – Arum Lilies and roses – and a few cards. The room smelled of lavender and a meadow. *Debra must have been here*, he thought.

SEVENTY ONE

A staccato rap on the door startled Jasper from his reading. In his trembling grasp he held the yellowed letters above the neatly starched linen of his hospital bed.

"Jasper, old boy, what the devil happened to you?" Merrill said, a cautious grin across his cherubic face as he stepped into the room.

Jasper was a little annoyed to see Merrill but he smiled in return and extended his hand warmly.

"Merrill, my china plate, good of you to call."

"It's not your ticker, is it?" Merrill said with concern etched into his face as he sat down, tapping a balled fist against his own chest.

"No, no, not at all," Jasper said quietly looking down at his hands, "It's far worse than that."

"Ah." Silence. "Well, as long as you're on the mend."

Jasper smiled unconvincingly and pushed the letters under his arm.

"I feel… a bit better, thank you."

"You look better," Merrill said nodding effusively. "I made an appointment to see you in the office, but Stacey told me you were in hospital again."

Jasper nodded submissively.

"Dr Montgolfier wants me here a few more days."

Merrill took a deep breath, opened his mouth and then stopped, angling his head to one side as if measuring something in his mind before beginning.

"You know the case of the little boy who died from measles?"

Jasper nodded, frowning ever so slightly.

"You were planning a suit against the parents alleging negligence, reckless endangerment of the public by failing to vaccinate their child with MMR…"

Jasper continued to nod. "Uh-huh."

Merrill sat back in the uncomfortable chair and took a deep breath.

"Well, the CPS has been looking into the case from a different angle and I thought you'd be very interested to know about this for two reasons."

Merrill paused for effect, but Jasper said nothing, merely holding his steady gaze and nodding.

"Firstly, we have you to thank for putting us onto this idea, and secondly our course of action may well influence how you choose to proceed with your own case."

Despite his mental exhaustion and emotional distraction, Jasper was more than a little intrigued, though it was the first time he had given a moment's thought to the Ollie Kowalski case for some time.

"But I thought you regarded my case as having more holes in it than a colander?" Jasper said.

Merrill narrowed his eyes as if sucking on something sour.

"You got me thinking, Jasper, recent developments have very much played into our hands."

"Another measles death?" Jasper said, sitting forward in bed.

"No, no, a GMC verdict."

Jasper's face displayed his confusion as a few tics tugged at his left eyelid.

"Dr Hans Isselbacher, who conducted and promoted the initial flawed research espousing the dangers of MMR and whose work has long since been discredited and rejected by the medical profession, has been struck off the General Medical Council register for misrepresentation, falsifying data and bringing the profession into disrepute."

Jasper twisted his hands palm up in a whole body shrug.

"The CPS is bringing charges against Dr Isselbacher for his pivotal role in the MMR vaccination scandal."

"What about Seamus Mallory and his parents?"

Merrill shook his head.

"The Mallorys are analogous to the small time drug dealer, Jasper. What we're going for here is the cocaine factory in Colombia. Dr Isselbacher's published research kick-started a media frenzy that put the MMR vaccine on the front pages of every national newspaper for all the wrong reasons, resulting directly in thousands of parents rejecting the vaccination for their children. They too are victims, like the Mallorys, and some of their children may also die from measles."

Jasper sat in silence, nodding his head rhythmically, his left eye flicking only slightly every now and then.

"We are building a case against Dr Isselbacher: criminal negligence, possibly involuntary manslaughter." Merrill paused, clearly pleased with himself. "I thought you'd like to know."

Jasper leaned back and rubbed his chin.

"My client very much regards the Mallorys as the direct cause of her son's death and I can sympathise with that point of view. You can't absolve the gunman just because a Mafia Don ordered the hit."

"If you'll forgive me, old boy, clients may be guilty of the lynch mob mentality – hang the first blameworthy person that comes along – but we lawyers must look deeper into the problem."

"I liked to think of it more as establishing a legal precedent, Merrill. If people know they can be prosecuted then they will think twice before refusing vaccinations. Problem solved."

Merrill shrugged and nodded simultaneously, then checked his wristwatch.

"As I said before, Jasper, it's not an argument without its merits, but I believe the judge will look further up the chain towards the end we're presently pursuing. As long as somebody is blamed for the death of her child, your client should be satisfied."

"You think that, do you?"

"That's your talent, Jasper, it's how you sell it, old boy. You've always told me that closure comes through apportioning blame. Well, just tell her that Dr Isselbacher is responsible for her son's death and that he will face criminal charges before the summer."

Jasper grimaced, realising he was being patronized but feeling suddenly as if Merrill's sentiments were resonating on a chord that he could not only hear but appreciate for its clarity. If only he could apply it to himself.

"I'll give it some thought."

Merrill left with a smile and a hand shake. Jasper wasn't sure how Debra Kowalski would react to this news. The echoing hollowness inside him still made it difficult to feel anything for himself, let alone for others.

After a few moments of thoughtful preparation, Jasper returned to the letters he had hidden beneath his elbow, extracting them slowly with a gentle tremble of his left hand that now seemed confined mostly to his thumb and index fingers.

Beside his bed stood the framed photograph of Jennifer, bearing a fine tear through the centre where the glass fragments had sliced into the emulsion.

SEVENTY TWO

Within a few days Jasper was back in his home. He spent much of his time sitting in the drawing room, looking through old photograph albums, ordering his thoughts and reconstructing his emotions and memories.

He was once again able to look up at the wooden model of HMS *Victory* where it occupied pride of place on the mahogany mantelpiece, to recall the memories it evoked and to enjoy the magnificence of its beauty and personal significance without regret.

The doorbell rang: it was Lazlo with a carry bag of takeaway chicken madras, lamb jalfrezi, coconut naan, and pilau rice.

"I was in the neighbourhood, guv," he said, swaggering past Jasper who stood in the entrance hall wearing tartan slippers and holding open the front door with a wry smile.

The aromatic smell of Indian spices and warm rice made Jasper's stomach rumble. He could not remember when last he had eaten.

"What have you there, Lazlo?"

"Indian – my favourite, guv."

"Let's eat in the kitchen."

They sat opposite each other around the rectangular

Provence style oak table, Lazlo with his legs wide apart to accommodate his belly.

"How's the matron?" Jasper asked, spooning rice and chicken on to his plate out of one of the styrofoam containers.

Lazlo nodded, licking his fingers appreciatively as he tore his naan bread into sections.

"Billie is very well, guv, thank you for asking. We're going away next week to the Lake District."

Jasper raised an eyebrow as he loaded his fork.

"Walking holiday, Lazlo, surely not?"

Lazlo chuckled and dribbled rice on to his plate, wiping his mouth with the back of his hand.

"No, guv, a gastro pub inn, small place near Buttermere – good food, good beer – just what we both like."

Jasper looked up as he chewed and contemplated the photographs of Charlie and Jack that hung skew on the fridge door. He could have removed them, he had been tempted, but decided to leave them as a reminder of something that Jennifer had cherished. He was perhaps trying to share a part of her that he had failed to do when she was alive.

"You know, when I think of what has happened to me, what I've lost, what has been done to me, all of which has left me with no reasonable alternative but to accept it and move on, or shrivel up and die, it makes me question… everything I stand for," Jasper said thoughtfully as he ever so slowly chewed a small mouthful of chicken.

Lazlo stopped eating and looked at Jasper over a loaded fork.

"It's a job, guv."

"What do you mean?"

"Well, there's life and there's work. They're separate. They don't have to make sense together."

Lazlo chewed energetically and appreciatively, lowering his head as he prepared another forkful.

"I don't know if I can do that. My life always exemplified what I did, my work, what I believed in. Now, I don't know how it will continue as the very foundations of that life have been shaken to expose their... their frailty, and... their failings."

Lazlo frowned as he ate, a sweat developing on his brow and upper lip.

"You're saying that life is not black and white, guv?"

Jasper pursed his lips and nodded slowly.

"Do you believe in fate, Lazlo, that some things just happen without cause, without reason, without blame?"

Lazlo shrugged and wiped his mouth with a paper serviette.

"You're losing me, guv, I'm just a simple investigator."

Jasper sat back and pushed his plate away with a snort.

"You know, you're full of Turkish Delight, Lazlo."

"Oh, that reminds me, I have post from Stacey," Lazlo said, reaching into his leather jacket and producing a brown manila envelope.

Jasper opened it with a kitchen knife and unfolded the letter.

"It's from Mr Ferret. Dear Mr Candle, blah blah, oh, listen to this, Lazlo, the hospital is offering a cash settlement for pain and undue suffering over the regrettable death of Edward Burns: no admission of wrongful actions... no individual culpability... bring the matter to a close..."

Jasper's eyes scanned the page energetically, then as he lowered the letter they met Lazlo's concentrated gaze.

"So no-one is specifically blamed, but a general apology and admission that Edward Burns' death was..." Lazlo said.

"'Extremely regrettable' are the words used." Jasper tapped the letter with his index finger.

Lazlo made a face and shrugged. They sat in silence for a few moments as Jasper read the letter again.

"What do you think, guv?"

Jasper took a deep breath and glanced at Jack and Charlie on the fridge.

"I'm no longer at all certain that I can do any better. I think I'll recommend the settlement to Magnus Burns and see what he says."

Jasper didn't make direct eye contact with Lazlo, but he could tell that a huge wave of anticipatory relief had washed over his great swede-like face as the big man's eyes closed momentarily.

Lazlo left soon after and Jasper watched him crunch down the gravel drive to his white van.

"Enjoy Buttermere, Lazlo, and thank you."

"For what, guv?"

"For everything."

Lazlo waved his huge arm dismissively without looking back.

SEVENTY THREE

Dr SP Whitehouse MB, PhD, FRCPath, LLM
Home Office Pathologist
Drury Lane
Durham

Dear Mr Candle,

Reference no 7318/10 – exhumation of the remains of
Jennifer Candle.

In accordance with Home Office and HM Coroner
procedure, the exhumation of Jennifer Candle was
undertaken to provide tissue and DNA samples for specific
genetic testing.

I am able to confirm that genetic tests for the HTT gene
on both Jennifer Candle and the foetus were negative,
confirming the absence of Huntingtons disease, either as a
carrier or major trait.

Yours sincerely,

SP Whitehouse

GLOSSARY OF COCKNEY RHYMING SLANG

artful dodger	*lodger (lover)*
Arthur Scargill	*gargle*
barb-wired	*tired*
bar steward	*bastard*
Bo Peep	*sleep*
bottle and glass	*arse*
bottomless pit	*shit*
Brad Pitt	*shit*
bread knife	*wife*
brown bread	*dead*
cheese and rice	*Jesus Christ*
chicken plucking	*fucking*
china plate	*mate*
cobblers	*bollocks, balls*
cream crackered	*knackered*
crust of bread	*head*
dental flosser	*tosser*
dicky dirt	*shirt*
Eddie Grundies	*underpants*
Engelbert Humperdink	*drink*
fit and spasm	*orgasm*
Frankie Dettori	*story*
Friar Tuck	*fuck*

gay and frisky	*whisky*
God forbids	*kids, children*
Jagger's lips	*chips*
jam tart	*heart*
hugs and kisses	*wife*
Khyber Pass	*arse*
lager and lime	*time*
Marquis de Sade	*hard*
mother of pearl	*girl*
panoramas	*pyjamas*
Partick Thistle	*whistle*
Patty Hearst	*first class (degree)*
pogo stick	*prick, penis*
Rolls Royce	*choice, first class*
Scooby Doo	*clue*
tent pegs	*eggs*
Tommy Dodd	*God*
tommy guns	*diarrhoea*
Tom Sawyer	*lawyer*
tomtit	*shit*
trouble and strife	*wife*
Turkish Delight	*shite*